Murder at the MLA

Murder at the
MLA

A Novel by

D. J. H. JONES

THE UNIVERSITY OF GEORGIA PRESS ☞ ATHENS AND LONDON

©1993 by D.J.H. Jones
All rights reserved
Published by the University of Georgia Press
Athens, Georgia 30602

Designed by Louise OFarrell
Set in ten on fourteen Galliard
by Tseng Information Systems, Inc.
The paper in this book meets the guidelines for
permanence and durability of the Committee on
Production Guidelines for Book Longevity of the
Council on Library Resources.

Printed in the United States of America
97 96 95 94 93   C   5 4 3
97 96 95 94 93   P   5 4 3 2 1

Library of Congress Cataloging in Publication Data
Jones, D.J.H.
Murder at the MLA/by DJH Jones.
   p. cm.
ISBN 0-8203-1502-8 (alk. paper)
ISBN 0-8203-1629-6 (pbk.: alk. paper)
I. Title.
PS3560.O474M87   1993
813´.54--dc20   92-22681

British Library Cataloging in Publication Data available

Acknowledgments

All characters in this book are entirely fictional. Although existing police facilities in Chicago have been cited with an attempt at accuracy, the names of academic institutions have been selected and cited at random. Any resemblance between a named university or college and the social evils and social virtues recounted in this book is purely coincidental. Titles of articles, panels, and books are likewise products of the imagination.

For several details and anecdotes concerning Chicago police work, I am indebted to Connie Fletcher's compilations, *What Cops Know* and *Pure Cop*. Both books were produced in New York in 1991 by Villard Books, a division of Random House.

I would also like to express my appreciation to Roy Dames, administrator of the Cook County Office of the Medical Examiner, and to members of the toxicology division of that facility. Their assistance was generous and invaluable.

1

"The irony of it all is . . ."

At the registration desk of the Hotel Fairfax, Professor Jonathan Kralleras was delivering some tumultuous news to his old friend from graduate school Martin Snave. They were two brunet and middle-aged units in a crowd of almost six thousand English professors and graduate students who, in various stages of arrival at Chicago, were converging for the Modern Language Association convention.

To hire, to be hired, to be free of the marriage for a few days, to gossip, to "network," and to present or listen to short papers by the dozen every hour: these events are annual and ordinary for the MLA. But not the event of earlier that morning, let alone the afternoon before.

". . . the irony of it all is that Susan Engleton never, and I mean *never* in her life, was seen in anything but perfect attire. She was born ironed. At her christening they slipped a Wellesley class ring on her finger, they say. But there she was, Martin, dead, can you believe it?, dead as her prose, face down on the rug, her skirt up and a run in her stocking."

"Wait a minute, Jon, wait a minute!" Professor Snave was pleading, as he tried to understand the last details of registration. "Sign where?" he called to the impassive clerk, who'd learned just to jab his finger at the bottom of the registration form, where block letters in twelve-point type said: SIGN HERE.

Kralleras continued, "Mitchell Bullard—you know, one of my students, he's at Rice now—Mitchell was going down the hall when the police were coming out the door. Saw the whole group in there. Seems that Susan was trying to get to the bathroom but didn't make it. Not that she'd have had a good time if she'd gotten in there. I gather the entire Wellesley committee got sick as rats, and there was some kind of mad scramble to get to the bathroom. Many an Armani jacket has been sent to the cleaners for *intense* attention."

"How many on the committee?"

"Four, plus Susan. Susan, who now rules the underworld."

Martin Snave, room key now in hand, had turned from the desk. With Kralleras at his ear and elbow, he maneuvered around a group of grad students in front of a tall, freestanding bulletin board. There, on computer-printout sheets, all MLA participants were listed by name and hotel. Snave had several people to look up on this directory, but he paused a moment to give Kralleras a high-eyebrowed look of protest.

"Oh, *Jon.* Jesus. I know you didn't like her, but she wasn't *that* bad. I mean, consider: the woman is *dead.* What are we talking about, anyway, food poisoning?"

Professor Kralleras nodded emphatically, as if knowledgeably. But his mind was hovering over Snave's summary of Susan Engleton. He now proceeded with as judicious an assessment as he required from his undergraduates' papers at Austin.

"Yes, she *was* that bad," he concluded. "You didn't interview for that senior position at Wellesley. I did, remember?"

Certain memories still rankled like medieval urticants. Before his interview, Kralleras had gone to the trouble and expense of obtaining a copy from Ann Arbor of Engleton's unpublished dissertation. And had read it. Then his humiliations in Massachusetts had included having to provide much of the introduction to his own talk, and having to ask Susan Engleton to reimburse the cab fare she'd promised—even as she'd made it clear she overlooked no detail of politesse for those she regarded as social equals.

Memory for a moment prevented Kralleras from moving on to the enormous other news for Snave; namely, that there had been another death at the Fairfax, an accident in the hotel lobby just the afternoon before. As he took up that topic now and Snave's mouth dropped in amazement (*"Alcott?!"*), the two of them merged with the stream of conventioneers headed across the wide atrium lobby. Halfway across, at the sunken octagon area, the stream forked and moved slowly toward two distant glass elevators.

Behind them, back at the desk area, a tall TV console with two opposite-facing screens flashed identical news toward the octagon and toward the east doors. The time, the screens said solemnly, was 2:30 P.M.; the MLA president's address by Josephine Horgan, previously scheduled for 8:00 P.M. tomorrow, would be presented at 4:30 P.M. today in the Regency Ballroom; and the Child Care Center could be found on the west wing of the second floor, in the Embassy Room. At five-minute intervals, all passersby were reminded that Hertz Car Rental and the Versailles Florist were at one's immediate disposal, and that anyone with information regarding Professors Michael Alcott or Susan Engleton should contact the police in room 210A.

That a rented car this afternoon would require chains on its tires was not alluded to. Dark weather was flowing into the hotel's east side with every revolution of its polished brass doors. Successive ice storms predicted for that Thursday morning had in fact arrived, with below-zero temperatures expected all day. The splendid and blasé resourcefulness of Chicago's city workers was being put to its severest test of the winter so far. Snow removal was still immediate and round-the-clock, but the storms had laid a dangerous coating on sidewalks, steps, and airport runways. More snow was forecast for midnight.

Chicago had been selected long ago for this convention. Its selection conformed, as site selection does for three years out of five, to the demented pattern of requiring thousands of people to convene in a desperately cold northern city during four days between Christmas and New Year's Eve. This year the six thousand, in their long, leaderless march, would be impeded by crushes of holiday travelers, by strandings in adjacent cities, by overworked air-traffic controllers at deteriorated facilities, and by barbaric weather that generates, right at the door of the hotel at last, the sidewalk glaze so effective at twisting the ankles of a woman in heels. It's rumored in the academy, it borders on mythic belief, that the MLA Site Selection Committee has never attended the convention itself, since no one who attended it would ever plan it this way.

This year, as late as Friday noon, many participants would still not have reached their hotels, their panel discussions, their scheduled interviews on which, for some of them, their careers depended. Arrivees would hear the news late, then, very late indeed, of death and more death in the hotel. Martin Snave was one of many hundreds who'd be educated over the next few days almost exclusively by rumor.

He and Jonathan Kralleras were now waiting for the glass elevator in the southwest corner of the atrium, adjacent to the south concourse. Like its glass twin in the southeast corner, and like the bank of standard elevators between them, the average wait for its opening door remained a reliable eight minutes.

Jonathan Kralleras was not mistaken now as he pointed out to Snave the floor area nearby where Michael Alcott's body had struck the terrazzo after a long, long fall. But Kralleras had been in error earlier when he'd nodded about food poisoning. That particular error would remain a widespread conviction. By now, Thursday, December 27, the "wretched conditions" of the Fairfax kitchens had already been embellished and propagated everywhere throughout the six hotels of MLA. ("Absolutely appalling hygiene, like something out of *The Decameron*," Philip Strees of Texas A&M had said that morning, over at the Marriott, to Beverly Snogg of Minnesota, who wondered what cameras had to do with it.)

From Thursday morning on, rumor-mongering would create a flourishing business for any restaurant in the Loop within half a mile of the Fairfax. A market in coffee and dinner specials would be particularly booming at the excellent family-style place, the Greek Taverna, just across Columbus Drive, whose ordinarily morose proprietor was now cheerfully convinced of the power of prayer.

4   Meanwhile, on the Fairfax thirty-third floor this Thursday, no

one was convinced, cheerfully or otherwise, of much of anything. By late morning, four detectives from Area One had finished their first rounds of questioning the surviving Wellesley committee. Susan Engleton, erstwhile English-department chair and an avid coffee drinker, had been dead since 8:30 A.M. Hieratic, zipped into a body bag and strapped upright on a gurney, she had descended the service elevator under the ministrations of the chief medical examiner and two assistants. Her long visit to the basement cutting room of the Cook County morgue was just beginning.

Rapid questioning by the hotel security officer and by Inspectors Malley, Hong, Halleran, and Dixon added up, without apparent conflict, to the following scenario:

Susan Engleton—regal, plump, red-headed, divorced, and fifty-seven—had checked into the 3321 suite at 8:15 P.M. the previous evening. Although there was an unused bedroom in her suite, the other members of the Wellesley committee had reserved rooms together elsewhere. Professor Herbert Gooch and Assistant Professor Lawrence Vaster were around the corner, in 3374, while two women, Associate Professor Muffie Murchison and Assistant Professor Jessica Griffith, shared a room farther up, in 3742.

At 9:15 Wednesday night, Susan Engleton had placed a room service order for a light supper (a BLT with broccoli soup). At 9:17, apparently on an afterthought, she'd phoned room service again to order the delivery of a full coffee service to her suite the next morning. Directing the hotel staff to leave the coffee cart outside her door at 7:15 A.M., she'd made it clear that she expected some means to be provided of keeping the coffee warm, "but not overcooked," for several hours.

Professor Engleton had then called her four colleagues with a reminding directive to be at her suite by 8:00 A.M. They'd set their travel alarm clocks accordingly. "Whatever Lola wants, Lola gets," Gooch was heard to remark drily to Vaster. Vaster, still untenured, had thought it politic not to reply.

On Thursday morning, Professors Gooch, Griffith, Murchison, and Vaster (in that order) had arrived at 3321 between 7:45 and 8:00 A.M. Only Lawrence Vaster had taken the time for breakfast.

Muffie Murchison would report later that she'd noticed Susan looking unwell and perspiring slightly. Engleton, however, was contemptuous of inquiries into her health and had made no complaint.

The four had helped themselves to coffee from the chrome urn on the wheeled cart that Susan had pushed to one side of the suite's living room. Herb Gooch had noted the bitterness of the brew: "Nasty stuff; really off." Engleton had agreed impatiently, noting that poor-quality coffee was known to be "a regional defect of the Midwest." She'd quickly drunk another large cupful nonetheless, hers being a life powered in part by the motor of caffeine.

Jessica Griffith, who didn't care for Herb Gooch, had defiantly gone back for another cup, possibly two. No one served refills to anyone else. Conversation had focused on the five job candidates Wellesley planned to interview that day, the first at 8:30 A.M.

It was at 8:25 that Herb Gooch had groaned, set his cup down, and lurched toward the main bathroom off the living room. The others were still looking around, baffled, when Susan Engleton had suddenly made an awful sound and stood up, "looking ghastly," according to Lawrence Vaster. She took a step away from the sofa, staggered (Vaster had half risen, extending his hand toward her, which she ignored), put her hand to her mouth, and a moment later had fallen to one knee.

Her face was putty-colored, her lips cyanotic. She was gasping for breath. As poor Engleton collapsed, clutching at an arm of an easy chair facing the sofa (a chair vacated by Muffie Murchison just moments before), a convulsive tremor went over her body. About sixty seconds later she was dead.

Muffie Murchison, terribly suggestible since her prep-school days to any scene of oral effluvia, had rushed to the bathroom in response to Gooch's noises. She hadn't remembered seeing Jessica Griffith getting sick, but there Jessica was, being exactly that and blocking Muffie's way into the bathroom's most important areas.

And so it was that at 8:30, the first scheduled interviewee, Annette Lisordi from Emory—dark, curly, and nervous—discovered a pale mayhem on the other side of the door. To Lisordi's repeated knocking, the door had opened finally as if by itself, with a gasping, doubled-over Muffie bunched on the other side. "Susan! Susan!" Larry Vaster was shouting. With a blinking look into the living room suite, Lisordi had run to the phone in the left bedroom and called for help.

Lifting the receiver, she did wonder for just a moment, though, as anyone at MLA would have to wonder, whether this was all a new kind of ruse. Testing the mettle of grad students somehow? Some new kind of role-playing introduced into the job interviews? Annette Lisordi could only hope she was doing what she was supposed to.

Dr. Jackfield Herd, the hotel physician, whose warm attentions had been directed to a colicky baby in the Child Care Center, arrived within minutes via the service elevator. Donny McGuire, the security officer, whose job it was to see to it that no incidents affected the hotel's public relations, came in with Dr. Herd. A 911 call was sent out and together they performed some long minutes of ineffectual CPR on Professor Engleton. Then the entire east wing of the thirty-third floor, suite 3321 in particular, became very crowded.

Two uniformed patrolmen from Area One arrived after leaving their squad car double-parked and enduring a long, chafing wait for an elevator. Behind them, out of an unmarked car, came Investigators Patrick Malley and Richard Hong, in plain clothes. These latter two had spent hours with the medical examiners in the Fairfax the day before, investigating the incident in the lobby.

When it became clear to the District One station lieutenant, Brendan Mulcahy, that two professional, out-of-town conventioneers had become violently dead within twenty-four hours, and both inside a major downtown hotel, Mulcahy had assigned two other, more experienced detectives, Boaz Dixon and Timmy Halleran, to take charge of the Fairfax investigations.

What with an evidence technician taking 35mm slides, and Pete Montenegro, the lay investigator from the morgue, overseeing the transferring of coffee urn and cups to evidence bags, 3321 offered few places to stand or sit when Boaz and Halleran arrived. The chief medical examiner, Russ De Bartolo, was on the carpet beside Engleton's body, while the hotel manager stood looking on.

At that point, the unused east bedroom in Engleton's suite was pressed into service as a temporary interrogation room—or "interview room," as the police prefer to call it. Jessica Griffith lay on the bedspread there, diaphanously pale and Edgar Allan Poe-ish. Her ashen colleagues were distributed in chairs here and there in the room, being fingerprinted and repeatedly questioned.

Dr. Herd, worried, moved from one to another, taking blood pressures and temperatures. Griffith he was particularly concerned about—she had low blood pressure and a light rash—but she refused to go to the hospital for the stomach pumping and EKG he wanted. Her body, weakened by dieting so rigorous that more than one acquaintance suspected her of bulimia, was not something she wanted inspected by hospital staff.

Other committee members were still dizzy and weak, although Lawrence Vaster had almost recovered. Vaster was now giving the second of many statements, this time to investigators Malley and Hong. Herb Gooch continued to complain of dry mouth, Muffie of more stomach cramps. Dr. Herd was writing multiple scripts for epinephrine and Demerol and slurry of activated charcoal.

Within an hour, the police had questioned Annette Lisordi in some detail. By 10:00 her room had been searched and the fluid found in her coffee cup there impounded for analysis.

"OK, I think you can close the scene, Boaz." It was the chief medical examiner. Peeling off his surgical gloves as he stood up, Russ De Bartolo was announcing in his quiet way that his first examination of Susan Engleton's body was complete. She could be taken now to the morgue for autopsy and toxicology workup.

It was then 11:15 A.M. Annette Lisordi had been released about an hour before. Two other bewildered job candidates who'd shown up for Wellesley interviews had been questioned and sent back to their rooms. The beat cops had gone to report to the district station on State Street, where the lieutenant was calling a press conference. Trace evidence, such as it was (considering that in a hotel room everything is evidential and everything is probably irrelevant), had been collected. Voices in the living room and back bedroom were now fewer and quieter. The swirling, chaotic data of the case were slowly funneling down onto the thoughtful personages of Boaz and Halleran.

Boaz Dixon was in his early forties. Angular and knobby, 175 pounds at six feet tall, he'd inherited the stubborn Ozarkan metabolism that doesn't put blobbiness onto a man regardless of the greasy food he ingests. His face preserved the shrewd boniness of men with Appalachia and the British highlands in their backgrounds. His medium-brown hair, longish, was combed straight back along a squared hairline, past large ears very close to his head. Environed by jutting eyebrows, jutting cheekbones, and a long nose narrow at the bridge, Boaz's eyes, surprisingly, were not a pale Ozarkan blue, but brown. His hollow cheeks emphasized a largish chin that was clean-shaven and a straight thin mouth that almost never laughed.

This was a long-limbed man with a prominent Adam's apple and bony knots for his elbows and knees. You expected him to bump into things and to look vaguely arthropodan when getting out of a car, say, or reaching for the phone—the kind of man who wears a green sweater at the risk of looking like a praying mantis.

But Boaz was surprisingly graceful. Now, as he stepped off the distance from the sofa to the bathroom with a characteristically alert and pursed-mouth look, he moved with an economy that had to do with learning to hunt at an early age. A nodding of his head, along with a sudden affability that arrived in the form of an anecdote or tale, were stable habits of the man.

Built-ins of Boaz's mind included the rhythms and verbal fretwork of the South, though usually those lay restrained beneath brusque, no-nonsense declaratives of the North. There was a twang, a memory of the old hills and the eccentrics they can produce, that would come and go across his vowels depending on his circumstance: sometimes when he was relaxed or tired, but especially when an accent might be useful to manipulate his listener's assumptions and prejudices. Many a defense attorney had made the dismaying error, hearing that accent, of thinking this man ill-equipped as a witness.

Aside from summers spent in the Ozarks, Boaz had grown up in the tense and dreary Uptown district of Chicago, along with several thousand southern whites whose families had immigrated after the Second World War. He'd taken two years at the University of Illinois in Chicago, and then, when his money ran low, had become a beat officer in Area Six. That notorious crime district north of the Loop had been his jurisdiction for twelve years, seven of them spent as a detective.

At forty-two now, Boaz was seven years divorced, and lately on such amicable terms with his ex-wife that it annoyed him a little. Just after that divorce, he'd transferred out of Area Six into a tactical unit working undercover, something to occupy his mind day and night. In that capacity he'd worked for the first time with another tac officer, Timmy Halleran. The two of them now worked out of Area One, often as partners, both as homicide specialists in the Violent Crimes Unit.

Timmy Halleran was forty, and six foot two, but in contradistinction to Boaz's general sleekness, Halleran had a lumpy look. Uncounted meals in diners and greasy spoons and riding around in a car all day had given him, as it gives most cops, the occupational outcomes of police life: fat rolls at the waist, hemorrhoids, and early hip-spread.

Halleran, in fact, looked a lot like most cops. He was clean-shaven and heavy-faced; his sandy hair was parted on the left with short back and sides; he could be seen chewing gum at eight o'clock in the morning. The scalloping around his middle lay in ever-widening cascades, the naked image of which the mind quickly turns from—the image a little too closely resembling that of the Venus of Willendorf.

Halleran also maintained, unintentionally, the tradition of police department haberdashery: polyester double-knit trousers with hideous plaid patterning; ill-fitting, mismatched jackets pulled out of shape in the back; lots of brown.

But there was a comfortable bagginess in clothing and facial flesh that gave this large man an immediate appeal. His was a body that, sitting or standing, looked as if it were sinking into immobility, and his blue-eyed Irish face looked sadly aware of this condition. His jowly cheeks, with sagging wrinkles around the mouth, and his heavy eyebrows sloping downward at the sides, gave him an easygoing, melancholy look. His voice was slow and deep. Most people felt drawn to him.

Some of the other hazards of police life—the "Three Ds" of divorce, drinking, and drug use—had found expression at one time in Halleran's career by enormous intakes of beer and brandies neat. For the last several years, though, Halleran's relaxation habit was to eat the best food he could find or prepare, eating it alone and in large quantities.

Distancing himself ever farther from his two ex-wives, Halleran had slowly become a secret gourmand. His drugs now, when he could get them, were wine and béchamel. It was a testimony to his stubbornness and ingenuity that he could manage to make food inquiries while enduring the long shifts and fast food and exhaustion of police work. Given his numerous socializing relatives, Halleran suffered often from the Irish allegiance to overdone meat and dull starch that he had no choice but to consume in tragic quantities. On the force it was known that he griped about food, but only Boaz was privy to the fact that Halleran saw a good reason for knowing the difference between the world's two cinnamons, that Halleran had twice prepared his own fresh ghee for Indian food, and that Halleran knew more uses for raspberry vinegar than as a sprinkled condiment on fresh strawberries.

It was not a part of memory at the District One station that Halleran had ever laughed out loud. Boaz a few times maybe, but Halleran never. When signaling amusement, his heavy eyelids narrowed in a lizardlike way and there was a brief movement of his mouth that made his jowls tremble. For this reason, a successful joke at the station was one that could "make Halleran have a jowl movement."

Boaz, some people had found tough and others had found

approachable. As his maternal grandmother, Laura Mae, had claimed, "Boaz could get a doorknob to talk." Still, it was Halleran, with the dour and patient face, who owned the reputation of eliciting confessions and extended statements.

During one long case in Area Two, Halleran had worked shift after shift and on his own time to bring in a certain killer, the bludgeoner of an old woman whose body he'd discovered in a basement. Toward the end of that investigation, when the leads were narrowing, he showed up for ten shifts in a row and would not let up. Cops around him began to wonder whether Halleran was getting paranoid, like the old Irish Catholic cops who worked homicide year in and year out until they were so spooked they wore their guns around the clock, even when taking out the garbage at home. One of those cops, it was said, went to Communion every day.

But Halleran simply wanted this guy and had made up his mind about it, the way all cops do on certain cases. And when the skinny little wretch was arrested at a laundromat and brought in to the station, where he wouldn't talk, it was Halleran who had put his warm arm, all sympathetic, around this guy's shoulders and said, "Well, I know how you feel. I just want you to know that I read the whole file on this. And I'll tell you, pal, if any old bag ever deserved killing, she did. What a bitch!"

"Yeah, I know, that's why I did it," the guy had said, slumping in relief onto Halleran's bulk. And Halleran had taken him off to a quiet room with a stenographer and gotten a complete confession, court-tight, before the end of the afternoon.

Halleran was next seen in the men's room, where he brushed his teeth. He was then seen at the sergeant's desk, where he announced loudly, in a room that got very quiet, "Nobody had better fuck up this case—nobody! Not with lost files or lousy paperwork. Anybody messes this up, I will personally stuff that asshole through a keyhole.

"I *want* this guy," he'd continued. "No fuck-ups!" And the sergeant had raised both hands with open palms and said, "OK, Timmy, OK."

Out the station door to take a couple of days off, the glowering Halleran had then told Boaz, "I'm going to go eat." And Boaz had dropped him at Carlucci's, where the maitre d' had also raised both hands with open palms, but in a gesture of smiling welcome. "Ah! Officer Halleran! Tonight the veal!"

Throughout Areas Six and One, Boaz was particularly valued for his hunches, for a memory for details that gave him a large overview of a case, and for his testimony in court. It was Halleran who was known for tenacity and the extraction of information. The two men quietly deferred to one another, depending on the area of expertise.

It was a habit of Boaz's to make a thoughtful nasal "Hunnh!" when presented with provocative information. He produced this small noise after Halleran called him aside, dipped a blunt finger into Vaster's cup, and tasted the coffee again.

"Ever had a case of food poisoning with coffee?" Halleran asked, with a melancholy look.

Boaz acknowledged the situation had a certain novelty. What with everybody's eagerness to get automatic weapons these days, he hadn't had a poison case of any kind for quite a while—not since that woman over in Cabrini-Green, the one who'd made her three kids drink pesticide.

"Well, if the kitchens are filthy, real latrines," Halleran said, "you can get salmonella into anything. Botulism, too. But it would take some real doing to get that crap into a pot of coffee and not in everything else."

"Salmonella might *be* in everything down in that kitchen," Boaz reminded him. "Could be Death Capital down there. I've looked at slides from restaurants where it's growin' like fur. Even on the wine glasses."

"Yeah, I know, but listen: the examiners are going down there, but I already checked with the desk. Nobody else has gotten sick in the hotel today. From coffee or anything else. Last food poisoning incident was about three years ago. Some tainted chicken salad. And nobody died."

Boaz looked around the emptied Wellesley suite in which there 13 was a sour, mixed odor of coffee and stomach acid and general crumminess. "You think maybe Mr. Stranger Danger made a little visit here?" he asked.

The part of Halleran's eyebrows nearest his nose moved upward in a kind of facial shrug. It was Halleran's version of "Who knows what evil lurks in the hearts of men?" "I want Mulcahy to get the lab on this right away," he said.

Boaz nodded. Within another few minutes he'd made arrangements with the lieutenant for top-priority status to be assigned to autopsy and toxicology workup on this case. Results would be forwarded to the station within twenty-four hours.

"Well, a little visit down to the kitchens is called for pretty quick," Boaz said, hanging up. "But I also want to set up a base right here in the hotel. I don't think we ought to waste time workin' out of the station. Where's the manager?"

"I am the concierge of the Hotel Fairfax, Officer," said a woman near the door. A thin, black-haired woman in her late thirties, crisp to the point of brittleness, she had already invested a good deal of her valuable time in this room and hallway today. With her assistant, Gerald, she'd been smoothing over appearances and pacifying hotel guests up and down the whole wing. Her smile was practiced and resolute and almost hid her annoyance at the disruption of her schedule.

"Ms. Carstairs-Norton. How may I help you?" with the same layer of a smile.

She had on a black skirt well below the knee and slit up one side, Boaz noted. A hip-emphasizing, black-and-white jacket nipped in at the waist; huge glass-and-metal earrings; precision haircut; platform heels: up-to-date and don't you forget it.

Having introduced himself and Halleran as the chief investigators, Boaz indicated that two or three measures would go a long way toward speeding up their work. One would be a set of passkeys for the service elevator and maintenance rooms. Another would be a brief tour of the layout of the hotel, conducted by herself and beginning with the kitchens. That tour might conclude, then, at some room in the hotel that would be set aside for their police work.

"You want a room in the hotel? *Now*, during the convention?" The woman's smile remained intact, a gleaming patina over her outrage. It was so inconvenient, another dead one in the hotel, *her* hotel. Her job and promotion might be on the line with the corporation.

"Oh, just some little spot in a broom closet would do," Boaz said, amiably and very firmly. "I didn't have in mind an executive suite. Of course, if you'd prefer for me to yank people out of this hotel to come down to the station to talk to me—and if you'd like to spend a lot of time at the station yourself . . . ?"

"I hardly think I have the time for that. Gerald!" And her tall, worried, vaguely avian assistant was put in charge of setting up a room on the second floor.

This meant, to her irritation, that Gerald could not be dispatched in time to raise the rinse-water temperature on the dishwashing equipment in the kitchens, where the evidence technicians were no doubt beginning to take samples of the Fairfax cookery. This was anything but a well-controlled day.

2

The four Wellesley survivors had now returned to their two respective rooms. The scene at the Engleton suite was officially closed when Boaz and Halleran applied the "police line," the eight-inch-wide medical examiner's room seal, across her hallway door.

During the next few midday hours, Hong and Malley made background checks. Among other facts, they determined the time when each committee person had checked into the Fairfax compared to the arrival time published on the plane ticket. Who, if anyone, had unusual opportunities? Annette Lisordi's story and registration would then be checked, as would those of all the Wellesley job candidates.

It was the kind of investigative work Malley and Hong excelled in. Patrick Malley, especially, enjoyed springing small discrepancies back onto a suspect like a mousetrap.

Malley was short, chunky, hardworking, vulgar, and suspicious. Thirty years old, with the blue eyes, curly dark hair, and square Irish features that are so often handsome but were not in his case, he wore, year round, one of two polyester sport coats. They were cheap and unwrinkled, and they hung open over his gut.

Malley derived from a sprawling and tentacular family in Chicago. Through them, in one way or another, he knew everybody in town. His capacity for "information discovery" was sometimes remarkable. His sources included a dozen reporters and every beat cop in every district, or seemed to.

Area One being what it is, its jurisdiction including not only the Loop but extremely violent and volatile south-side regions as well, certain ambiguities of character in part of the police force can be useful in the *realpolitik* of Chicago neighborhoods. And Malley was an ambiguous cop, a dirty-work cop, known as a tough go-getter. If not many actual arrests were made by him, it was because the emergency rooms of more than one hospital had seen the results of Malley's interactions with pimps and drug lords and various sociopathic players. In uniform, Malley had been up once before the Office of Professional Standards because of excessive use of force. He'd been a detective now for less than a year and was never all that far from being busted back into uniform.

For the last several months, Malley had been exercising a new and specific hobby. It involved a 35mm Nikon with Nikkor zoom and partial fish lenses, which traveled on the front seat of his un-marked car like an arrogant and large-snouted pet. The fact that on a detective's salary Malley could possess such an aristocratic instrument either was a testimony to his splendid self-denial for the sake of his savings account, or else it was not. The fact of it remained uninquired-into. Something else that was not inquired into was the fact that Malley's original partner, a cop so clean he wouldn't accept a free cup of coffee, had been quietly mated up by the sergeant with another clean cop after about two weeks in Malley's car. This was, after all, Chicago, a city that is pragmatic about itself.

Richard Hong had been Malley's partner now for eight months. Hong was twenty-eight and five feet eleven, tall for his Singapore family background. He had straight black hair, the ability to keep his own counsel, and the third-generation acquisition of occidental pimple problems. On the force for seven years, Hong was developing into a specialist in gangs and organized crime. Fluent in two Chinese dialects, he had numerous contacts among the organized crime units from Singapore and a couple of mainland areas, units whose extortion rackets in the United States were as entrenched and ruthless as in their cities of origin.

Hong was also familiar with the signals and high signs of every juvenile gang on the South Side. They in turn feared his reprisals and called him, among other things, "Fu Manchu." Once, when a fifteen-year-old named Jube, known to have committed two knifing murders as well as multiple rapes, eluded serious prosecution yet another time on the grounds of his being a juvenile, Hong and his partner at the time picked up the noble youth very late at night. Jube had jeered at the police on his way out of the courtroom earlier that afternoon. He had also told the frightened sister of one of his victims, "I'm gonna *get* you, baby bitch, you're next."

It was at gunpoint that night that he was cornered and put into the squad. Blue-and-red strobe flashing, they'd driven him deep into the territory of a rival gang. The siren, which they left on, created quite a bit of attention in the street where they stopped. It was 2:30 A.M. and five blocks to the boundary of this particular gang's turf. For some reason, Jube no longer wanted to leave the squad car. At gunpoint they kicked him out. Up from the pavement a moment later, he was running for his life. Hong turned off the siren and drove the other way. It was on the next shift that a body was reported in that part of town.

While Hong and Malley now proceeded with investigations into a world very far from their usual interests, Boaz and Halleran began their tour with the concierge. Donny McGuire, the security officer, joined them at the registration desk.

Staying out of the way of the sample takers, Boaz and Halleran moved methodically through the storage rooms, maintenance closets, and cooking areas. Smells of Pine Sol, murky water, old dark frying oils, and basement damp replaced one another in turn. Past fifty-pound bags of monosodium glutamate, into walk-in storage refrigerators with open bowls of sauces, past an almost-deceased mouse, its four paws stuck onto adhesive rodent paper: it was a fairly typical restaurant milieu, offering nothing much surprising. Neither investigator made a remark.

The kitchen staff was nervous and confused. Rumors of Engleton's death had flowed to the basement floor, of course, and one rumor had it that these people taking samples were connected with the health department. In which case, why hadn't they gotten a warning call in advance, the way they always had before?

18   The basement was separated efficiently into areas for preparing

salads, cooking entrées, and deploying wheeled carts for coffee delivery. The busboy who'd assembled the Wellesley coffee service was now requested and produced. As Boaz began jotting a few notes, the concierge spoke.

"There has been *no* food poisoning at the Fairfax," she asserted categorically. To Boaz's "What do you think happened, then?" she truculently murmured something about the guest having suffered an aneurism, perhaps.

"Why have I got four other sick people from that same suite?" Boaz asked patiently.

"I'm sure I don't know. Maybe someone brought in coffee from somewhere else . . ." Her overall attitude was consistent, that she was an important person beset by trivial passing events. Her under-attitude, coloring a few words here and there, was that police are public servants—emphasis on the word *servants*. Boaz and Halleran ignored both attitudinal aspects. They'd looked after such individuals more than a few times, when those people's pressured lives had imploded toward suicide.

Now Halleran picked up a small, souvenir baseball bat emblemed with "Chicago Cubs." It had been propped on a shelf near a walk-in storage unit. This, he learned from a reluctant worker who kept glancing at the baleful concierge, was for the night shift. They made use of it sometimes on emerging nocturnal animals, the largest and furriest one of which the staff had named Rommel. Halleran's eyelids narrowed and his jowls twitched slightly as he replaced the bat.

He asked, then, that a copy be made immediately of the chart pushpinned to the door of the service-management office. This chart blocked out the daily shifts of every hotel worker that week. "I want to see the charts for last week and the next week's schedule, too," he said. "And I want to see the records of who's been hired and fired over the last year."

"I'd like to see where that coffee came from," put in Boaz, who'd noticed in storage the hundred-pound bags of French Roast beans. "Receipts for the most recent deliveries—say, over the last six months. I want to know the supplier's name, address. And I want to see any and all complaints about food service since, oh, last summer. All that can be put in our headquarters room— which will be where, exactly?"

"Gerald is setting up a room on the second floor, 210A. It's the best we can do on such short notice."

"Well, I think that'll probably be fine. Maybe McGuire here could give you some help. And meanwhile . . ." Boaz suggested now that since the concierge would be busy for a while assembling the information they wanted, he and Halleran would like to talk with the busboy "more private-like."

"Perhaps you would not mind meeting us again at the desk after a bit, say, forty-five minutes from now?"

The concierge recognized manipulation when she heard it, but hers was also a hierarchical mind that recognized an order when it was issued. "Whatever will bring this to a speedy conclusion, Officer," she smiled, and went off with McGuire.

The busboy was now told to repeat every step of coffee-cart preparation. For a moment, Bobby Firtch just blinked and stood still. He was a short, twenty-year-old blond from the grime and dolor of Gary, Indiana, whose smallest requests from life had to date been ignored. He was so frightened he just stood where he was. When Boaz asked whether he understood what was wanted, Firtch stammered, his face flaming.

"Why don't you just tell me yes or no to a few things, OK?" This was Boaz's last try. If this didn't work, he'd turn the kid over to Halleran, in which case they'd have to hear the boy's entire life story, probably.

Bobby was able to indicate that his own shift, beginning at 6:00 A.M., normally would have ended at 2:00 P.M. Room service is available, yes, twenty-four hours a day. Morning coffee service is delivered by a busboy who gets the order in the form of a check-list from the desk. A coffee cart is then set up with pink linen, a coffee service with sugar and creamer, and whatever individual food items have been ordered. The coffee itself is brewed in a multiple-gallon unit dispenser in one corner of the basement. Out of that the Wellesley urn had been filled, along with several other morning orders, none of which had provoked a problem.

For the last step, the coffee service is wheeled onto the service elevator and delivered by the same busboy. At no time was the Wellesley cart left unattended or out of sight during these steps.

Boaz and Halleran walked the boy through a reenactment. Mouth open a little, Bobby Firtch pushed another coffee cart into the service elevator and with uncertain fingers pressed the wafer-sized button for the thirty-third floor. From there the east wing extended to the left, down a long hallway. Several of the guests in that hall, knowing of a link between a coffee cart and room 3321, watched in fascinated horror as another cart rolled up to that door. Bobby Firtch would look at none of them.

Boaz and Halleran learned, monosyllabically, that Firtch had parked the original outside the Wellesley door at 7:15 that morning, that he'd looked at his watch and knocked. Receiving no answer, he'd waited, then knocked again. Finally he had heard a woman's voice saying, "Fine! Just leave it." He'd seen no one in the hallway as he left, but he'd been in a hurry and hadn't paid much attention.

"Was anyone in the hall when you first got off the elevator?" Halleran asked.

Firtch, still a little wide-eyed, shook his head. He was the very picture of guilt, which is to say, the picture of innocence.

"That's all, that's all I did. I didn't do *anything*. I just went back down. I didn't even get a tip." A nodding Boaz patted his shoulder firmly and back they went.

They found the kitchen areas crowded near the service door with people from both shifts. The morning staff hadn't been allowed to leave until questioned by the lay investigator, the examiners, and the police. This break from routine was much appreciated, since they all remained on payroll. There was a holiday atmosphere. Gossiping and group discussion were ongoing near the door.

Billy-T, another busboy, his voice heavy with mock amazement, announced, "I can't believe it! An English teacher broke down and gave me three dollars. A real goddam tip for a change. That has gotta be a first. Third floor, on the west wing. I was gonna put a plaque on the wall."

Contributing murmurs and short sarcastic snorts, the others agreed, one woman remarking that the only people worse to work for than the "snooty teachers" were the nurses' convention.

At the word *nurses* a groan went up, along with "Oh God!"s of various intensities. One voice opined that you might as well take your vacation during *that* convention since "you can't make a dime offa *them*"—this to more agreement.

The staff's mood of solidarity led them to feel cooperative with the police. Boaz's and Halleran's inquiries as to whether anything unusual had happened that day or during the week before (unusual orders, unusual people, unusual arguments)—these would lead, over the next few days, to several drop-ins at 210A as some staff members tried to be helpful. A few would vent their personal dislikes and feelings of persecution. All their information would be followed up. None of it would take the investigations anywhere.

Boaz and Halleran now rendezvoused with Ms. Carstairs-Norton, whose suspicions about the deportment of her staff when out of her sight were not so great as to force a question from her.

"First to your headquarters room, I thought," she said. "Then the quick tour of the hotel which I believe you requested, Officer?" Boaz nodded patiently. He and Halleran were led off then by their impatient Virgil, her right arm around a stack of charts and personnel records.

The three proceeded along the mirrored west wall of the lobby, which reflected the central sunken octagon with its numerous chairs and small tables that collected glassware all day. This long west wall sank open at one point, Boaz noticed, to reveal the Fairfax Gift Shop. It was a spot featuring T-shirts, doodads, newspapers, and Chicago memorabilia. Galoshes and black umbrellas of Woolworthian $4.00 quality were also available, repriced here for your convenience at $19.95. For this proprietor, too, the MLA events and weather were perfect.

Five sizable conference rooms encircled the atrium around the second floor. As the concierge pointed out, the Gold Coast Ballroom had been pressed into service for something called "The Book Exhibition." The smaller Crystal Room had been rented as a cash bar (by academic Marxists, as Boaz would later learn). It would open late that afternoon. Adjacent to it, as if to invite comparison, was the Child Care Center, in the Embassy Room. At the moment the Du Sable Ballroom was empty, and off the Du Sable was 210A.

In here the concierge dumped her first batch of materials on a card table and looked around. Another busy clerk was snapping open some folding metal chairs. Boaz pointed out at this time the advantage to the hotel of the police keeping very low profiles during their investigations. Commandeering the telephones in the hallways and lobby, where the lines were as long as the lines to the rest rooms, might rankle the guests.

"See that Mr. Vixon has telephone service immediately. I want two phones for the two jacks. And see that any information he wants is provided to him as soon as possible. Mr. Vixon . . ."

"*Dixon*. Dixon."

". . . Mr. Dixon and Mr. Halleran are our VIPs." The concierge's smile could have been a tool for industrial diamond cutting. "Any questions, you see me." The clerk got moving.

Halleran opted to start on paperwork, first sending McGuire to modify the TV announcement in the lobby to include Susan Engleton's name. Boaz, for his part, indicated to the concierge that she could continue the hotel tour for him.

Out the headquarters door, the hallway speakers, sometimes drowned out in the lobby, informed them that "the ox and lamb kept time, pa-rump-pa-pump-pump." A part of Boaz's mind, an unfriendly part, nudged him into noticing that he'd heard that song a couple of times through already.

At that moment, a couple of women, rounding the corner from the Book Exhibition, accelerated past the cop and concierge. One was beating the air of the hallway with an extended open palm in time to her habitual phrase, "there is a way *in which*." A name

23

tag on, evidently a teacher of something, the woman concluded, "There is a way *in which* methodology replicates mythology within all narration." Halleran, had he heard this, would have given the woman a basilisk glare. But Boaz grew thoughtful.

The service elevator brought them quickly to the tenth floor, which was ordinarily a business floor, having only a few individual suites but five more conference rooms (the Diplomat, the Erie, the Alpine, the Ogden, and the Ambassador rooms). Now the tenth floor had also acquired the lurid distinction of being Michael Alcott's former address. At some position not precisely known, but along the east marble balcony with its occasional columns, he had departed this floor and this life on Wednesday afternoon.

The intent of the design for the hotel was more easily readable from this height. The Fairfax (part of the 1970s depredations in the Loop) was a forty-story "renovation" preserving only part of the shell of a 1920s masterpiece of steel-frame construction. Seen from the outside, what once had been a thirty-four-story example of the Vertical Style, setback designs of Holabird and Root, now stood sheared of its original top ten stories. Upon the old base were now sixteen floors of much simpler theme, with oversized aluminum windows that stammered up to a brutal cornice and then stopped. Overall, the exterior elevations brought to mind the disappointing offspring of a gifted parent.

Seen from within, the Fairfax looked as if a tubular space had been gutted out by a giant apple corer. Thanks to cantilevered trusses and clever grade-level reinforcements, an inner atrium lobby now occupied ten stories in the center of the building. Hanging vines and plants depended, floor after floor. Two glass elevators constantly in motion descended and ascended the southeast and southwest sides of this space.

Above the tenth floor, four clerestory floors circled the atrium with slim, Deco-ized columns. Just above those was a cleaned and rejuvenated ceiling fresco.

The concierge provided a quick, curt summary. The Fairfax contained seven hundred guest rooms. Of these, sixty-six were suites.

These were distributed on thirty-six floors and had been assigned on a first-come-first-served basis to schools putting in their reservations last October. The topmost floor contained an athletic spa and two indoor pools.

Boaz, nodding, rubbed a knobby hand down a nearby marble column, and looked down.

The concierge, a bit tired, succumbed for a moment to her desire for sympathy. She lamented to Boaz that the tenth-floor parapet was so low. "It puts the hotel at considerable litigational risk," she observed, with a wringing of hands in the tone of her voice. She recalled that a ten-year-old boy had been seen walking along the seventh floor balustrade only a few months ago. She was waiting, she told Boaz, for advice from the hotel chain's legal office in New York about putting up some signs advising that the Fairfax cannot be responsible for any accidents.

"How about putting up some railing, instead?"

"Thirteen floors of railing? Can you imagine the expense? But of course, the hotel understands that it has some exposure in this matter." Boaz remained noncommittal. The concierge abandoned hope of finding understanding from a man of his class. Soon after, Boaz thanked her for her time and proceeded alone to the base room with a good deal on his mind.

Back at the registration desk, Ms. Carstairs-Norton (checking off items on her invisible Things to Do list) would now complete the entries for some new room arrangements. Among other things, she shuffled two distraught guests on the thirty-third floor—a honeymooning couple in 3323 who had seen a little too much of their neighbor, Susan Engleton, out on her gurney.

"Why anyone would go to an English convention for their honeymoon is beyond me," the concierge opined. "I never saw so many dweebs in my life." She touched two manicured fingers to her left temple.

For the nth time that day, Gerald received a snapped command. This time it was to send flowers and chocolates, along with an apologetic note for the inconvenience, to each of the Fairfax guests on that wing. It was terribly important that the Fairfax hold its own against the other hotels hosting this convention, particularly the Palmer House.

Ensconced now in 210A, Boaz reviewed the Wellesley statements collected by Malley and Hong. Halleran had spread out the schedules of workers' names and shifts across three card tables pushed together. Leaving Halleran bent over those tables, and Malley and Hong developing lists of follow-up questions, Boaz went to take his turn at interrogation.

It was a little before 3:00 P.M. The Wellesley people, Boaz thought, would probably be exhausted. The first shocks of death and examiners and police interrogations would be wearing off, leaving fatigue. Typically that would be followed by emotional tremulousness and uncertainty. They'd be vulnerable, then. Under repeated pressure, a lie, some previously prepared story, might reveal its clumsy stitching at the seams.

Along the hallways what Boaz was noticing now were more of the kinds of crowds he'd scanned earlier with the concierge: crowds in every wing, crowds in long lines for the public facilities, more crowds in the lobby and elevator areas.

And the women in these crowds, he noted: they hadn't been shopping at Water Tower Place. On the whole, their faces had a different kind of intentness, their bodies less confidence. As a group, they didn't remotely resemble the striding, arrogant women of wealth of Chicago (keen-eyed, coursing the Loop boulevards and long linkages of shops underground, women who in pagan times would have been devotees of the goddess of the hunt).

With some reluctance, Boaz had tried to learn to read clothes. That wasn't something always emphasized in the Violent Crimes Unit, but you were a better investigator if you could.

These women were hard to read. Some kinds of clothes were repeated in various groups. Boots under long skirts, for instance. And a prevalence of light-colored suits and dresses even though this was Chicago in the very bottom of winter. Oddest of all were the flat, gopher-colored, Birkenstock sandals worn by women in suits or under dresses that had jackets on top. It was as if the woman had suddenly given up all decision-making at the point of the knees.

As for the men: well . . .

Not for nothing had Boaz worked those years in Area Six, "the Hollywood division," notorious for the variety of its wacky crimes, and where the homicide cops were snappy dressers. Or sometimes were, at least. Boaz had come under the influence of that dashing style, but it was at odds with the Ozarkan training that had taught him to blend into the woods when you're hunting. He resolved this conflict with restrained, well-cut suits and a collection of splashy off-duty ties. At the moment his dark, flecked sport coat, his dark blue wool trousers, his blue button-down shirt, and silk windsor-striped tie blended into the surroundings well enough to please him.

In fact, he noticed, these teacher-guys in the halls looked a lot like what plainclothes cops always used to look like: polyester suits with white shirts, jacket sleeves too short, a rep tie with slanted stripes of blue or red.

Even the well-dressed men here managed to look alike. It had to do with the way they walked and stood around with the same mannerisms. He hadn't seen that much constant self-consciousness since he'd watched, one by one, a column of black ants cross the back-yard concrete when he was a kid.

Now and then one of them—they looked like maybe the arty types—tried to do the David Lynch look, with dark shirts buttoned at the throat and no tie. But they'd have on the wrong shoes. He saw one or two turtlenecks that didn't make sense. The men on the whole weren't easier to read than the women.

It was with a silent "Hunnh" that Boaz squeezed onto the elevator. "I have no gift to bring, pa-rump-a-pump-pump," said the elevator speaker.

What Boaz also heard, going up to the thirty-third floor again and again for days, was a certain lilting tone of voice. Convention women produced this sound when they were talking to men—

rarely when talking to another woman. By the end of the convention, he'd think to himself that if he heard it one more time he'd break out in a rash.

The woman's voice would go along normally until she got near the end of the sentence. Then there'd be this lilting lift that changed everything she'd said before into a question. All of a sudden she'd be tentative-sounding, as if she didn't *really* know a thing in the world—just a little dingbat. Sometimes she'd even say, brightly, "Am I making any sense?"

To which Boaz would grow increasingly inclined to tell her, "No, ma'am, not a speck of it."

Off the elevator, the occupants of the Gooch-Vaster rooms on the thirty-third floor provided no new revelations. They were remote with exhaustion. After listening for almost two more hours and hearing no important discrepancies in the four people's stories, Boaz left them all for the day and headed for the base room again.

Halleran was assembling more detail work, at the moment with Malley. Hong, checklist on his lap, was on the phone with United Airlines. Restless, Boaz proceeded down a flight of stairs to the lobby. He was looking for food, but he also wanted to mingle with the convention habitués. It was the overview he was after, a summary of these people. He did not like the feel of these inexplicable falls and illnesses among them.

3

Just inside the lobby, Boaz paused by the stairway door. Beyond a potted palm a male academic (it was Jonathan Kralleras, back downstairs again), evidently continuing a discussion begun earlier, inquired of a man standing beside him (it was Martin Snave), "How many lines do you have?"

"Thank God, just two," was the reply. "I hear Purdue's got nine."

Boaz, to whom the noun "lines" had several meanings, a couple of them criminal, had the uneasy feeling again that he and his partners were fishbowled in the Fairfax, inside some systematic and intricate world of its own, complete with its own language.

The good investigator, as he knew, is the detective with good sources of information, good informants. It worried him that these people hereabouts were not going to inform him of much. If the hotel events developed into a homicide investigation, which this Engleton thing was promising to do, he had to hope the player turned out to be somebody on the hotel staff. Staff he could talk to. Anybody else here, he'd be in some trouble. He was going to need someone who spoke this dialect, a kind of interpreter, to help him.

This was another problem with a certain novelty. What was known as "getting your street degree" or learning to "read the street" hadn't been that difficult for Boaz, raised in Uptown and having in his background various hawkeyed southern hunters and fishermen, not to mention hawkeyed southern women. No one ever finished street school completely, of course, as he was aware. As soon as you thought you had, your body was likely to be found with a peculiar new hole in it. Still, he was as fluent in that particular language as anyone.

There had been, he recalled, that case at a Madison Street construction site two years ago, when his teenage experience on summer jobs had stood him in good stead. Questioning sub-contractors and design engineers, with their casual references to laydown areas, to ductbank and conduit installations, blowers and rotometers and submersible propeller pumps, then their descriptions of the headache ball, the socket orientation of a crane arm, and a body in a manbasket—all those had been less opaque to him than what he was hearing here. His two years at Illinois would give him a starting point, but . . .

"Polyvocal narrativities," someone asserted with vigorous head-nodding to her companion in the TV area of the lobby. Not far from her, someone "deployed" something about "representativity and alterity."

This, he thought, was sort of like the noise of constantly moving, constantly flapping birds (the image of his second cousin's four-story chicken house came to mind)—these people whose dialect was as specific (and, he suspected, as much about power) as is the language of all poultry.

Boaz crossed the busy atrium. Down the north concourse, which extended behind the registration desk, two restaurant-cum-cocktail-lounges confronted each other rebarbatively. Hoping for food, Boaz glanced into both. One, the Chez Toi, relied usually on power lunches conducted by upscale businessmen—men who expected, evidently, large chunks of maroon, pink, and gray décor under nouveau-Holophane fixtures. Other than the fact that it could not sell coffee at any price today, let alone for the usual three dollars per cup, Chez Toi was doing a crowded late-afternoon business.

Opposite, in contrast, the Perfect Square offered aggressively stripped sophistication. A tall, square, gunmetal bar suggesting the shoulders of a great robot stood in the center of a large square room of silver-gray. The room was dotted with round metal tables with gunmetal piers and, beside them, square-backed brown leather chairs having rounded seats and more gunmetal legs.

The surroundings departed from modern cliché only by being consistently geometrical down to the last details: the silver-on-brown wallpaper included little compasses, various angle measurements, and locus-of-points diagrams of cones and tesseracts. A right triangle, c^2 along its hypotenuse, demurely graced the elegantly brown bar napkins. All these designs were small enough to remain overwhelmed by richer backgrounds. They would not, then, intimidate the business-minded or the English-business-minded visitants of such a hotel, to whom the dark beauties of geometry remained a darkness indeed, and among whom the name of Euclid was known only to crossword enthusiasts.

From the door of the Perfect Square, Boaz could see near the bar a group of half a dozen men in self-aware poses, standing close to the figure of an imposing blonde woman in her mid-thirties. In here, before the 5:15 P.M. opening of the Marxist and other cash bars, the representatives of various fashionable academic creeds gathered to drink either white wine or the butch, "in" beer of the moment. Potential male and female partners in the room were being appraised, of course, but by wearers of what was, evidently, the *echt* costume for any and all sexual persuasions among the men: blue jeans, white T-shirts, genuine leather jackets, expensive running shoes, and an impressive single earring, usually in the pierced right ear.

Although this establishment was specifically the hangout of the Marxist-materialists (groups of whom at several tables were now making up in advance for the weak drinks that would be poured at their cash bar), the cluster of six men by the bar, a group egregiously gay, was intent upon the extremely tall, extremely pretty-faced, and extremely pear-shaped Joan Mellish, an academic fashion unto herself. From her upraised elbow, which formed a right triangle with her head, hung a large charm bracelet from which dangled a long gold diaper pin. At that elbow leaned her inseparable and very thin companion, Jason Keggo. From the perspective of the doorway, he looked something like a straight line tangential to an inverse-napiform oblate spheroid.

Boaz sighed. More noise.

Some distance behind him in the lobby, a certain Nancy Cook also sighed, but for a different set of reasons. Assistant Professor Cook, thirty-one and a dark-streaked blonde, had felt unnerved and baffled all afternoon by these weird deaths in the hotel. They'd given her a recurring mortality *frisson*. Something about the proximity of death had made her feel stymied, too, as if the life she did have left were going nowhere.

That notion for her was a product unique to this convention. But Nancy was also bored and frazzled, and those are typical MLA modes of feelings.

MLA is hectic. Even if you're not caught up in the interviewing mills, it is difficult, day after day, to arrange even half-hour meetings with friends and colleagues. "Let's have dinner Thursday night at the hotel" is an optimistic proposal that must be scheduled well in advance. Everyone's day is condensed, overworked, and subject to last-minute schedule explosion.

It is a law, then, of MLA (Cook's Law, Nancy thought) that you're sure to run across someone you never want to see in your life again. That was the one you'd see three or four times, in every elevator, whereas the face of a good pal would be hard to find.

The pal she particularly wanted to connect with was poor Annette Lisordi, old friend from Providence and now here from Emory. It had been around ten o'clock that morning when Nancy had heard a rumor that an accident had happened in the Wellesley suite and that "all kinds of bodies" were being taken out of the room. Appalled, she'd dashed to the lobby to learn the suite number, then flown to the thirty-third floor to look for her friend.

Annette was just being released from questioning when Nancy arrived. Professor Cook had shepherded the stunned woman ("Oh, Nancy!") off to her own room for half an hour but hadn't been able to talk with her since.

Oddly, something about all these events had increased Nancy Cook's worry about an undergraduate student of hers at Yale. A brainy, original young woman from Montana who'd written for her a description of the aurora borealis forming a Maltese cross that touched all four horizons of the Montana night—this vivid freshman was floundering. Whether from "culture shock"—whatever that might be, considering the non-culture of New Haven, Nancy thought—or from unguessable personal restructurings was hard to know.

It was trying for this young teacher, how limited her resources were for this problem. Her attempts to arrange a meeting in Linsley-Chittenden Hall with her student's other Yale professors had fallen through. They weren't interested. Professor Cook had all but decided simply to give away the highest possible grade, if that could rescue her student's grade-point average and keep the woman in school.

What with these multiple issues moving their gears, Nancy Cook was considering a phone call to Mark Reese back in New Haven. But their relationship, after two years, was fast becoming a past-tense event. Worn down by Mark's vacillations between importunity and then robust indifference, Nancy had decided, grimly and sadly, that he was not what the doctor ordered, not Doctor Cook. Still, she could call him up and have a few complicated moments, and maybe he'd make her feel better. She wanted to talk.

All in all, Nancy Cook was a puddingstone of low-level irritations and lonesomeness. In no mood, then, for tableaux, she had backed away a few moments before from the silvered room of the Perfect Square.

Partway across the lobby, however, looking back around, she noticed an old ally from Providence, Professor Jack Fullerton, standing at the door of that same bar. Relieved—good old Jack!— she moved up behind him.

"Oh, you don't want to drink in there," Nancy said to the man's back. "Not without your white T-shirt. Do you have on your very best white T-shirt?"

Boaz turned. Nancy was still prattling away: "No, I see that you don't. Fashion error."

Boaz looked down onto a five-foot-seven, brown-eyed blonde who was smiling amiably up at him. Then he saw her blink.

This was not, Nancy realized, Professor Fullerton. Wasn't this man the policeman she'd seen for a second at the Wellesley door? (Standing in the 3321 doorway, a tall man with brown eyes and slicked-back hair had caught and held her eyes speculatively for a moment, then stepped aside to let Annette pass into the hall.) Yes, it was the same man, and still looking at her speculatively.

"Oh, I'm sorry, excuse me." Nancy laughed briefly at herself and made a gesture of what-can-I-do-with-myself that invited him to laugh at her if he cared to. "I thought you were someone else. Sorry."

Boaz had a number of things on his mind. He was about to make the usual social murmurs and move on, when he had a sudden thought. Wasn't this the woman who'd met Annette Lisordi in the hall?

She was striking, this blonde, with her good figure and long curly hair that lifted around her face to heights that suggested good-humored wildness. And you don't often see really brown-eyed blondes. From the general look of her, she was in the category of Possible Professor.

Only "possible" professor, because she wasn't wearing a name tag and because her outfit wasn't loud or dowdy: no huge sprig of red and green holly on the lapel of a green and red suit. This woman had on a very dark gray dress. Over that, some kind of wide-shouldered, olive-green jacket, long. Big gray purse. (Details he didn't exactly identify included the fact that the dress was knit, the jacket gabardine from the late 1940s, and the pumps deep olive.) The woman's earrings, three inches long, were wispy gold metal shapes, vaguely sculptural. Very nice.

"Are you checked into this hotel, ma'am?" he asked brusquely. "You a member of this convention?"

Taken aback a little, Nancy Cook replied in the affirmative.

"And you're a professor?"

34   Nancy did not answer. She looked at him.

Boaz produced the requisites. "I'm a police officer, ma'am. An investigator. And if you're a part of this convention, I wonder if you'd mind answering a few questions for me? If you have the time."

He was, as almost always, very polite when presenting the star. To his surprise, the woman actually looked at his badge number and checked his ID photograph against the face in front of her. It was an unapologetic, quick assessment, followed by a friendly, if slightly brisk, professionalism.

"I *do* have some time. I'm an *assistant* professor, though." Then seeing his confusion at the distinction, which is made only in the academy, she added, "I'm a *new* professor. Cook. Nancy Cook. I don't have my name tag on. By the way, am I under arrest?"

"No, ma'am, no. I'd just like to get some information about this convention if I could. But if you have, oh, maybe a driver's license I could see for just a second?"

The license photo, of course, was a grotesque caricature—as always, as if required by law. Making Nancy look brunette instead of blonde, the photo held no hint of her vivacity. What was simply her poise had been deftly transformed into sullen hunkering.

"I know," she said, "it looks like a mug shot. Like I've been hanging out with Johnny Dillinger. Actually, though, I just teach English."

Boaz nodded, with a slight twitch at his mouth. He'd never met a woman yet who didn't feel put out about her driver's license photo. Too, like most Chicagoans, he approved of women with moxie, liked the way they talked.

Behind them people were milling in the concourse noisily. Boaz suggested "a cup of coffee, maybe?" and looked around. "Not in here," he said, indicating the Perfect Square. "Looks like what they serve in here is mostly bullets. Across the way?"

But the Chez Toi was also very noisy, with a waiting period now of twenty minutes. Finally they set out for Slade's, a little-frequented coffee shop at the far end of the north concourse. It was one of those unexpected, leftover Chicago eateries of long 35 ago that can still be found here and there in the Loop. It lacked the slightest bit of ego-flattering cachet.

Comfortably dirty stools stood at a chrome-edged counter, with a short stack of booths along one wall. No concessions had yet been made to the possible existence of nonsmokers. Brownish nicotine deposits lay so thick on the walls by the counter area that one of the regulars referred to the place as "The Suede Room."

Leaving Nancy in a booth for a moment, Boaz made a reconnoitering call to Halleran from a pay phone in one corner. Halleran and Malley were still comparing pieces of the Wellesley information. Mainly they were waiting for preliminary lab results about the coffee, findings that might get called over from the morgue tonight. Both investigations were more or less halted now, pending Forensic Institute contributions.

Back at the booth, there was a sudden new awkwardness, something Nancy found interesting in itself. (This definitely beats going to the president's address, she told herself.) For his part, Boaz wasn't sure this was a great idea, but there wasn't much to lose. Their coffee arrived in sturdy, chipped white mugs on small white saucers.

"Well, like I said, I think I need some information, Professor Cook. Because I expect I'll be looking into some things here for a while."

"All right." Nancy's brown eyes were alert, but at no point had she seemed very surprised, Boaz noted. Her coming over to him in the hallway—was this a setup?

Boaz pressed his sport-coated shoulders against the booth and quickly memorized this woman. Regular features, straight forehead. Heavy straight brown eyebrows. Those and the brown eyelashes and brown eyes were a little surprising since all that streaked curly hair was clearly blonde. Nice skin, a nose very pointed, a chin just a shade too short, considering the wideness of her mouth. The mouth was interestingly squared at the corners. A couple of moles on her left jawline. Her eyes were very warm, but changeable. Evidently, pretty much her own woman.

Her figure, he'd noticed, had the economy of line you see over in the preppy regions of north Chicago, say over at the Latin School. It was a body that suggested New England somehow— maybe a New England reticence.

(Nancy, in fact, was a woman who, like many academic women, had looks notable enough to excite the energies of make-over artists behind counters in department stores. They saw, in Nancy especially, a beauty *in potentia,* if only she'd put on some Mulberry Crush eyeshadow and get rid of that preoccupied air.)

Shifting again in his coat—a new habit acquired since the belt clip of his short-barreled magnum had begun to scrape his spine— Boaz tapped his coffee mug with his knobby right hand.

("These hands are gonna look like chicken feet one of these days," he had mused to his wife, now ex-wife, one morning. "My dad's and my mother's both did." His wife, with whom there'd been no physical events that morning, had continued dressing and made no remark. It was a moment that told him something. He had gone on to have a bloody and terrible day which, when he came home, he did not tell her about.)

More of Boaz's Missourian twang was in evidence now, as was a slightly puzzled tone. "It might not be *information,* exactly, that I'm lookin' for, but I don't know yet. First I gotta find out if I need it. This convention . . ."

Boaz gave up for now the attempt to be general. "For starters: what does it mean if somebody says, 'How many lines have you got?' Some guy in the lobby is talking to another guy, they both look like teachers, and one guy says, 'How many lines have you got?'"

"Oh. Sure," Nancy said promptly. "That just means, 'How many positions are you interviewing for at your school?' It was shop talk, what you heard. A 'line' is a job opening. It could be for a tenured position or for somebody at the junior level, either one."

"Hunnh. OK. Thank you. Well—I wish you'd tell me what some other things mean here, too." Boaz paused again.

Nancy, meanwhile, had just figured something out. Hoagy Car- 37 michael, that was it. This man looked like a craggy version of Hoagy Carmichael—of whom, incidentally, she was a fan. He did not look at all like crewcutted, blond Mark Reese.

"I guess what I want to know is," Boaz said, "who exactly *are* all these people? I mean, what was it made you all decide to have a convention this year? What's goin' on?"

"*This* year? Oh no, there's an MLA convention *every* year. In fact, I think this is the 108th MLA."

Boaz remained unenlightened, and looked it. At this point, Nancy Cook, who was not surprised at being approached with questions and who was an excellent teacher—which is to say, adroit in her ability to guess the location of her students' confusion, to sense the context that might have prompted a question— Professor Cook hazarded a shaping question of her own.

"I gather—is this right?—that maybe what you need, Mr. Nixon . . ."

"*Dixon,*" Boaz interjected. "Boaz Dixon." He waited a beat, for the usual response. He was used to people's raised eyebrows and incredulous "Boaz?"—followed by some less-than-hilarious question about Ruth.

But Nancy was a teacher, with a volunteer background. What with high schools and community colleges, she had roll-called, by the age of thirty-one, everything from Jenny Clinkpenny to Morning Waters to Clitoris Brown.

"Yes, I thought I saw that on your photo," she said, "but—I'm sorry—I misread your last name."

Boaz pursed his mouth a little. She had disarmed him a bit.

"By the way, are you a native of Chicago?" she interjected out of nowhere. Knowing a little about him, she told herself, she might be able to guess what he needed. (But that wasn't why she'd asked him, not really. Mark Reese absolutely hated a sudden swerve of conversation into the personal.)

Boaz, trained to give a lot of conversational rope, answered, "Yes and no. Three-quarters native, I guess." And after another moment's effort to read the blank page of this woman, he decided

to elaborate on his background.

The Dixons had come from central and southern Missouri, where multiple cousins and step-uncles and one of his brothers still lived. He'd spent almost every summer of his childhood with relatives in two or three small towns in the Missouri Ozarks. Many a Greyhound bus he'd ridden in early June, alone or with his older siblings, Belle and Zeph, down to Rolla, there to spend early mornings in the limestone caves and shallow streams and oak forests that lie mostly out of sight, invisible from the plateaus of U.S. 44.

"I don't know if you're familiar with the way a small town can go right on, inside a big city?" Boaz's left hand smoothed his hair back above his large left ear.

"Well, my mother maintained the little town of Jane, Missouri, right inside a pretty tough area of Chicago. Had all her kids here in the city. But she was—well, you could say she was an *enthusiast* for religion. Various Baptist types of churches. So she named her boys out of the Bible. Came up with Micah and Boaz and Zephaniah. The girls got off, I don't know why. Lynette and Belle. Didn't make the two of them any less peculiar, though."

Boaz's mouth had pursed a little. He invariably spoke of his family with amused and exasperated affection.

What Boaz's maternal parent had also done (though he did not go into this) was give all her children not her religion but a distaste for pointless swearing, as well as a self-possession that is part of the riches of southern courtesy. These had made Boaz the butt of savage jeering some years ago, when he was a beat cop in Area Six. Another patrolman, Terry Riley, had insisted for months on calling him "Mr. Manners," along with other implications. He had done so loudly, in public places.

This had resulted in a wonderful off-duty fight one night that was still remembered in a couple of the district stations of Area Six. A dozen cops showed up to watch it. Three or four of them had heard Boaz slam his helmet on Riley's table that noon at the Billy Goat Tavern, under Wacker Drive.

Boaz had ended his remarks to Riley by mentioning a certain parking lot behind a certain bar on the near West Side. "Five o'clock. Anything lookin' like you shows up in that parkin' lot, I'm gonna take that rotten son of a bitch and I'm gonna spread him in a thin film."

Riley was bulky, strong, and experienced. So the dismantling of Riley had taken a satisfyingly long time. He failed to make roll call for two days, then missed more time to go get his stitches removed.

"Anyhow, that's the story of the name," Boaz concluded. He was not talking for nothing. Halleran got people to talk by looking like Halleran. Boaz got people to talk by doing some talking first and watching all responses. He continued, stirring his coffee.

"I thought for a while I'd change that name soon as I could. But nobody ever did in the family, except my big sister, Belle. She took a notion she liked the name Dixie. I said to her, 'You are actually gonna go out of your way to change your name to Dixie Dixon?' And I accused her of losing something important, like her mind. But she went off and did it, anyway."

Boaz smiled a little at the professor who'd lifted her cup with a laugh. Nancy had been digging casually through her big shoulder bag—a gray-leather, brass-grommeted item—to pull out a pen.

"Well, 'Nancy Cook' doesn't offer much I can tell anyone about," she said, doodling on her napkin. "Not even the elegance of an *e* at the end of 'Cook.' And I'm afraid the only local color my background has is white. It's dull, but there you are: white clapboard houses and white, white people."

She'd grown up in Deerfield, Massachusetts, in a house that looked a lot, she said, like the house in *The Trouble with Harry*.

"You like Hitchcock, I take it?" Boaz asked, having taken into custody once a man who'd replicated a murder in *Frenzy*.

"Oh, sure." Her family's house had been in a small, personable, New England crossroads community not very different from Hitchcock's pastel town. Then she'd lived in Providence while going to Brown. No siblings, both parents still alive.

(It was a background Nancy had worked very hard to get away from, though she didn't fool herself into thinking she'd moved very far. Airless conformity remained anathema to her. Throughout her late girlhood and adolescence, she'd looked at her mother's life and been afraid.)

Nancy was working now as an assistant professor at Yale, without tenure. It was her first job since taking her doctorate at Princeton. Boaz, blessedly unfamiliar with the arch, affected Princetonian air that can seem so often like an adhesive membrane over the lives of its graduates, did not know that Nancy lacked that air.

What he learned from his questions instead was this: Nancy had been teaching at Yale for three semesters, with three to go. A temporary appointment. It wasn't just Yale, she explained, but also Stanford, Harvard, lots of schools, even small colleges like Wheaton or Kenyon, that will use young teachers for just a one-to-four-year stint.

"After that, it's discard time. Unless you're at some little place where your contract might get renewed, the temporary job's over, and you're out. They believe this method saves them money. They get good teachers, and they can just fire the old group after a few years and hire another set." For the first time, Nancy's tone was edged with sarcasm and something like weariness, too.

"It's a throw of the dice with this kind of job," she noted. "You make a gamble. And it's not as if I didn't know what to expect. What you hope is that you won't turn into a little academic Kelly Girl. You hope the school's name will look good on your résumé later. You hope you can get a book written fast enough that you can get another job. You try to counter-manipulate the fact of your being manipulated, I guess." She smiled, her brown eyes direct.

Part of Nancy's tone was bravado, an attempt at self-reassurance. Soon enough, she knew, she'd be on the mean streets of MLA, very probably at the convention next year. Boaz gathered that part of her reason for coming this year was to look over the scene.

Meanwhile, Nancy continued doodling on her napkin, an inveterate habit. Her fingers, blunt-nailed like a child's, were nevertheless long and sophisticated. The sideways tilt of her head while doodling could also look naive, belied by intelligent preoccupation in her face.

Looking up at him at an angle and pushing back a wad of curly hair, Nancy asked him lightly (it was a teacher's effort again to define the parameters) whether it was the accidents in the hotel that he was investigating. She'd been to two MLAs so far and "this is the first time there've been any deaths I've heard about. Just the law of averages catching up with the convention?" Her face was guileless.

Boaz didn't answer. His face didn't change, but her inquiry bothered him. No one in the citizenry asks a cop what that cop is doing. The people who want to know are generally people who already know. With upright citizens, a cop comes up to one of them, what he gets is hostility. Boaz was used to that; it made sense. Somebody coming over and talking to a cop, though . . .

Besides: why was she talking so personally? Was she hunting for information? Was he going to get a come-on soon, part of a little game with the police? Were she and Lisordi up to something? How long had Nancy Cook been waiting on the thirty-third floor, and why?

Boaz had observed that this woman's scrawling sometimes included the repeated letters BCV. A lover's initials? Anything else? To encourage monologue, he did not reply.

Mark Reese sometimes didn't answer questions either, Nancy recalled.

"Anyway," she concluded, "I'm sort of thinking about other things to do if I can't get another teaching job. Maybe I'll join the circus. *Another* circus."

Interlacing her fingers around her cup, Nancy added, "I'd like to do something different, maybe. I warn my classes about turning into cut-paper dolls. Just living out stereotypes. Most of them don't know what I'm talking about, but they might eventually. Of course, the worst was Princeton. Killer school."

"Princeton, New Jersey? Saw a picture of that place once." Boaz shifted in his jacket. "Looked like nothin' but coffee houses and dog shops."

Nancy assented with a short laugh.

"A Lake Forest kind of place," Boaz went on. "Not a pinch of dust, even on the fence around the train station. No pigeons, either, but you never see the exterminator. Squeaky clean. Not too much in the way of violent activity there, I imagine."

"Not the visible, physical kind, no. Just the occasional soul murder—of babies of a very advanced age."

"You didn't like it there."

"No."

Boaz, like all cops, was used to being lied to. He expected it. Candor, therefore (and he had to admit this did sound like candor), interested him. He always wondered when—not really whether, but when—it was going to slither off and turn into a lie.

Sitting up straight in the booth, Professor Cook decided to bring this divagating conversation into line. It had been a relief to chat, but it was time to get back to the invisible syllabus, whatever that was.

"I gather now—is this right?—that what you're looking for is something like 'An Introduction to the MLA'?"

"Yes, ma'am, that is indeed what I need," Boaz said firmly.

Nancy thought a moment. This man very likely didn't know a thing about MLA. Who would? A four-day convention of research chemists would be news; the Chicago papers would cover it daily. Ditto for R&D people or origami enthusiasts. But a convention of English teachers? It would arrive on little cat feet and then silently move on.

"OK," she said, putting her fingertips together and marshalling her thoughts, "an orientation course."

Boaz then learned that the Fairfax was the main hotel of the convention for the English departments, the "main hotel" having a bulletin board with computer lists in its lobby, the largest number of registrants, and the president's address and organizational meetings within its domain.

"But," Nancy cautioned, "MLA sessions will be over at the Hyatt, too, at the same time. And people are in lots of hotels. But is this useful at all, is it news?"

Boaz nodded. "What are the other hotels?"

He was jotting notes in a small notebook. (Like all people with excellent memories, he took a lot of notes.) He'd returned to the working position of taking this woman at face value.

"Oh, let me think. There's the Palmer House, and the Swissotel, and the Westin. You could find out all of them at the registration desk."

"But all the hotels are in the Loop?"

"Well, I don't know exactly where the Loop ends. The hotels are all close together, though. They have to be. Because—well, say you've got an interview at one hotel. If you've got another interview, chances are good it will be in a different hotel an hour later. So you run out and get the shuttle bus or a cab. And maybe you run over to *another* hotel an hour after that."

"Well, *maybe* I'd be doin' that, if I could think of a *real* good reason. Why would I be running around to these 'interviews'?"

Nancy smiled at him. Her teeth were individually squared off, like the squaring at the corners of her mouth. Not unattractive, not beautiful, but interesting.

"To get a job, any job, maybe even the job you really want," she told him. "How to summarize this . . ."

With her back against the booth, Nancy could have been before her blackboard. The expression in her eyes shifted readily from warmth and openness to something that was more self-contained and appraising. She was all organization now.

"Overall, think of MLA as having just a few functions."

Boaz was now apprised that a major function of MLA is to provide a site for job interviews for universities and colleges throughout the U.S. And that the way you experience that function depends on which side of the interview you're sitting, as interviewer or candidate.

"The other function is to present the panels. A panel is where some short papers are read about, oh, ghosts in nineteenth-century poetry, or—well, all kinds of things. They're held at the Fairfax or the Hyatt, in the big conference rooms.

"And the panel schedule is absolutely jammed: this year MLA has—I think it's 650 panels, all packed into four days. That's why you'll see people pouring in and out of the conference rooms all day."

Boaz cocked his sleek head to one side. His attention seemed not to have faded. He never interrupted. In fact, Nancy noticed, whether talking or quiet, this man never opened his mouth very far. (Mark Reese, you saw a lot of teeth all the time.)

Nancy's observation was correct. What with two slightly overlapping front teeth and some crooked lower teeth as well, Boaz had long ago acquired the closed-mouth habit.

Crooked teeth, of course, are a great asset to a young man. They're seldom appreciated as such; Boaz had never appreciated them. Such dentition, however, can and often does prevent the growth of bloated male egotisms. They promote the effort in a man to become attractive in other ways, in patience maybe, or in conversational dexterity, including the ability to listen.

Now, with Boaz in early middle age, the teeth had done all they could for him. Nancy found herself now, as many people had, able to hold forth in front of as absorbed a listener as she would ever talk to.

Nancy explained now that a long-standing precedent of MLA had been broken this year. Because the Fairfax (in an effort to one-up the competing hotels) had offered extremely low post-Christmas rates, some schools had opted to one-up their competition for candidates by holding interviews a day early. Hence the early arrival of the Wellesley committee, for instance.

"I don't imagine they think that was such a good idea now," Nancy noted. Boaz watched her narrowly.

"Anyway, the whole thing is *officially* just getting started now," Nancy went on. "The first panels are scheduled later tonight. There was a 'preconvention workshop' at 1:30 P.M. Frankly, I've never understood what that is. And at 4:30"—Nancy glanced at her watch—"she should just be finishing, in fact: the president's address, by Josephine Horgan. I hear she moved her speech a full day earlier because of all the upset in the hotel."

(Coterminously, as it happened, with Nancy's remark, Professor Horgan in the Grand Ballroom was indeed acknowledging, in stentorian tones, "While it is true that two terrible accidents *have* occurred"—and her arms suddenly burst away from her body in inexplicable and characteristic waving motions—"it is my hope that we will all carry on with the spirit of professionalism that is a mark of the greatness of the academy," et cetera.)

"So," Nancy said, pushing back another hank of unruly blonde hair, "that's pretty much what all these people are up to, hiring and paneling. Unless you count 'networking' and social climbing. Consider those a sort of third function." Her voice had a clear mockery.

"OK," Boaz said. "So I can assume that everybody I set eyes on around here is an English teacher?"

"Yes. Well, no, not quite. Language teachers and comparative literature people have their interviews here, too. I gather there's some horrible huge hall over at the Marriott where the candidates have to get interviewed at little tables, like at a flea market. And your competition for the same job is standing in line right behind you."

At the Fairfax, Boaz now learned, the big ballrooms had been set aside for large meetings or displays such as the Book Exhibition. Some smaller halls were rented as cash bars by a few of the schools.

"If you go to a cash bar, that's where your interview continues, in an unofficial way. But I'd better start at the beginning about this interviewing stuff."

Nancy paused for coffee reinforcements from the waitress, a lanky, galumphing woman without animosity or pretension, whose seriousness was appealing. Boaz glanced around the room, as he'd done a time or two before, giving it a rapid checkout—a very old, ingrained habit.

"Let's say," Nancy proceeded, "for the sake of example, let's say you're in graduate school somewhere." Nancy's eyes narrowed at him. "Where should that be? Let's say—oh, Stanford."

In a testing way, Nancy was edging near the subject of class, the most sensitive sore on the American corpus. Mark Reese was always protective of the acknowledgment of his class.

Boaz shifted in his jacket, his mouth pursed. His brown eyes were amused. "Well, all right. I did have my heart set on Advanced Dancing School, but all right. Stanford."

There was such a sudden warmth in Nancy's smile at him that the cop ignored for a moment that part of his mind reminding him to check back with the base room soon.

"So let's say you've put in six years of graduate study after college," Nancy invited him. "It's early September and you're getting ready to go on the market."

"Go on the market?"

"That's what they call it. 'Going on the market.' Picturesque, isn't it? Brings to mind a cattle drive or something."

Nancy explained then that in a certain autumn of life, a graduate student sends out upwards of fifty letters of application to schools advertising for a teacher in his or her "field."

"A field might be Victorian novels or medieval literature or feminist theory"—Nancy's parallel hands defined a small sandwich of space—"usually some little region of prose or poetry."

"What's your field?" Boaz immediately inquired.

"Modernism. But let's say your field is—oh, Americanist stuff: nineteenth-century novels. Emphasis on Mark Twain.

"Well," she continued, "you don't just jump in your car and come to MLA and have a Mark Twain party. It's all by special invitation. First, if some school were interested in you, then they'd have asked you for a 'writing sample.' That little document is probably a chapter from your Ph.D. dissertation. It's definitely something you've sweated blood over. You try to get it polished to a high shine."

Boaz smiled. He had the southerner's ear and love for all tropes.

Nancy, ticking more items off her fingers, explained that the writing sample, along with a dossier with letters of recommendation, "all telling the schools that you're the greatest thing in Western culture since Saint Paul"—all that gets mailed out by the clenched, hopeful candidate in the fall.

"This is very boring for normal people, I know," Nancy smiled. The skin just under her dark brows was very delicate.

"But for you as a job hunter from Stanford, it's not so boring. Unless you get bored by insomnia and anxiety that have gone on

for about a year before you even get to the convention. Where you get to have some moments of really *big* panic. Even as a star student."

"Were you a star?"

"Yes, I guess so. Sort of. I had a lot of interviews. But then I got just one job offer."

Nancy summarized that, at last, if some school's hiring committee agrees to interview you (and the debate over you at their school might be a nasty one, with power struggles in the department being bitterly thrashed out)—then you'll be invited to meet the committee in a hotel room for about forty-five minutes during one of the four days of MLA.

"On that one interview hangs everything. Really, your whole future career. So, of course, life plays a joke on you. You can be sure that there'll be something going on among the people on the committee. Competition about turf, maybe; or an affair between two of the committee members; or somebody's got the flu. Some agenda you can't guess: Professor X hates blue shirts and you've got a blue shirt on. Sometimes you find out about it later through the grapevine."

Nancy straightened the left sleeve of her gray knit dress. "I found out later that there'd been a love triangle going on at my Dartmouth interview. Husband, wife, and girlfriend, all in one department and all on my committee. Whatever candidate one woman voted for, the other woman would vote against. Great, huh? Dartmouth didn't hire many people that year."

"Who thought up this system?" Boaz frowned.

"Beats me," Nancy smiled. "But anyway," she said briskly, "for the grad student, it's over then and you just wait. If a school really liked you, they might contact you again at the convention. But more likely the school calls you when you're back home, maybe a week or a month after the convention.

"Needless to say, that's an interesting month for you. You notice how high your phone bill is for giving you so few calls. I finally couldn't stand it. I bought an answering machine and I just stayed in the library."

Nancy looked warmly over at Boaz, his long arms at ease on the 49 table top. It was easier to think of him relaxed on a piano stool in a smoky room than tense on a sofa in an interview.

"Well, that pretty much introduces you to The World According to the Grad Student of English. Or part of that world, anyway. There's more—about power."

Nancy opened both hands in a casually inviting gesture. "Questions so far?"

"Hunnh." Boaz's bony face was a study in neutrality. Who was this woman with the sort-of-sarcastic talk, now bringing up "power"? How discontented was she? He believed her descriptions—these folks sounded like human beings, all right—but who else was she? He flipped over a fresh page and flagged it; pretty soon, her alibi information would go there.

"Well, I'm obliged to you, uh, Professor Cook." Boaz, like most cops, tended to use people's first names, in deliberate over-familiarity. That aggravated people and could be an effective move during questioning. But not, he thought, here and now.

"'Nancy,' if you like," she said. "It's shorter."

"All right. Nancy. Thank you. And I'm obliged to you for your time. I'd like to hear whatever else you can tell me. If you're still free—?"

Boaz glanced at his watch. 6:16 P.M. "I've got a call to make, but then I'd be pleased to get us some supper. If you've got a mind to eat?"

Nancy glanced at her watch, too. "Sure, let's eat."

It was puzzling to her, pleasantly, that her companion let her talk and opine without male vanity rushing in, waving its frantic arms. Who was this guy?

Boaz, having checked in again with the base room, where nothing had been heard yet from the lab, slid back into the booth in a smooth single motion. Nancy smiled toward their ectomorphic, no-nonsense waitress who was approaching their table with fresh determination.

"You wanta order dinner now," the woman inquired, posing all interrogatory sentences in firmly declarative mode, Chicago-style.

50   Boaz reached for the plastic-covered menus, suspiciously slick,

behind the sugar dispenser. But Nancy had an intuition about the fried pork chops special with white gravy and biscuits, chalked up on a board by the cash register. It included cherry pie.

Nodding, Boaz held up a couple of fingers toward the waitress and firmly said, "Two." Soon the woman returned to slam down paper napkins wrapped around ancient flatware. The long afternoon was over.

It would not have surprised Nancy, nor any other MLA veteran (nor, at this point, would it have surprised the student of MLA, Boaz Dixon), to learn that Annette Lisordi, who'd knocked at the Wellesley suite at 8:30 A.M., had continued to have a dismal morning at the convention.

Lisordi, dark-curled, stocky, and twenty-nine, had been questioned by cops in Engleton's private bedroom until almost 10:00. Once, with a start, she'd asked if she could use the phone. Contacting Purdue University, she'd explained her circumstances and asked to reschedule her 11:00 A.M. appointment time. The Purdue committee had coldly reassigned her time slot to 11:30 A.M. and warned her to be on time. Annette had had time only for a brief venting of emotion with her friend Nancy, over chilled fruit juice in Nancy's room, before heading once more into the fray.

On time she was at the Purdue suite, if a bit annoyed by their callousness. What she discovered was a committee of five, one of whom, Brent Bunt, was the newly tenured and swaggering factotum.

All that morning, Bunt had been overriding other committee members' remarks and questions to various candidates. Relying unconsciously on the polite reluctance of his midwestern colleagues to make scenes or start arguments, the insensible Bunt conducted all interviews in his own manner. He'd been the one to reschedule the Lisordi appointment.

He now motioned her to a single chair facing the pillows of the bed. Other members of the department—Professors Dunst, Bugg, Waterman, and Wheeling—continued to sit or stand quietly around the walls. Bunt stayed where he had been when Annette entered the room: reclining on the bed, his head propped on two pillows, his legs spread-eagled but occasionally in motion on the spread.

Annette close in front of him, Bunt proceeded to pose a few languidly aggressive questions about other approaches she might have taken with the seventeenth-century subject matter of her dissertation. Ms. Lisordi, forced to address the Bunt face by way of the Bunt crotch, became, to her own secret astonishment, professionally enraged. She watched herself uncross her arms and assume a posture of extreme relaxation, including looking for a moment at her fingernails.

She then informed Professor Bunt that his observations on what she *might* have written were surely irrelevant, and his questions were "in any case not very interesting." Sharp uneasiness then registered itself among the vertical committee members, since this candidate was one they'd wanted very much to woo. Even so, they did not intervene.

Annette Lisordi's Purdue interview would join, among many others, the invisible annals of MLA Nightmare Interviews, of which every member of every English department in the United States can recount at least one.

There was the experience, for instance, of Anne Erlich, from Syracuse, one of whose three interviews had been for a position at a Baptist school in North Carolina. There had been another woman in the room, but that dim creature had scarcely spoken and had taken up what evidently was a familiar posture, sitting in silence with her hands in her lap.

Professor Nelson, the middle-aged interviewer and only other person in the room, had pushed some questions toward Ms. Erlich with little movements of his head, but what had most preoccupied him was the picking of his nose. At no time during the brief interview did his left index finger leave the interior of his left nostril. He twisted it and talked under it, and was so busy with it that he did not stand up when the interview concluded. However, to be fair to him, it must be added that he did not display to her the results of his narine investigations.

Then there was Mark Mayer, from Washington University in St.

Louis. While he stood waiting in a side bedroom for his 1:00 P.M. interview with a group from George Mason, a female professor had called out to him—it was a peremptory tone from the living room—saying please pick up her baby. There in his room an infant a few months old had started fussing in the middle of the bed.

Eager to oblige, Mr. Mayer had lifted the infant to his suited shoulder and patted its back. Whereupon, of course, the baby's milky contents had distributed themselves down and over Mark Mayer's arm. He received a hurried apology from the mother, but no offer to have his jacket cleaned—Mr. Mayer, who owned no other good suit and who had an interview with Harvard in an hour.

And there is always, at any MLA, at least one grad student who suffers from acute acrophobia. Invariably, this person has an interview schedule so clustered at one-hour intervals that he or she cannot attempt to use the stairs between appointments and has to make use of the elevators, which are more and more frequently glass. You see these children, green and golden, following people out of the whizzing boxes with their eyes still closed. You see them going down hallways with one shoulder or fingertip discreetly touching the wall.

Except for Annette Lisordi's, all these experiences had been lived through during an MLA convention in gelid New York. At this moment, in gelid Chicago, up on the fourteenth floor, a certain Assistant Professor Christopher Crozon was prosecuting his position with a woman near the elevator bank.

Thirty-seven, short, red-haired and rapidly balding, Crozon was a member of a rare academic species: the prowling, rootless, amoral entity who takes no pains to disguise his urges. Because he'd lived in England for only a short part of his childhood, it was puzzling to one or two of the departmental souls with him at Michigan that his high-pitched accent became more pronounced with every passing year.

Thanks to that accent, and to having a book in press (on Dante Rossetti's juvenilia), Crozon's tenure was assured. By early in his third year, he'd become famous (not for his book, which in a year's time had sold, apart from library purchases, six copies), but for his predations on undergraduate women taking his classes. There'd been a flutter of trouble when it came to light that he'd advised a sophomore that she could blow up her grade by blowing him. But complaints from the department's women had been waved aside by his drinking buddy, the department vice-chair, as "female overreaction."

Crozon was now wearing his round-eyed, capuchin-monkey, aren't-I-adorable look, talking with great *sprezzatura* to the engrossed job candidate. The woman had interviewed that morning for a position at Michigan. "Shall I play for him? pa-rump-a-pump-pump," commented the speaker above the elevator.

Crozon's smiling message to her now was divided *in partes tres,* but very simple: that he was available, that the job might also be available, provided that she were available. The young woman blinked. She felt so indecisive. After all, he was just an *assistant* professor. Not tenured, and not in her field: How much good could he really do her?

Meanwhile, back at Slade's, Nancy had eaten quickly and was now emptying a little trapehedron of half-and-half into her coffee, pleased, as anyone is who passes through the Midwest, that she didn't have to try to dissolve some godawful powder.

Her dinner, a wide and high production of white gravy all over white pork, white biscuits and whitish limas, had been excellent, if over-heaped. (Chicago retains a subconscious regional memory of terrible Depression and southern poverties, and it still measures the quality of a meal by the quantity of meat provided. Restaurants, aware of this, are afraid not to deliver.)

This woman ate too fast, Boaz thought. East Coast again. He still had a quarter of his meal in front of him.

Being a proficient fixer of all things mechanical, Boaz had recognized in Nancy's layout of MLA reality the presence of machinery. He'd posited a sensible question during their dinner chat.

"Why don't you people just set up some kind of proficiency test? Other employers don't find their people this way. You could still arrange it so that whoever wanted to go off and prance around a hotel for a while could do that."

"Because you do want to meet the school's committee in person," Nancy told him. "And they want to meet you. Besides, there are a lot of people who really enjoy this power system. They *like* being on these committees that decide people's lives in just an hour.

"And there are social climbers, people who come every year because they get a kick out of all the 'networking.' You have to realize it's been a long time since anyone teaching English could feel that he or she was important, really respected. I sometimes think the MLA system is one of our power-substitutes to make up for feeling so—well, insignificant."

"I don't know about that 'insignificant,'" Boaz put in. "Taken for granted, yeah, I suppose." This word *power* keeps coming up, he thought.

The waitress was removing Nancy's plate. "Good food," Nancy told her in a friendly way. The woman blinked, taken aback. Then to Boaz, who'd liked the niceness of her style, Nancy went on.

"You see, in English now . . . well, let me think." Getting organized again, Nancy began doodling on her napkin some more. She would, over the next few minutes, slowly sketch and block in the letters BCV on the corner of a fresh napkin.

"I'm really simplifying now," she said. "But if you're a grad student looking for a job tomorrow, then you'd better know in advance that there are two main divisions out there on those committees. Athens and Sparta. Both pretty powerful.

"The old guard, the Tweeds, that's one group. I'm sure they'd like to think of themselves as Athenians. The other group, they're the Spartans, or the young Turks, maybe. They see themselves as revisionists or revolutionaries. They definitely include the new hotshots in critical theory—what I call the Trendies."

Nancy's tone had a mordant edge as she explained how common it is these days for there to be Athenians and Spartans at war within the same department.   55

"God knows they're at war at Yale: big cliques and nasty moves against each other. Before I leave I ought to write it all down, I guess; be a new Thucydides."

Boaz made a mental note that this woman kept making references to leaving her job. What was she planning? And who were these folks she disliked? He finished his last biscuit.

"The Tweeds you'd recognize. They're the gentlemanly professoriate, straight out of the movies—Frank Capra stuff. They're smoking pipes and wearing tweed jackets with leather patches on the elbow. Or even if they're not, somehow they've still got the *attitude* of a pipe and jacket." Boaz, having already seen a good deal of that in the hallways, nodded.

"For me," Nancy said, "the Tweeds are sort of like lounge lizards. You talk to one of them and it seems as if this guy were born on a sofa, with loafers on: I mean, they try to be professionally relaxed.

"I know a lot of tweedy types at Yale. They can be charming and intelligent and impressive. But the new people coming into the academy—well, they look at those guys and what they see are white men over fifty who have been *very* comfortable for a very long time. So comfortable that their point of view is defective, and oppressive.

"The tweedy guys are accused of being, and they *are*, just armchair scholars. They sort of *chat* about books. They go on teaching the same literature that was taught forty years ago, and little else. Maybe they write up biographies of poets, like William Rickerts at Williams, or they edit a few essays written by other people.

"But the secret fact is that a lot of them haven't been very productive at all. A lot of Tweeds have never written a book in their lives. They didn't have to. They were able to get tenure without that in the old days."

(How much *will* he listen to? Nancy wondered. No one in the real world thinks that problems in the academy are important. By now, too, Mark would have changed the subject even if he needed to know what she knew.)

Boaz, lifting a craggy eyebrow now and then, went on monitoring for tone. Hearing long, embittered outpourings was standard stuff in a detective's week. At what point did she act on it?

Nancy now outlined the sad fact that for years the number of college teaching jobs has been small. Worse, while budget freezes have made for department cutbacks down to the baseline, the number of grad students has stayed high off the chart.

"About one out of every four people you'll see here is a grad student looking for a job. That's an all-time high. So real power has stayed in the hands of the Tweeds, because MLA is such a buyer's market.

"So here you are, let's say, as that star grad student from Stanford," Nancy went on, her tone returning to near-jauntiness. "You're one of the new people, say. You're not a Trendy exactly, but you're familiar with the new thinking, and you've had an article published in some journal. Now you have to come here and be interrogated by tenured old men who've published zip, from schools that maybe aren't even very good. Schools that have mixed feelings about whether they want to 'upgrade' their departments with pushy, hotshot types like you."

Boaz laughed a little and held her brown eyes with his own, but disclosed nothing. That imperturbability and self-control had been frustrating, then infuriating, to his ex-wife.

Nancy smiled at him. "If life plays some more jokes on you here," she said, "then you'll have to sit in a hotel room with some Old Boy who despises everything later than criticism of the 1940s. But here he is, shopping with great disdain among 'poststructuralists' and 'Marxist-materialists' and 'cultural critics,' every one of whom has written a lot, maybe even whole books. Feelings can run pretty high."

"How high?"

Nancy addressed her newly-delivered wedge of cherry pie, so congealed with cornstarch she wondered whether it could stand on its point by itself.

"I don't know how high. Nobody knows what to do with this situation. In the old days, say in the 1950s" (Nancy's voice was wistful, though that era was before her time), "the old guard 57 was—well, in the best cases, they put together the Great Books Foundation and *The Book of Knowledge*. They were good teachers and were honored for it. I mean, as long as they could stay out of the way of the HUAC witch-hunters.

"But the old guard doesn't have so many fine teachers any more. They tend to be arrogant and aloof. And they get more dismissive about their students every year. You should hear how they talk about students in the faculty lounge at Yale."

Nancy laughed shortly. "Prosser Devereau, for one. He's famous for a few things, one of them being a novel about his girlfriend. In which he described all her failures, including in bed. Then he published it using her real name. He thinks people admire him, but actually the thing he's famous for is how badly he treats people. He told one freshman right in class that the kid wasn't smart enough to be taking his course. I can just hear him saying it. The boy was just about devastated."

Nancy shook her head. Disapproving curls moved here and there. "Devereau fascinates me. I wonder if his voice is arrogant even in his dreams."

"What do you mean, fascinates you?"

"Oh . . . I keep wanting to ask him what his first words were. Probably something like, 'Oh *really*? I *doubt* it.' I was talking to a counselor once from the mental health center, at a dinner party— this was at Yale. And I brought up Devereau because he's a real type in the academy: someone who thinks he's established as a singularity, but really he's just another mean, small guy.

"Dr. Styte's position was that we just have to be philosophical about it. That the Prosser Devereaus of this world probably do less harm by going into academics than if they'd gone into politics, for instance. He told me, 'Imagine what would happen if Devereau had an army at his disposal. Or if he'd gone into business, how much dirty work he could have done.' Dr. Styte thinks that Devereau's damage is sort of circumscribed and controlled at Yale.

"Well, but that bothers me," Nancy continued. "So, see, I guess I use him as an example of how not to be alive. Teachers should set an example, and he certainly does. I know that I don't want to turn into tweedy Prosser Devereau of Yale University. But I know people who do. Some of them are here." She gestured toward the Fairfax.

Boaz now flipped back to his flagged page, some distance toward the front of his notebook. Nancy realized she'd been discoursing quite a bit.

"I talk too much, I know," she said straightforwardly. "It's a teacher's vice."

"What were Susan Engleton's vices? You know her? Conservative type? Tweed?"

"The Wellesley chair? I never met her." Nancy paused, thoughtfully. "Conservative, probably, yes. That's Wellesley's reputation in general. But I've never heard anything specific about Susan Engleton. It's really too bad about her."

In an even tone, jotting as if just for the record, Boaz asked Nancy her room number and where she'd been early that morning. Nancy had been in her room, 311, on the third floor. She'd gotten up at about 7:30 A.M., and an hour later was just about ready to go out to breakfast.

"Did you have breakfast with anyone?"

"No."

"And where'd you eat?"

"Here."

"You see anybody here you recognized?"

"No. I was reading the paper. I was pretty tired and not paying a lot of attention."

As for her registration, Nancy explained that she'd flown into Chicago last weekend, on Sunday evening, and had stayed with a friend in Hyde Park for two days over Christmas. She hadn't checked into the Fairfax until Wednesday around noon.

"Did you leave the hotel Wednesday afternoon?"

"No, I took a nap and did some reading. Dina and I went out to some clubs that night."

"Dina?"

"Dina Marinetti, the friend I stayed with. I knew her in Providence. She's on Greenwood, if you want to check it out."

Nancy cheerfully showed him the "M" page in her address book. Boaz jotted the data and would indeed have it checked out.

The pie, meanwhile, was not the pie he'd hoped for, having eaten cherry pie worth the name in Missouri. He moved it to one side. The waitress stacked it on other plates with studied concentration, but neglected to return to wipe the table. Boaz and Nancy watched their elbow placements.

"OK," he demanded, "so you don't want to turn into Devereau. Good. So what is it—oh, I remember now: you're gonna join the circus."

(This was one of the most unlikely interviews Boaz had had for some time. Nancy was opening up a new region and rivaling that long talk he'd had years ago with the cat burglar from the Gold Coast. Guy knew everything there was to know about carpets. Went on long riffs about them: Persian, Turkish, Indian, Romanian. Could have been a museum curator. Trouble was, he'd always leave a pile of personal fecal material some place special in the house. A kind of calling card at the end of his robbery. Once he'd left it on a doctor's dinner table. The evidence technicians had gotten pretty tired of him.)

Nancy, enjoying the light mockery in this cop's tone, pushed back some hair with mock defiance.

"What do I want to turn into? I want to be Nancy, the Sacred River.

"At East High School," she explained, "my junior year: that's 'where Ralph, the sacred river, ran.' We said that behind his back, about Ralph Dunnston. We were making fun of his way of putting 'Kubla Khan' on your desk when he thought you were ready for it.

"Of course, we were trying to deny that he had any power over us, some of us. But he did have it. You'd go out of Ralph's class, and some assumption you'd walked into that class with had just sort of cracked open. And there was all this air around, and you didn't say a thing about it to anybody. It made you feel kind of wobbly, all this new space you had.

"All he'd done, really, was let you know some basic, organizing idea. Once he compared the Parthenon to some Greek vases. Sounds boring, but that was news to me. I mean, if you can compare a building to a little piece of pottery, then you can compare anything to anything else. I really wobbled after *that* class.

"Then I went around comparing everything. I compared insects to cars for a while. And one day I even compared myself to my mother—pretty preposterous, huh? What I got out of *that* was pretty interesting.

"Ralph was a great teacher. Because of his timing. Teaching's all about timing, of course: when does this kid need what. So what you are, if you're a teacher, is what you can empathize, what you can guess. Which means keeping your own ego out of the picture.

"I know this is all obvious stuff, but I don't hear it acknowledged any more. And you won't hear it acknowledged *here*, in this hotel. Here there's nothing *but* ego.

"Almost none of the panels, you know, are about teaching," Nancy emphasized. "That's too unfashionable. Your colleagues would sneer at you if you went to those panels. I can just hear the hallway remarks. Teaching has zero prestige now; it's beneath the Olympian intellects here."

Boaz was looking at her with an assessing frown. Was she exaggerating?

"At MLA, and back at our schools, what you *write* is what you are. Your writing defines your little pigeonhole. It's your reputation, it's your salary, it's your power. *Scribo, ergo sum.* I write, therefore . . .

"Well, but I'm talking too much again," Nancy interrupted herself. Boaz was looking off into the distance.

"*Scribo?*" he said. "My baby sister had a 'scribo.' That was Lynette. Cute kid. When she was about three—let's see, I was about sixteen—she got herself a guinea pig. Maybe I got it for her, I don't remember. All the kids had these guinea pigs for a while. And they all got good guinea-pig names like Blackie and Spot. Peaches. But not Lynette. No, she's got to go and name hers Screebo. And wouldn't tell anybody why.

"Turns out—when she could talk a little better and somebody figured it out—turns out that was her way of sayin' Screwball. That's when I knew she was on to the family, they didn't fool her any more. Buncha nuts.

"And she stayed just like that, smart-alecky and stubborn every day. She's a grade-school teacher now, by the way." Boaz's brown eyes were cheerful and teasing, both.

"Are you making that up?" Nancy demanded.

"No, ma'am."

"Lynette? Well, maybe I'd like her."

"I expect you might." For a moment, each smiled at the other without an agenda of distraction or reservation.

5

The pager that went off inside Boaz's jacket wasn't loud, but it was insistent. When Boaz dialed up to the base room again (much of a cop's day is spent on the phone), Halleran let him know that at 4:00 P.M. the toxicologists at the Forensic Institute had handed on the coffee samples to the evening shift.

This was unusual. Toxicology workup was usually rapid and routine. At 7:00 Chuck Metek, chief toxicologist and a friend of Halleran's from high school, had taken a break from his protocols to give Halleran a call. It was especially unusual for the chief toxicologist to be putting in overtime. But the cause-of-death determination for Susan Engleton still lay under "deferred" status, which was interesting to Metek.

"Unless the hotel's getting real sloppy and putting gravel in the pots," Metek had told Halleran, "you've got yourself a homicide case. But I can't say that officially yet."

A residue of "gritty stuff" had been found at the bottom of the coffee urn from the Wellesley suite. Small, dark bits. No way they were coffee grounds.

"Offhand, they look like seeds," Metek had said. "Definitely some organic. Not an inorganic like arsenic." The lab was closing in on it but would have to consult the regional Poison Control Center tonight. Firm results probably by morning.

"Hunnh," said Boaz, down in Slade's. "So no easy fishin' on this one, Timmy. You know, there might be some real heat on this pretty soon, if the press gets tired of Happy New Year stuff."

Halleran put in a fervent remark regarding the sexual proclivities of the Chicago press. It was a sentiment with which Boaz was in agreement. Halleran was likely to make a remark next about the lieutenant's sexual proclivities *with* the Chicago press. Boaz interrupted.

"Listen, Timmy, that woman's still here, the one that came up to me in the lobby. She's still talking a lot."

"About how lonely she is at this great big convention in this great big city?"

"No, she's talking about the convention and I want her to go *on* talking. She knows procedures here, and people. A lot's goin' on here, Timmy. People are at each other's throats. After a while, I want her to go on up and look at the Wellesley rooms. Maybe she can spot something."

"Suspect?"

"Dunno. Informant. Maybe nothin', but it's what I got right now. I'll give you a call to meet us up there."

"Well, give me a half hour or so," Halleran said. "I got a couple of airlines to clear up with."

"Right. And see if that princess manager can get a cot into that room there, will you? I'm gonna sleep over, I think. It's time for me to look real close at the statements. You know, Vaster's not real sick. I also want to see who's been fired from the hotel lately. Whether we got somethin' in that area."

"Yeah, I know. Malley's still here and he's looking at some of that. Hong's gone home. Call when you're ready."

Back at the booth, Boaz found Nancy regarding him cheerfully. But it was a different man, with a hard expression, who picked up his coffee cup again. He did not speak for a moment, and she did not inquire. A cop isn't always somebody you ask questions of, she thought.

"If you have a little *more* time," Boaz said finally, "there's something I'd like for you to look at, in half an hour or so." He paused. "On the thirty-third floor." There was not a nanosecond when his eyes left her face. "The Wellesley rooms."

Startled, Nancy was silent. It was with a curiosity she hoped wasn't just morbid that she said she'd try to help however she could.

"Well, meantime," Boaz said, "we have a little time 'til my partner's ready. Maybe we could finish up about—what'd you call 'em—'the two groups'?"

"Oh, I might have known you'd remember that," Nancy sighed. "I was thinking of skipping it. The New Killer-Dillers in the Academy: the territories they defend. But I guess if you want to know MLA and who hates whom . . ."

Boaz, regarding her with an uninterpretable look, nodded slowly.

"OK. You know about the Tweeds. And you know there are big differences inside departments these days about ideology."

Nancy sighed again. "Oh, this is such a drag to make any sense of," she said, leaning on a gray-knit elbow. "Because a lot of academics aren't in just one camp, of course. It's easier, in a way, if you *are*. The rest of us are just lost, frankly. We teach a little of this theory and a little of that. And we tell our students and we tell each other that we don't have to choose sides. We say that books have 'a richness that can be taught from many points of view.' Et cetera.

"Meanwhile, though"—Nancy straightened her back reluctantly against the backboard of the booth—"the lines between the little groups go on hardening. And nobody knows what to do to fix the main split. Which is between those people who think 'the Anglo-American tradition,' as it's called, is valuable and wonderful, and those who think it should be trashed. I'm putting it crudely, but that's really how it breaks down.

"The Anglo-American tradition," Nancy responded to Boaz's quizzical look: "I know of two professors who refuse to teach Milton or Shakespeare because both of them are 'sexist' and 'racist' and because they supposedly lure people into an acceptance of war. I know teachers who've taken *Huckleberry Finn* off their reading lists because some of the characters are slaves.

"So these little groups I'm going to tell you about—their impact has been pretty large. I should warn you, too: lots more of this is going to sound like *Ripley's Believe It or Not*.

"And believe it or not, I'll have more coffee, yes," she assented to the lanky waitress, whose symbolic icon, were she to appear in an old mosaic, would surely have been that round glass pot, perennially half full, that she carried everywhere.

"If you were going to go around visiting all the Trendy camps here" (A little touch of Boaz in the night?, Nancy thought, admonishing herself at once to straighten up), "the main factions you'd see would be, oh, the radical feminists, the gay studies activists, the academic Marxists, the ethnic studies people—who else? The 'new historicists' and what's left of the deconstructionists. There are subsets, like the psychoanalytic literary theorists' group and maybe a group you could just call multiculturalists."

Boaz had his notebook turned to a new page but was not writing. He listened with a frown. Where was she goin'?

"So: radical feminists and gays and minorities—their positions you're probably somewhat familiar with?"

"Oh yes," replied the public servant, with a wry, closed-mouth smile. "They all just love me to pieces."

"When they're calling you for help, I suppose." Nancy gave a short laugh. "Well, I wish that loving anything was part of any of the current thinking." That thinking was something Nancy had given a great deal of thought to lately.

"Here at MLA, those particular groups do argue, but they manage to agree that white male hegemony and 'heterosexism' in the academy are cultural prejudices that need to be corrected, period. With which, you might as well know, I am in full agreement."

Professor Cook gave Boaz an eye-to-eye look, then surprised him with a look away, a look of weariness.

"The charges being made against that position—that the slant of courses in women's studies and black studies and gay studies is always dogmatic, and the bias in the reading lists is so extreme as to amount to censorship—well, I wish I could say that I've seen those charges refuted. I'd like to say I've seen wide reading assignments and dialogue being encouraged in the classes I've sat in on. But to tell you the truth, I *haven't* seen a lot of that yet. Which is not to be repeated, please, until I have a tenured job. Freedom of speech is not what it once was.

"But moving right along," Nancy continued, breaking the surface tension of a tiny water puddle with the tip of her pen, "what's another maniac group? I'd agree that the source group, the energy, for the people who'd like to trash the Western tradition, came from the deconstructionists.

"Those people, when they're not busy defending their main guy, Paul de Man, from charges of being a Nazi sympathizer, they write books, using words, telling us that words have no meaning we can rely on, really. That meaning is always contradicting itself so much, language can't be thought of as trustworthy at all. The 'signifier' does not necessarily refer to a 'signified' and other phrases like that from structuralism, which I am *not* going to go into.

"What's important to go into is this: 'meaning,' if it exists in a book such as, oh—well, it can't be *Huckleberry Finn*, can it? We already know that has to be eliminated and never spoken of again until there is perfect racial equality. But a book like—what's your favorite book?"

"I don't have a lotta time to read, ma'am."

"What did you like to read down in Rolla?"

For a moment, a green wind blew across a wood-slatted porch in Boaz's memory. An entire summer of fishing skills and sunburn and pampered box turtles and approaching manhood lay condensed in a volume on a table on that porch in his mind.

"*The Call of the Wild.*"

"Oh, *yes*," said Nancy, smiling. "Well now, the 'decon' people would like you to realize that there is no meaning in that book, or that any meaning in it does not point outward, away from the book, to anything or anyone. You have to think of language as being a kind of world of its own, regardless of the author's intentions. In fact, whatever meaning a book has, has been sort of pushed onto it, partly, by the reader's response.

"So, you see, according to this view, the reader is equal to the author in authority and creativity. Unless, of course, the reader just so happens to be an academic literary critic. In *that* case the reader of Jack London is *superior* to Jack London, because the 67 critic knows more about what's going on in *The Call of the Wild* than Jack London ever dreamed of.

"Nifty, huh?" Nancy laughed, noting her pupil's exasperated look. "Of course, decon theory has no interest in the fact that no one knows very much about language yet. About how it's acquired, or how the brain does its mapping of meaning—whether from the world or from texts or from someplace in the middle of its own neurons. Deconstructionists *could* find out what's known about that, but that would take them into introductory neurology or some other field, and that's beyond them."

Nancy's tone had been fed up. Now it was acidic. "Meanwhile, here at MLA, there couldn't possibly be anything *personal* in the deconstruction agenda—which has contaminated new historicist and Marxist positions, both. Oh no, nothing personal. Their positions have nothing to do with English academics wanting to feel empowered for a change. With the fact that if you asked anyone in this restaurant to name a powerful person, the *last* thing named would be an English professor.

"No, envy's got *nothing* to do with MLA. It's always dismissed as an operating principle. Because it's too painful, I suppose. After all, not one of the decon people or 'reader response theorists' or any other Trendy could create in ten years what a good novelist can put together in a week."

Professor Nancy Cook, Boaz noticed, was not attractive when she was mad. She was very nearly beautiful. Wisely, he did not share this observation.

Boaz's square chin had been propped on his left palm and forearm. He now nodded the entire unit. "Is that all of the gangland divisions here?" he asked. "Or am I gonna have to go get myself another little notebook?"

"Almost all. I've saved the best for last. The Marxists. Some of them were in that bar you were looking in, the 'Square' thing. Harold Snaff from UCLA was at one of the tables."

"Those guys were Marxists? In hundred-and-fifty-dollar gym shoes?"

"And real leather jackets. Absolutely. Now what they'd have to tell you is that everything that's ever been written has been shaped by the writer's prejudices having to do with race and class and sex. The works we've been teaching for so long—Chaucer, Wordsworth—were deformed so much by those prejudices that what they amount to now is 'instruments of cultural domination.'

"Western culture—what we're sitting in right here—that culture is more or less defunct, they say. And its products, such as Shakespeare, should not be taught as being beautiful or important. Certainly not more important than a product of any other culture. Otherwise, you're making 'elitist' distinctions and being oppressive, yourself.

"What we have to do as teachers now, according to Marxists, is show all the naive children in our classrooms . . . Do you *have* any children, by the way?" Nancy interrupted herself. She made her question sound purely informational.

"No, no kids. Just as well, I guess: no wife any more." Boaz made his reply sound noncommittal.

"Oh. Well, anyway, to finish with Marxists: what we need to do, they say, is show our students every shade of oppression and bigotry that's secretly hidden—hidden in the books we used to love and value. Either that or just don't teach the old texts.

"Makes you wonder why send a kid to college at all, doesn't it? But enough," Nancy said, determinedly putting down her pen. "I will rant no more."

"Wait a minute. What's *your* book about, then?" Boaz demanded. "Said you're writin' a book?"

"Yes. I'm in modernism, but I'm using some of the work I did for my master's degree in Chaucer. There are some new ways to talk about narrative, some new thinking that isn't *too* demented, I hope. I'm applying some of that to Chaucer's *Tales*. By the way, you can't say the word *story* any more. Or *theme*. Those are just hopelessly out of date."

"No more stories?"

"No more stories. Only *narratives,* and *narrativity,* and *narratology.* Now you know. If you want to go ahead and use the word, it'd be pretty bold these days."

Earlier, Boaz's assessment-apparatus had racheted up a notch at Nancy's repeated choice of the word *power*. Now, with her talking about stories, his attention racheted up again. What story did she really want to tell him? *Was* there another story behind her mockeries?

"Go on," he said simply, glancing at his watch. "We got a minute."

Nancy gave this wonderfully attentive, if unfathomable, man a quick smile. Why was he spending so much time with her? she wondered. Men. They made no sense.

"I'm revising the last part of my book now," Nancy resumed. "I've sent the first chapters out to a few places, publishers. Little samples of the ultimate Cook book."

Nancy spread her hands apart in an apologetic gesture for the pun, a kind of shrugging of the hands. She added, "That's probably the reason I'm so bitchy lately. A pre-crone."

"Pre-crone?"

"I'm afraid so, yes. I mean, I *know* I am. If I can't find a publisher for my book—well, it's not just that I'll be fired at Yale. I'll be fired at Yale, anyway. But I won't be hired anywhere *else*, or not without some fancy maneuvering."

Pushing back some long curls that insisted on behaving like stolons and rhizomes, Nancy acknowledged that even without a book publication, she'd still be in better shape than the people "who spend ten years getting a doctorate and then get *some* kind of teaching job, then come up one day for pretenure review and are out on the street with nothing.

"Well, I refuse to crone it up any longer," Nancy said decidedly, and replaced the pen in her gray bag. How vapid the ideas and concerns of her compeers could sound, she thought. It was salutary, this exercise of presenting the MLA before someone with the intelligence and commitment of the solid, transacademic world. Not pleasant, but salutary.

"If it's a useful distinction," Nancy concluded, "I mean, if you're investigating all these awful deaths here . . ." Boaz frowned.

". . . well, then," she went on, "you could think of Michael

Alcott as a representative Trendy. He was a very typical Marxist-materialist in thought, word, and deed."

Boaz's silent alarm system went off again. Without a leading question, this woman had brought up the dead again and asked him about the investigation. Just when he was feeling relaxed about her, she bothered him afresh.

Getting up to call Halleran, Boaz reviewed his uneasiness. What exactly did Nancy know? Could she be one of those weirdos who commit a crime, or more likely know about a crime, then go and hang around the cops? Cop-seeker-outers were intelligent manipulators but were not usually women. Usually. Women were changing lately, though, showing up as perpetrators of the most godawful stuff these days. Choppin' people to flinders.

(Not that murder statistics had changed all that much yet. It was still the case that the most common form of female homicide was that of mothers killing their children: the hallucinating, schizophrenic woman who murders her offspring "for their own good," and then does something like wash them and put them in bed with flowers on them. As a beat cop, one of Boaz's mornings had included the experience of carrying such an eight-year-old victim to the squadrol wagon. He was helping the medical examiners, whose arms were similarly full. Two had been smothered and one drowned by their mother, who then stood preaching from her Kenwood apartment window. The limpness of the little girl's weight he could still feel sometimes across his forearms. He was not a hard-drinking man, but he'd drunk like a shark that night. He and Janie, his wife, had been thinking then about having a child—mostly his idea.)

In homicide investigations—which aren't difficult, as a rule, murder having the highest clearance rate of all violent crime—what detectives do is pay attention to three people: the person who found the body, the person who reported the crime, and the person who keeps talking about it. Those are often the same one person, the killer.

The problem here in Slade's, Boaz knew, was the thrills aspect. The sociopath approaching the police (the volunteer for the search party: "I'll help you look for the body, Officer") is, in a quiet way, a thrill seeker. Manipulating the police, he relives a little of the control and the kick of power that the murder gave him.

A couple of those wretched faces from Boaz's professional history, one a woman, floated to his mind. Their sketches did not match well the poised woman talking about power and control in the academy. Of course, she could be working with some creep of a partner. In which case, though, she probably would've come on to him right away, made a big invitation.

Boaz doubted his small, recrudescent doubts about this blonde. But then, he always did doubt his assessments. That was a reason why his hunches were reliable.

Putting hunches on hold, Boaz notified Halleran that they'd meet him with keys at 3321. Back at the booth, he reached for the check. Arriving coffee-stained, it lay face down on the table melodramatically, like a victim from the population of paper.

"Well, Nancy, I appreciate your help. And I will count myself a lucky man having a simple life, just getting shot at from time to time." Boaz turned toward the register easily and unselfconsciously.

It would be a shame, Nancy thought, if this man got shot. He was nice looking. No. Not nice looking. Well . . . he *became* nice looking when he was doing things. She tried not to clamber out of the booth.

With a pause at the door of Slade's, Boaz checked up and down the concourse before looking back for his companion: old Homicide Unit habits. Straight across the concourse was a plainclothes cop. A couple of these units Mulcahy had sent over. Meeting Jimmy Duffy's eye for a moment, Boaz nodded toward Nancy inconspicuously. From now on, that particular cop would follow her.

The concourse was hectic. People were maneuvering in the two-way stream like cars in a traffic jam. Boaz and Nancy negotiated the openings and emerged into the lobby. "I am a poor boy, too, pa-rump-pa-pump-pump," greeted them faintly.

Nancy's original plans had included going to the Harvey Boule panel at 8:00 P.M. It had started already and Nancy found she didn't much care. She decided not to elaborate about it to Boaz, either. It would just take too long, maybe forever, to explain why the panel discussion would center on Boule's most recent contribution to civilized thought, *The Book of G*.

Interpreting a new translation of the Sumerian epic, *Gilgamesh*, Boule at this very moment was repeating his assertion that this ancient work, possibly composed in the city of Ur, was almost certainly composed by a captured Pygmy.

To support this, *The Book of G* meticulously identified every instance in the cuneiform of statements related to measurements and size. Because Gilgamesh, Enkidu, and their monstrous opponents are consistently described as having great physical strength and height, the six stone tablets must, then, have been tapped out by a single remarkable Pygmy. Lamentably, the name of this ancient writer has been lost, but he or she stands tall in the history of literature, certainly as one of the greatest writers of all time.

Nancy felt relieved in general that Boaz hadn't pursued her passing remarks about panel discussions. Having to read out some of those panel titles (the November *PMLA* program issue, listing them all, was in her ample purse) would have been too much like assuming the role of sidewalk huckster outside an adult bookstore.

Tonight at the Hyatt, for instance, there would be "A Bard in the Hand: Masturbatory Arcs in *As You Like It*," and "Sex-textualities: The Erotics of Early Irish Manuscript Study." (However, if you preferred to avoid all suggestion of a physical world, there was "Primatology, Immunology, and Cyborg Praxis.")

Meanwhile, the Fairfax would be featuring, along with Harvey Boule, "Maternal Incest in the Novels of Jane Austen," followed by, at 10:00, "Lesbians at the Race Track: Toward a Queer Theory of Gambling."

("'Queer Theory!' Jennifer!" Nancy had groaned to a Yale grad-school friend last November, as they were perusing the list of panels. "What's next? 'Spic Theory'? 'Kike Theory'? I don't understand this. How can you force a word of hatred into another person's mouth and expect it to turn into a word of acceptance?" 73

"It's pretty queer, all right," Jennifer assayed. "Weirdosity-laden.")

Friday at MLA, two other "Queer Theory" panels would proceed, but also, as if pulled up overnight in front of the adult bookstore, other hucksters would hawk their different wares from the back steps of their snake-oil wagons. Besides Sarton P. Mudge's panel in the morning, which would center on his new book, *Learning to Parse*, there would be a panel led by Gerald Merk of Boston University addressing his renowned work on Saint Augustine. Merk's tightly argued premise, much admired, was that Augustine's intentions in the *Confessions* and *The City of God* are "linguistically subverted on every page" (Merk providing lists of puns and ironies and other "subtextual sabotage"), so that "both texts are merely repeated examples of language languaging."

The atrium lobby was very noisy. Boaz and Nancy moved from the desk toward the southeast elevator through waves of talk. More MLA registrants were just now learning of Alcott's accident and the Wellesley "food poisoning" events. More upwellings of gossip kept converting the forty-story Fairfax into a Tower of Babel.

The elevator door squeezed closed in front of their noses. "I mean, they were throwing up in the wastebaskets and in their coffee mugs!" Behind them, Professor Walter Yisseldack, tightly suited in a beige summer jacket, with the stuffed-toad self-importance of a TV newscaster, was sharing the late-breaking news with a small group around him from Fairleigh Dickinson.

"A couple of them, Herb Gooch I know was one of them, they were vomiting right into the bathtub! And Muffie Murchison filled up the entire sink and *then* some—according to Andrew, anyway. And some hotel maid said it wasn't her job to clean that sort of thing off the phone. If you can believe *that*."

Nancy wondered with some apprehension what she was going to have to look at in these Wellesley rooms, but she said nothing.

Someone else in the elevator—it was Brook Branstool from Louisiana State—summarized sarcastically that "Susan, as usual, was leaning on everybody. Hotel coffee wasn't good enough for *her*. I hear they offered her Hawaiian Kona blend, but she wouldn't take it. Said it had to be Jamaican Blue beans and nothing else. I hear the hotel spent hours trying to find it. I guess what they found was rotten or something," he concluded, with a shrug that implied that Susan Engleton had gotten what she deserved.

Nancy wondered what he deserved. She was tired. She wondered what she herself deserved.

Moments later, out in the hall of the thirty-third floor, two professors from U.C. Riverside moved slowly past them. "Well," said Kevin Pill, "I guess Alcott's had his last *big* fall off the wagon, huh? Just kidding."

"Well, but really, about Alcott," said Drew Polkinghorne, "Wasn't he known to have a drinking problem? I've heard he bathed in the stuff . . ."

Professor Cook, who'd been feeling (except when describing current ideologies) like something of an ambassador for her profession, found herself wishing someone would come along and issue a few pink slips to the principal's office.

Halleran was waiting at the 3321 door. He and Nancy proceeded to perform discreet and rapid mutual readings. Halleran, Nancy thought, had a big old basset-hound look. If you were in terrible trouble, trapped in your car, this would be the guy you'd want to see coming to help you. She wasn't surprised that Halleran was regarding her with a certain undisguiseable skepticism. Why shouldn't he, after all? And how many first days of class had she entered her classroom and met, at first, that kind of look?

Halleran for his part had had a long, long day and was now, like Boaz, well into his second shift. What was a professor going to do for him? He *did* like curly women, though. Always had; couldn't help himself. Both his wives had had curly hair. Not that it had done him any good. He looked at Boaz.

Then Halleran looked *behind* Boaz, the way cops in public do not look at each other directly for more than a glance. One is always looking behind the other, surveilling, just to check out what might be coming at them.

Boaz, having scanned the hallway behind Halleran, introduced 75

Nancy with more deliberate good manners. Nancy extended her hand without flirtatiousness or condescension, simply as one professional to another. Halleran took it briefly and thought maybe she wasn't so bad.

"Nancy's been in MLA interviews before, she knows this kind of setup," Boaz said.

Turning to Nancy, he went on, "What I'd like for you to do is look around these rooms in here and let us know if you notice anything unusual. Something you'd expect to be there that isn't there. Or if you see something there that shouldn't be. Anything at all. A lamp. A piece of paper. Anything."

"All right," Nancy nodded. "But . . . is Susan Engleton still in there?"

"No. No one's in there. The rooms are empty." Boaz was peeling back the police line taped across the door.

Nancy nodded. She turned to Halleran, her voice quietly firm. "I've never been in a room where someone's just died. And I've never been in a police investigation. Is there something I should do that I ought to know about? Should I just stand at the door?"

Not bad at all, Halleran thought, seeing as how a lot of teachers act like they already know everything. He advised her not to touch any surface whatsoever. Then, in a spirit of friendliness, or the beginning of that, Halleran did something for Nancy he wouldn't have considered doing for an English professor with "attitude." He warned her these rooms had been closed all day and that the windows could not be opened now.

"It's not going to smell so great in there," he told her. "It might be rough. You let me know if it gets to be too much." Nancy nodded, with more dread.

The Wellesley suite, opening to a tiny foyer, had doors to the left and right. What had been Susan Engleton's bedroom and bath were to the left. To the right was the living room, beyond which was the second bedroom, originally unused. Invisible from the front door, off the living room to the right, was the second, infamously overused bathroom to which the coffee sufferers had staggered.

Directed to look around Engleton's bedroom first, Nancy saw nothing out of the ordinary. Three chairs were in place around the double bed. A freestanding suit caddy complete with electric shoeshiner stood near its foot. The usual appointments: desk table with lamp, end tables by the double bed, a vanity with matching stool. A tiny refrigerator stood in a corner with an ice bucket on top.

Boaz opened the refrigerator carefully and Nancy took a look at the hotel's provisions. Besides the standard carafe of chilled red wine that so appalled the hotel's California and New York guests, there were Toblerone chocolates, a jar of dried nuts, assorted juices and drink mixes, along with shot bottles of Jack Daniels, Absolut, Cutty Sark, and other liquor.

Nancy shrugged and shook her head. This was kind of creepy and she didn't feel very talkative.

There was a phone by the bed, another on the desk table, another in the small bathroom beyond the vanity. There was a strange air of expectancy about the phones. Nancy felt grateful the little red Message Waiting button was not shining on any of them. If it had been—oh God, who would it be? she wondered. Cerberus barking?

The three went into the living room. A low sofa against the left-hand wall faced a couple of aggressive easy chairs and two smaller chairs as well. No coffee table interfered with this confrontation.

Various other tables and chairs stood propped around the walls with another desk and a sizeable TV. The coffee cart, now dusted with dark powder and minus its chrome tureen, stood in conspicuous silence across the room. The cart had been pushed by Susan Engleton to a spot at some distance from the sofa. Nancy glanced into the bathroom, but did not enter it. The emetic odor was fairly strong but not too unsettling.

Through the half-open door of the unused bedroom, Nancy could see a leaning philodendron. Throughout the suite, enormous plants in pastel pots were being asked to perform the functions of furniture. The monstera and faded crotons in the living room looked stoic and all but gasping in the dryness; they stretched their wide-fingered leaves and etiolated petioles toward the windows as if remembering the humid La Selva slopes of Costa Rica.

Aside from the faint identity of the plants, however, the room was sinister with anonymity. Nancy tried to figure out why. The *faux marbre* beige veneer on the tables, the chairs vaguely French provincial, the sentimental prints (here, from Picasso's Rose Period), the pinkish upholstery: all these were cloned throughout the hotel—in her own room, too.

But the beige drapes, pulled half open by Susan Engleton that morning, stood where she left them. And the odor, sour in the room, seemed to emanate from the very walls and furnishings. The message of the room, despite its attempt to be innocuous, was that what is mysterious is right in front of you—also what is dangerous.

There was no view now from the sealed, oxygen-repelling windows that had been dark since four o'clock. In daylight what they would have shown was a lake-facing vista over a sunken section of Grant Park, out to Chicago Harbor as far as the breakwater for the Columbia Yacht Club and the tip of Navy Pier. The great stone pylons of the Randolph Street Bridge and the dark single pylon of Mies van der Rohe's Lake Point Tower framed this invisible view. Nancy knew that the Chicago River ran like so much melted ice just to the north, where the masterpiece buildings of the Magnificent Mile were standing in their Zen silence, indifferent to the snow on their steel and travertine and terra cotta shoulders. Day or night, immobile or in motion, the snow everywhere was both unpretty and unapologetic about it.

Propped on the arm of one of the easy chairs was a room service menu. Boaz picked it up. Susan Engleton had not had time to place an order. Just as well. The "Continental Breakfast" (at nine dollars, plus room-service charge and a 20 percent gratuity) would have provided her with one croissant and a three-ounce glass of orange juice, neither of which would have absorbed enough to save her anyway.

Halleran leaned, brown hill–like, on one side of the sofa, and was quietly watching Nancy's moves in the room. She stepped very gingerly everywhere, touching nothing.

"These plants need watering pretty badly," she murmured at one point. Halleran asked in a low-voiced, friendly way if she grew a lot of plants herself. Preoccupied with the room, Nancy shook her head, saying she avoided large tropicals for houseplants now, that she just did outdoor gardening.

Boaz put down the menu and looked over the room. "What I'm wonderin' is how come Susan Engleton put the coffee cart way over there, across the room. Would have been easier to have it right here by the couch."

"Oh," said Nancy, standing by a fake-marble table, "that looks like Princeton's old trick. I've heard that Wellesley does it, too."

Glad to have her attention focused on something specific in this awful, blank room, Nancy explained that most schools will provide coffee in the room or suite. The style of that presentation will vary, but only in a few schools is it used as a test. At Ohio, Penn, Berkeley, and most places, coffee will be part of an effort at relaxation. Mugs and rolled-up sleeves kind of thing. Somebody will just pour you a cup and hand it to you.

"But at some of the Ivy schools, or places like Virginia"—Nancy gave a short sigh—"what they'll do is, they'll wait until you're sitting down, probably on the sofa, some place that's not an easy place to get up from. Then one of them will smile and ask you if you'd like to *help yourself* to coffee or tea.

"Even if you don't really want any," Nancy smiled a little over at Halleran, who didn't mind, "there's something about the way it's offered that is an order, really. See, they want to watch you: they want to see how gracefully you get up from that sofa, and whether you can walk around the furniture without bumping into anything. They know you're nervous. They want to see how you *handle* that nervousness, physically.

"It's all about details," Nancy went on. "Can you pour your coffee without spilling any? Will you have the nerve to take sugar and cream? Did your spoon make a scraping sound? And see, there's no table here at the sofa. They don't *want* you to have a table. They want to see how you're going to sit down with that cup and how you're going to hold it."

Halleran looked disgusted. So did his partner.

"It's a test of *savoir faire,* or the kind of suavity they think they need in a teacher." Nancy gave a short exasperated laugh. "After all, at Wellesley, they still have cocktail parties for parents and teachers. Kind of a PTA with booze. So the committee here has to find people they think are suitable to teach the daughters of ascendant businessmen and the daughters of decrepit monarchs."

Halleran hauled his shoulders from right to left. "Is that what happened to you? What *you* had to go through?" In his low tone, full of sympathy, Boaz recognized Halleran's interrogation mode.

"No, not really," Nancy said openly. "Yale's interview was more like taking an SAT test. They want to know what your views are. Whether you're combative and interesting. They're more concerned about getting people who're on the cutting edge of new theories and stuff. They couldn't care less about coddling their rich students.

"You see, not *all* the Ivy League schools do this coffee thing," Nancy said. "I don't think Vassar does. Or Radcliffe, either. But I know Princeton does; I hear stories about it."

In addition to providing no place to put a cup, Princeton uses another trick, of never asking the candidate any important questions. As a way of off-balancing the candidate to see how well he or she can socialize, just a little chat will happen, confusing and aloof, during which the most substantial question will be something like, "And how would you feel about a move to the East?" Or, "I understand Fred Crews is still at Berkeley. Did you know him?" Half an hour later they thank you, you leave, and you probably never know what they'd been looking for.

Nancy drummed her fingers on the table, then looked guiltily down and moved her hand away. She hadn't meant to touch anything. To Halleran again she said, "I don't know which is better or worse, really. Wellesley babies their young women and forces their faculty to be something like glorified baby-sitters. But their students do tend to be alive at graduation time. Yale averages about two undergraduate suicides every year. That's been true for decades. So maybe they ought to set up a coffee test? I don't know."

Halleran didn't look over at Boaz. But Boaz, his arms folded on the top of an easy chair, could tell that his partner felt this woman hadn't been killing many folks lately.

Then Nancy brought up the dead. "Is it true what we heard in the elevator?" she asked. "I heard someone else say something like that. That Susan Engleton demanded some special coffee, and there was something wrong with the beans? Is that right?"

Boaz unfolded his arms and turned to confront her. "Susan Engleton was poisoned. And not with blue coffee beans. The autopsy's being done right now. By now, they've cut out everything that was in her stomach and her stomach's in a jar."

Boaz watched Nancy Cook flinch a little from the image he'd forced on her. Her eyes traveled around the room. The smell seemed to be a little stronger.

"How awful!" she said. "Poor woman!" She put her hand down again on the table. "Oh, my God, and Annette! She might have been poisoned, too, if she'd drunk anything!"

"She *would* have been poisoned, yes, if she'd *had* any coffee," Boaz confirmed. "Now what *about* Annette? What should we know about her, Nancy?"

In these surroundings, Nancy considered her friend with some confusion. What was there to tell about the peasant-solid and good-hearted Annette who'd been in danger here? The idea of that pert, curly intelligence getting poisoned in this room made Nancy restless with helplessness. She moved around the table a few steps.

"She's been a good friend to me. We were at Brown together. Then she lived with her family in Italy for a couple of years—before she came back and went to grad school. At Emory. Now she's looking for a job here. I don't know what else you need to know."

Boaz spread his hands. "You got any idea why the Wellesley people were singled out?" he asked. "You know anybody who was mad at them, maybe?" Then, feeling a little too close to the fuzzy interrogation limit imposed by Miranda, he softened his question.

"What I mean is, did Engleton have any arguments with other professors, anything real hateful, anything you heard about?"

Nancy frowned down at the flat, pileless, blue-gray carpet. "No. Wellesley's a low-profile place you don't hear much about these days. No scandals I've heard of. No critics of big trendy importance. No."

She looked at them with a touch of defiance. "And Annette, if that's what you're getting at, did not come here with a grudge against Wellesley. She'd never laid eyes on any of them before. Besides, Annette is not a vindictive person." Nancy laughed at little at the thought. "If anything, she lets people walk over her too much."

Halleran shrugged. For the time being, too, Boaz gave up. "Well, we might as well go on out. Nancy, I'll take you to your room. Timmy, you goin' home?"

The weary Halleran nodded and tossed Boaz a roll of adhesive tape out of his pocket. Somehow it was not surprising that Halleran's shapeless and comfortable brown suit would produce such an object.

"I'll bet the concierge, bless her little heart, was real glad to give you this," Boaz said, as he locked the Wellesley suite and reinforced the police-line tape across the door.

"Oh yeah. Real glad. All I have to do is put my hand on my gun."

Nancy stayed quiet in the hall. She couldn't quite read these guys.

"I think the tenth-floor room can wait 'til tomorrow, what do you think?" Boaz was indicating to his partner that he still intended to take this professor to Alcott's room.

Halleran nodded, bleary with fatigue, said good night to the woman who'd maybe changed his mind a *little* about professors, and went off to the service elevator.

Boaz, still trying to put together an overview, chose the public elevators. It was a long ride down to the third floor, with many stops. Nancy felt somewhat at a loss.

Does he like me at all? she wondered. She couldn't help it; she did want him to. No big deal, of course. Just . . .

Boaz seemed lost in thought. And he was. He was considering Mr. Miranda.

Boaz had decided not to take Nancy to Alcott's room tonight, because, for one thing, he wanted to talk privately with Halleran first. For another, nothing about today's information would stand up in court if he ever needed it to, since he hadn't officially informed Nancy of her rights.

There was a way around all that, of course, as Boaz knew from many a session in the interview areas in the district station. It was a matter of repeating pertinent questions inside a room so small and windowless that it felt not only unreal, but cut off permanently from all other rooms in the world. People tended to talk in that circumstance, Miranda or no.

Boaz told himself he didn't want to Mirandize Nancy yet because of the strain it would make—that he'd found it helpful talking with her about the shape of things relevant to this case. What he preferred to ignore was that he liked talking with Nancy, period.

Finally, with a frown and a nod as if he'd decided something, he looked over at her. The elevator doors closed behind them on the relatively quiet third floor.

"Professor Cook: somethin' my Grandma Laura Mae took a notion to tell me, when I was little, was that if you want to steal a chicken, never mind lookin' at the chicken house. Just find out all you can about the farm."

"Now I appreciate your taking the time to tell me about the farm here," he continued, with a gesturing hand that took in all the hotel. "But I get the feelin' there might be something else you can tell me?"

He looked at her with eyebrows raised. "And there's also another room I'd like you to take a look at tomorrow, if you don't mind."

"Michael Alcott's room?"

Boaz nodded, watching her.

"Well—OK. I don't know how much help I can be. I mean, I

don't know how much you can tell *me* about what you're doing. But—sure. And I guess, as far as orientation goes, there *are* other power issues you could know about: money stuff."

Then, with oddly emphasized professionalism on both sides, Boaz Dixon and Nancy Cook compared morning schedules and, at Nancy's suggestion, arranged to meet at 11:00 by the TV console in the lobby.

"Maybe I should also take you to look at the Book Exhibition," Nancy added. "That's definitely part of the farm."

"All right, that'd be fine." Boaz left her at her door.

Nancy was a little crestfallen at the "Professor Cook" and at the general coolness of tone. Shrugging away the image of a little midnight supper, she went to read some papers apposite the Mudge panel tomorrow morning, at which she hoped to pose a crabby question or two. Before going to bed, she watered the plants in her room.

6

Boaz, meanwhile, had dropped back down to the second floor. Maneuvering past the bar crowd toward the Du Sable Ballroom and its 210A appendage, he overheard two women, both nice looking, evidently grad-school candidates, recapping their day's experiences.

"I still can't believe it!" one said. That afternoon, Shirley Lafarge had encountered a cowboy-booted, string-tied version of the academy as represented by the University of New Mexico at Gallup.

"I mean, there I was. Everything had gone pretty well, no big problem. There were these three guys on the committee. And at first I thought, 'This is great!' Because they kept asking me questions about my project, and it was very easy stuff.

"So then at some point I asked *them* a question, about how many grad students go into my field there. And things got kind of weird: they were almost defensive. Finally one of them tells me they haven't read my writing sample yet. Not one of them had any idea what my field was, even!"

Her friend, Abby Fraker, gave her the teacher's incredulous "Oh-really" look over her glasses.

"And *then*, get this: I'm getting my stuff together and I'm just about to leave when this jerk with this string tie on, he actually asks me, 'Oh, by the way, can you cook?'"

Boaz, for whom the word *cook* had acquired a new resonance all its own, listened with extra interest.

"I couldn't believe it. I said, 'What do you mean, can I cook?' *85*

And I said something like, 'That's a totally irrelevant question' and 'Have you been asking all your women candidates that?'

"And he looked flabbergasted. Honest to God, he really *was surprised*. Then he got real huffy and he tells me, 'Nobody else ever objected to that question'—like there was something the matter with *me*. He mentioned something about how the women at New Mexico do little potlucks and cooking activities for the department. I can just *see* them. Little aprons, right?"

"Oh, yeah," her friend put in. "With lots of turquoise jewelry."

"Right. Hopi patterns on the aprons. Well, I told him I don't *do* potlucks. I do professional teaching and research."

Agreeing, then, that Mr. String Tie had won, as Abby said, "the Gaping Asshole Award for the Day," they moved off for a consolation drink in the Diplomat Room on the tenth floor, where the University of Virginia offered its cash bar. UVA was known for the heavy-handedness of its bartenders, particularly if predictably with bourbon.

Boaz wondered what Nancy might have to encounter at the next MLA, at her interviews. He made a mental note to ask if that would be held in Chicago again.

The flimsy door to the base room opened with a nudge, since no attempt had been made here to disguise the cheapness of the wall construction. In this shelter Boaz was up until midnight, addressing details of the Fairfax staff schedule sheets and jotting notes.

On the cot he'd demanded delivered to the room, he slept some five hours before driving to his apartment in Andersonville. There he showered, shaved, and brought back a small suitcase with a change of shirt, tie, and toiletries to the hotel, just in case. The concierge, at the door of the base room at 7:30 A.M. Friday, spotted his suitcase on a folding chair and felt further aggrieved. Was he moving in?

She'd just stopped by, she said crisply, to ask if his accommodations here in the hotel were useful, were producing any progress?

"All the time, ma'am. All the time. Thank you." He looked down again at the schedule sheets. Ms. Carstairs-Norton closed the door firmly.

Boaz adjusted his tie. He had on his dark blue wool suit, nothing emphatic, but with a more vivid tie. It displayed indigo-blue tablets on a dark charcoal ground, against a button-down blue-and-gray plaid shirt. There were cases—long, dirty cases—during which you resolutely stayed clean and fed and kept your tie knotted, to remind yourself of your professionalism, to keep alert.

Halleran, Malley, and Hong, pulling up in their unmarked cars at about the same time, shoved the base door open at 8:00 A.M. Boaz lost the coin toss with Halleran and had to call in their four names for the morning roll call at the district station. The briefing after that with the lieutenant was as lengthy and roughshod as he'd expected.

"The loo," as he was known, was not cheerful about the lab findings, which he'd had copied and sent to the hotel under a siren. Homicide was going to be tough to investigate in these circumstances. The police could hardly search every hotel room in the Fairfax or bind over for questioning the thousands of conventioneers. Fingerprinting the various suites was next to useless: any hotel room was bound to have dozens of partials and no fast way of sorting them out. Just checking out alibis and backgrounds of the committees was going to be a labor, and not of love. Worse, the hotel staff numbered in the multiple dozens. Layoffs had been heavy in the last twelve months, for a variety of reasons.

"Without a confession or a witness, we're basically fucked," Mulcahy said. "Or have you got a different assessment, Dixon?"

"Not yet, Mulcahy," Boaz said, with a slight underlining of the word "yet." He persuaded the lieutenant, who was a showboater with the press, to tell the reporters as little as possible for now—no lab findings, if he could lid them. Also to let him keep Malley and Hong until further notice, and to send over another unit to help with the checkout work. Top-priority status of all lab work would remain in place if he and Halleran could come up with something else to be tested.

At 8:35, Chuck Metek phoned. It was not an obligatory phone call. But Metek, one of the few evidence technicians to know any cops personally, had details for Boaz to supplement the issued report. He sounded tired. His toxicology division's night shift was about to go treat itself to a mega-breakfast at Lou Mitchell's on Jackson Street, where the double-yolk eggs and fresh orange juice would be well earned.

"That was a helluva pot of coffee, Boaz," Metek began. "Let me tell you a little story about yesterday afternoon. About 12:30, we're running acidity tests and ruling out some inorganic stuff, and we went ahead and asked the computer the fifty-thousand-dollar question." (The Chicago morgue's toxicology computer has a database with chemical fingerprints of fifty thousand organic compounds.)

"A three-hour search later, all we could get it narrowed down to was 'taxine alkaloid.' Which might be any one of ten or a dozen different plants."

But the morgue is required to determine cause of death for all eighteen thousand customers in need of its services each year in Chicago. Not who did it, but only what did it is the preoccupation, then.

An extra difficulty about "what did it" arises in the case of toxins. The mere fact of there being a poison in Susan Engleton's digestive system was not, in itself, sufficient evidence that what did it was that poison. The lab must be able to show that the amount of poison found was sufficient to kill a human being of that particular age and weight. Comparison has to be made to an "authentic reference standard" for that toxin, even though not all plant toxins have been standardized.

Problems of seed identification and then of locating an authentic reference standard were what had kept Metek up most of the night, as well as the deputy chief toxicologist, Mary Ann Wu, and an evidence technician who'd carried samples with them to the Poison Control Center. Some slides had been prepared and squinted at. Pages had been turned in illustrated tomes such as the *AMA Handbook of Poisonous and Injurious Plants*. Eventually, two members of the plant science department at the University of Illinois had been rousted out of bed for their input.

The gritty stuff in the Wellesley coffee sediment proved to be remnants of "dozens and dozens, maybe originally ten dozen" crushed yew seeds. The concentration of toxin was such that respiratory failure and/or arrhythmia of the victim's heart would have been produced "probably within an hour, maybe within half an hour" after ingestion, Metek said.

"Since everybody else just got nauseated," he continued, "probably the victim drank a lot more than anybody else did. My guess would be, she got up early and drank a couple or three cups before anybody else got there. Of course, she might also have had a heart condition. That would have made her more susceptible. You might check the autopsy pages for that. And if you're going to call down to the cutting room now, tell Russ to let me know, will you? I'm kind of curious. This is weird."

"Never heard of this poison, Chuck," Boaz said. "How's it classified?"

"Herbal, buddy, herbal."

And Boaz, jotting down notes, was provided with another crash course, this time on the subject of the ubiquity and propinquity of yew shrubs, particularly *Taxus cuspidata*, Japanese yew, and *Taxus baccata*, English yew.

"As a planted ornamental in the United States" ("Get on with it, Chuck," Boaz told him), "there are four species of yew, all evergreens. Here, they're used a lot for hedges. In England you see it as a single tree, usually in cemeteries. Japanese yew is pretty typical: needles about an inch long, yellowish on the underside, each with a sharp little point."

"Could you maybe pick up a step, Chuck? This feels like church."

"It's the dumb green bush that everybody's got right by the front door out in all the subdivisions, OK, Bo? What's more . . ."

And Boaz continued to be instructed, with an occasional "Hunnh," that in addition to having a taproot and an ability to grow in virtually every plant zone in the Northern Hemisphere, the yew produces soft red berries every autumn, about the size of peas. Each has a single seed inside, greenish-black.

"These are eventually eaten by birds. Without ensuing problems," Chuck Metek added. "Or without problems that we know of."

"Chuck . . ."

But Metek, who knew Boaz through Halleran and had last seen him at a wedding whereat Metek's second cousin had joined Halleran's enormous family, enjoyed hassling both detectives just a little.

"Goats and deer have big problems with this plant, Bo. Several have been reported dead in this country. Also a dead burro and some reindeer have been reported. Usually they die with the leaves right in their mouths. The whole plant is poisonous, *except* for the fleshy berry part. Where you get the most poison is in the seeds.

"A yew-berry dosage lethal to a human child could be harvested from, oh, just one long hedge, maybe. The Poison Center gets called about a sick kid or two every year." For an adult, as Metek indicated, a lot more berries would be necessary.

"Now the principle here—since you asked—is an alkaloid, rather than a polypeptoid or an amine or a resin or maybe an oxalate."

"So?"

"So the poison would taste bitter; all alkaloids do. Which probably accounts for the huge concentration of liquid sweetener we also found in that pot. That was probably added in advance to the toxin to disguise the taste. Ordinarily an alkaloid would be too bitter to drink, even in something bitter like French Roast, if that's what it was."

"Yeah, that's the house blend. Saw it in the kitchen."

"OK, now," Chuck proceeded briskly. "The taxine alkaloid in the yew plant happens to be what we call an 'uncharacterized or incompletely characterized' alkaloid."

"Meaning?"

"Meaning that its crystal structure is sort of indefinite. We know, though, that alkaloids are insoluble in water. So if you're going to get poisoned by them, you'll need an organic solvent, like your stomach acids when you eat the seeds. But the victims didn't eat the seeds. The seeds sank to the bottom of the pot; they wouldn't come out the spigot. No seeds were found in any of the cups.

"Besides *that*," Metek continued, "if you just threw the seeds we found into a big coffee pot for a few minutes, you wouldn't get a strong enough poison. It takes longer than that. So somebody must have prepared a very strong extract in advance, using a lot more seeds than what we found.

"The easiest thing to do would be to use more coffee as your solvent," he went on. "That's my guess, anyway. The seeds had been partially crushed, by a mortar or something, to release the toxin. And all the seeds we found were soft; they'd been steeping for a while."

"Hours?"

"Maybe. Maybe days. And so, to summarize, ossifer . . ."

"I'm right here."

"You got premeditation, buddy. You got Murder One. Have a nice day. Oh, and hey! Give me a call later next week, Bo. Sherrie tells me we're putting together a little picnic on Saturday. Catch you later."

At Boaz's request, Metek transferred the call to the morgue's lay investigator, Pete Montenegro, who put him briefly on hold. Boaz pushed his note pad over for Halleran and the others to read.

He and Montenegro discussed details. As summarized in Engleton's autopsy report, Russ De Bartolo had discovered a minor malformation of the victim's heart indicating a long-standing heart murmur. (This was confirmed by Hong later that day, when Susan Engleton's physician in Massachusetts told him a mild murmur had been diagnosed in Susan's early twenties.)

Nothing additionally toxic had been found: not in Annette Lisordi's coffee cup, nor in containers of any kind in the searched rooms. No apparatus had been found to concoct a poison. However, any of the immediate suspects or someone else in the hotel could have prepared a poison before the convention and brought it in with the luggage.

Smudgy fingerprints were found, as expected, near the spigot of the coffee tureen. One light set of Engleton's prints, a three-finger partial, was on the left side of the tureen, as if she'd touched the metal lightly to see if it were still hot. As for the lid of the tureen: absolutely clean.

"Well, of course it was," Boaz remarked drily. "When do we ever get a clear set of prints in a murder case?" Halleran, beside him, nodded gloomily. Hanging up, Boaz briefed the detectives around him on the Engleton lab results. Digestion on Malley's part was somewhat slow.

"This bush is in Chicago?" he asked.

"This bush is everywhere. But there's no special reason why the poison would have to be made here, anyway. Might have, might not."

Another search through the hotel kitchens, this time for evidence of a specific red berry and/or greenish-black seeds, was begun. Two arriving beat cops were sent down to take up that tedium. Meanwhile, informing the conventioneers about this possible hazard would serve no purpose, it was decided. The halls were as crowded as ever with people, but morning or night, no wheeled coffee carts were to be seen. No one was ordering it.

Boaz turned now to Malley and Hong. "OK, alibis. What went down?"

The overall answer was, not much. According to Malley, Nancy Cook's friend, Dina Marinetti on Greenwood, giving sleepy answers to a cop this morning, had corroborated that Nancy had stayed with her for three nights before leaving to check in at the Fairfax. But Professor Cook's opportunities for mayhem were still wide open on Wednesday afternoon and on Thursday morning. Nobody at Slade's could remember seeing her at breakfast on Thursday.

"Which means exactly zip," Malley noted. "Fuckers forgot my potatoes *and* my rolls, too, last night."

"But I'm sure they'll remember *you* a long, long time," Halleran put in.

"Flying fuck time, Halleran," Malley said, with terse amiability.

(Halleran didn't care much for Malley. Malley was too quick, too sleazy, and had too big a grin on his face when he was needling another cop. But as Halleran had said to Boaz one day, "A good thing about Malley, one good thing: he hates people. Really *hates* them. Makes him a good man to have at your back if you get a call into Grant Park some night. Goddam cat wouldn't get past him.")

Turning now to the Wellesley statements, Boaz wanted input and reactions about where the committee people had been on the Wednesday when Alcott died, and how their statements compared to registration listings.

Hong reported that everyone in the Wellesley group had checked into the Fairfax on Wednesday night, after Alcott's death, except for Jessica Griffith, who'd checked in at 1:00 Wednesday afternoon.

"Why'd they all show up so early?" Boaz asked, jotting notes. "How many positions they looking for?"

Halleran and the other detectives were a little surprised at this swerve, but they hadn't attended Nancy's orientation course.

By way of answer, Hong said he'd picked up that Wellesley had just one job to fill. Competition for the job they expected to be pretty heavy. Something about Sarah Lawrence and Bryn Mawr also looking for a professor out of the same group Wellesley was going to talk to. Vaster had said something about the committee's plan to get a head start with early interviews and make a job offer to somebody right on the spot. Susan Engleton's death had put them off schedule now.

"OK. So Jessica Griffith's here on Wednesday afternoon," Boaz noted.

"Yeah," said Hong, "but she called the desk at about 1:15. Had a complaint about the plumbing. She stayed in her room the whole time the plumber took the elbow pipe out. And he didn't get finished 'til about 5:00."

"Four hours just to change out an elbow?"

Halleran's mouth twitched a little. "Union pay, Boaz. Be a good brother. He'd still be in there if he hadn't wanted his dinner."

"Yeah. OK, Thursday morning now."

Malley said Thursday morning was wide open for all the Wellesley committee. Not one of the two men and two women had an
alibi that could be verified. There was a window of time of ten to
fifteen minutes when any of the four could have poured a poison
into the coffee cart standing in the hall. Two or three of them could
even have been in a conspiracy to kill off the Engleton woman.

"We got to check into their connections some more today,"
Malley said. "How they get along, what they do with each other"
—Malley showed some teeth—"I mean, besides telling each other
how fucking smart they are all the time."

Individually, each person in the Wellesley group "has got the
intelligence profile of a poisoner," Hong pointed out. Malley put
in at this point that it wouldn't have been hard to figure out how
to drink just enough to get sick, but not dead-sick. "Or maybe just
fake being sick."

"When was the last time you faked it, throwing up, Malley?"
Halleran asked.

"You back so soon? I thought I told you it's takeoff time."

"What about the staff?" Boaz put in.

Halleran had followed up on Boaz's first inquiries among the
hotel staff the day before. Nothing had turned up yet in the way
of grudges or vendettas in the employee-management relations.
People couldn't remember any threats being made, or hard feelings about layoffs. The union was pretty quiet, and fairly good at
checking out people they put on the job. Still, in Halleran's opin-
ion, it couldn't be ruled out that some disgruntled employee, past
or present, was trying to discredit the hotel with a deliberately
created scandal.

Boaz, getting up to walk around the base room, ticked off the
difficulties of questioning these committee people. Ordinarily in
investigations, you start looking at all the people the victim knew
or recently came into contact with. You look at the address book,
recent letters, personal calendar dates. All that was impossible at a
hiring convention. In a way, Susan Engleton's "address book" was
the entire MLA registration list. Her personal calendar was not
just the interviewees, but any of the 650 panels she might have had

some personal reason for going to. "Or there could be problems back in the department we don't know about."

Boaz then speculated whether Susan Engleton might have poisoned the coffee herself. She was the one who'd wheeled the coffee service into the suite. An elaborate suicide, could it have been? Meant to kill other people in the school with her, too?

Halleran in his brown suit lifted his head impatiently. It was not unlike a groundhog popping up from a mound of earth.

"No, I know, Timmy, don't tell me," Boaz said to him with a lifted hand. "It'd be a whole brand new way to go."

And suicide methods, as cops know, are emphatically conservative. When a plan is under way for self-annihilation, the planner does not become experimental. Suicides rely on history, staying with the tried and true methods they've heard about.

"Would you add an unpredictable poison to a pot of coffee and then go get dressed and let everybody in the room?" Boaz posed, then sighed. "About as likely as Oklahoma rain having more than dust and bugs in it.

"OK." He slid gracefully onto his folding chair again. "So we're gonna go on plowin' this straight-up-and-down field for a while." Halleran heaved his bulk about and grunted.

Boaz shoved the staff schedule sheets to one side. Halleran would disagree, but they struck him as unpromising leads at the moment. No one Boaz had interviewed on the kitchen or maintenance staffs had struck him as having a poisoner's resourcefulness and general wherewithal. The concierge, though, yes, and with another phone call he put a tail on her.

"I don't want her to take a pee in this hotel or anywhere else without you knowing about it, Joey. And find out if you can if she does any gardening. Or does she just walk around the neighborhood and breathe on things and they die? No, no, I'm not seri . . . never mind, Joey. Just tail her."

Boaz hung up and rubbed his forehead. "OK, now. Alcott." He turned to the other detectives. "What have we got?"

"Well, I got some shots of the crowd," Malley said. "Half a dozen. But they aren't blown up." 95

These snapshots were the result of Malley's 35mm hobby. During their partnership so far, Malley and Hong had worked out a kind of routine when first arriving at a scene, provided other cops had arrived and chase activity wasn't required. For a few moments, Malley would move around the edges of the scene, shooting a quick set of wide-angle lens shots, regardless of the fact that the morgue would send an ET to take slides of the body and adjacent area. According to Malley, what that technician couldn't help but miss was the arrangement of John Q. Public; that is, the first curious crowds to gather at the scene.

It was these bystanders Malley recorded whenever possible. Full-lengths of faces and feet: just a fast few shots. Only once so far had this actually helped to clear a case. On that occasion, the perpetrator had lingered at the scene to relish the attention paid to his bloody handiwork on the street. Malley's crowd-scene photos had been developed and checked against mug shots of convicted felons, with an arrest made shortly thereafter.

After that, Malley was unstoppable. Patrolmen and wagon men were more or less used to it now, the sight of Hong standing behind Malley, covering him, Hong's eyes scanning everything, making occasional stabbing glances behind himself, moving around with his snapping partner as if in a dance.

Malley now fanned out his Fairfax lobby shots on the table. The detectives looked them over, seeing no unusual details and no one they recognized. At least, as Halleran pointed out, none of the onlookers was smiling in these shots. Usually some wiseacre thinks the whole mess is funny.

The Wednesday afternoon statements by the University of Arizona committee, taken by the lay investigator, by Malley, Hong, and then later by Halleran, provided the following information:

Four people made up the Arizona group this year: Jerry Sprague, the department chair, and associate professors Blackwell, Esposito, and Pogue, Pogue being a woman. They'd come to hire for four positions.

"But Alcott was *not* part of their committee," Malley said. "He came solo to this place, on his own. Had a lot of connections he wanted to touch base with here. 'He liked to mingle'—that's according to Sprague."

As for Michael Alcott personally: age thirty-six. A tall guy, kind of thin. Thought of himself as a real player with women. Appeared to be uninvolved in any present relationship. Sometimes made moves on the graduate-student women, but no one had been seen with him for quite some time, months. Some angry women in his life, according to Blackwell and Pogue, but no ex-wife. No heirs who could be interested in much. The insurance package provided by Arizona listed his mother as beneficiary.

"OK, so Alcott checks in on Wednesday, in the morning," Malley went on. "Aw, what's this?" he added, looking at another note. "Oh yeah: Alcott's background was Johns Hopkins University. That's where he got his doctor degree. Cornell before that. They called him a Marxist. I got the idea he was some kind of a big deal. Sprague talked about him like he was some kind of prize."

"A communist?" Halleran asked.

"More'n likely he wasn't anything near a communist, Timmy," Boaz said. "If Nancy's description's right, then the Marxists here like to talk big, but they wouldn't know a 'worker' in a room with ten lights on. They'd all do real well in a tall-tale competition."

"Alcott used to teach at the University of Georgia," Hong put in. "Then Arizona bought him away from there. Sprague was really bragging about that; I guess he had something to do with it. Even with Alcott dead, he seemed to think Arizona's reputation is big-time now. Gave the impression the guy could pitch a no-hitter or something."

"Pitched bullshit," Malley put in bitterly. Malley had never done well in school.

Hong and the others ignored Malley's contribution this time. Hong continued, "They're pretty out front, all four of them, especially Esposito, that Alcott was a real son of a bitch. But they knew that about him before they made him their big job offer. I got the idea he had professional connections, but not really any friends."

"Enemies?"

"Unknown. Probably."

"OK, so he checks in Wednesday morning, about 10 A.M.," Malley piped up, shuffling his notes. "Not many people were here then. The convention didn't really get started 'til last night."

Boaz nodded. This matched Nancy's orientation information.

"Hong's still waiting to hear about a couple of the plane tickets and registration times we're checking out. But it looks like nobody in the Arizona group got to the hotel 'til Thursday afternoon. They found out about Alcott's swan dive into the lobby like everybody else."

After registering on Wednesday morning, Alcott had come across Dennis Doog from the University of Connecticut. Doog was someone he'd been to school with long ago at Cornell. According to Doog and other restaurant witnesses, the two of them had eaten an early lunch at the Chez Toi.

The appalled and rattled Professor Doog had a solid alibi for the rest of the afternoon. He'd gone to the Art Institute with a woman from Swarthmore ("Are you going to tell my wife about this?" he'd asked several times during Halleran's late-afternoon visit to his room). Then Doog and the woman had taken an architecture tour down Michigan Avenue.

"They did it on the tour bus?" Malley asked, grinning.

"They did it in the back of your old squad car, Malley," Halleran answered impassively. "The squad you're going to be busted back to one of these days."

"What else was in Doog's statement?" Boaz asked.

Alcott had kept looking around the restaurant and making comments about the women, Doog had said. He hadn't seemed particularly nervous or worried, though. He'd had several drinks, whisky sours, confirmed by the Chez Toi bartender, who put the number at three.

Mostly Alcott had talked to Doog about how much money he, Alcott, was making now, and how *Critical Inquiry* had just solicited an article from him, and how the Arizona women were really hot, not like the Georgia ball-breakers.

After lunch, Doog and Alcott had gone their separate ways.

Doog maintained they hadn't arranged to meet again and he didn't know where Michael had gone after that.

That was the extent of witness information. No one else from the convention had come forward about Alcott, Halleran reported, even though his revised TV message on the lobby console was still running every five minutes. (IF YOU DRINK, DON'T DIVE was another message Halleran had proposed, to the snorts of Malley and Hong, though the concierge had been anything but amused.)

"Doog came forward all on his own?" Boaz asked.

"Scared shitless," Malley said. "Came up to me at the desk Wednesday. He's next door at the Hyatt, if you want another statement. But I don't think he knows jack. Just another jerk at college. Couldn't find his butt with both hands."

Boaz nodded, and, since Halleran was stimulating Malley like a cattle prod, Boaz chose not to inform Malley at this time that the correct phrase, which is Ozarkan, is, "couldn't find his butt with both hands in broad daylight."

"What else you got, Timmy?" he asked Halleran.

"Well, it looks like Alcott was heading back to his room on the tenth floor after he'd boozed it up at lunch. Evidence we have seems to indicate he didn't make it. The morgue figured the probable trajectory put him just past the elevator on the tenth floor when he went over."

"Also," put in Hong, "three of the shot bottles in Alcott's refrigerator were empty. Found them in the wastebasket in his bedroom. Looks like he'd helped himself to a few ounces before he even saw Doog in the bar."

"Right. So this guy was tanked," Malley proceeded, somewhat loud-voiced. "Lab says his blood alcohol level was—where is that?—0.31 percent. Three times the legal limit. Even with the food he ate, he would have been feeling it. We're talking about spazzed-out walking, eyes real wide, probably couldn't talk worth shit, maybe couldn't see straight.

"So he gets off at the tenth floor," Malley went on. "There's a 99 good chance nobody saw this guy at all after he got off the elevator up there." Alcott's single room, 1012, was located on one of the conference-room floors, and the conference rooms were not in use on Wednesday afternoon.

"I think he got off balance when he came out of the elevator," Malley concluded. "He was turning to the right to go down the hall to his room, but he tripped up and started staggering some more, and hit the balcony and went over."

"The balcony's at the left in that hallway," Boaz pointed out. "Why would he stagger left if he was turning to the right?" Boaz inquired.

Halleran said nothing but rolled his big head in Malley's direction. He squinted at the younger detective as if looking at something unexpected in a petri dish.

"The morgue establish a scenario on this thing?" Boaz demanded of Malley, who shook his head.

"Not exactly, but they think it was an accident."

"Any bruises on Alcott's left leg? From hitting the side of the balcony?"

"I don't know," Malley admitted sullenly. "I don't think so."

"Who's going to find fresh bruises, Bo, when you're looking at fresh massive injuries?" Halleran put in. "Here's De Bartolo's report. They spent a lot of time here with this." With that, Halleran pushed the file folder with its looseleaf pages over to Boaz. In it were the Alcott autopsy and toxicology report.

"*But,*" said Malley, "so what if Alcott didn't stagger to the left, the way I said? Maybe he had some other reason for being next to the balcony. Maybe he was looking around for that bar up there. Maybe he'd just decided to take a piss down the atrium. And don't ask me was his fly unzipped. It wasn't, OK? But the guy lost his balance, that's all."

Boaz riffed the five pages of the examiners' report thoughtfully. He'd know them thoroughly very soon, along with the pages of the Engleton report. Leaning back on his folding chair, he gestured now to Halleran, Hong, and Malley together.

"Why don't you all just tell me that Susan Engleton was the

secret lover of Michael Alcott and they put together a suicide pact?" he said. "Older woman, younger man. He jumps, she drinks—right?"

Hong smiled.

"No way, Bo," Malley said.

"OK, then, tell me they were secret kin," Boaz said. "Double cousins and secret kin. Their rich uncle died and some in-law came here and did them in."

"Why do you keep thinking there's a connection, Bo?" Halleran asked.

Boaz shrugged. "By the way, what all was Alcott wearing? You remember?"

Malley glanced at Hong and looked irritated anew. "What do you mean, do I remember? He had leather pants on, tight stuff. Black leather . . ."

"A white T-shirt?"

Malley produced a toothy smile. "Well, I guess it was white to begin with, yeah."

"One earring?"

"Yeah, I think so."

"One earring," said Hong. "His right ear."

"But Engleton, if I recall, was partial to silk," Boaz said. To Halleran he asked, "Wasn't that a silk blouse? Designer-clothes kind of thing?"

Halleran nodded.

"So what?" asked Hong.

"So they were in different worlds, that's what," Boaz told him. "Might as well have been at two different conventions. No Arizona-Wellesley connection. None. Trouble is, I don't truly believe that. Just doesn't feel right."

Halleran moved his bulk backwards carefully in his chair, as if adjusting a patient in bed.

"Poisoners don't push people, Bo. They aren't muscle guys, they're brain guys, you know that. Now we have evidence that Alcott was a boozer and that he was pretty well zapped. We don't have *any* evidence that he was anything except a clumsy asshole. 101

The morgue's ready to assume jurisdiction over it as an accident and close out the case."

Boaz, however, did not nod. Halleran became more emphatic.

"There aren't any witnesses of *anything*, Bo. We even talked to the people in the elevator. The glass one. Asked them if they noticed anything unusual about Alcott when he went by." Hong and Malley laughed. Halleran had paused, his eyelids narrowing until he looked lacertilian.

"Couple of them said Alcott seemed like he was twisting in the air. So he was probably alive the whole way down. But nobody saw anything on him, and he didn't wave or signal anything. He was just a guy in the air out there, and moving fast.

"And what was left of him—well, you can read it: no twist burns on the wrists, his clothes aren't torn, no signs of struggle. Rolex still on. Plus: his wallet was full of credit cards, and he had about two hundred, three hundred dollars on him."

Malley spoke up, "Yeah, his financial condition was pretty solid. No big debts, just car payments. No gambling anybody's heard of. Good credit rating. Ditto for Engleton, too. No money sweat in her life."

But Boaz was still frowning heavily. The other cops watched him for a moment. He made a brief "thch" sound off a front tooth and his mouth pursed. But he did not nod.

The elevator door had opened all but soundlessly. There he is. *Michael Alcott was standing as if confused or undecided, near the atrium balcony ledge.* He's turning around.

No one else had gotten off the elevator, and the tenth floor hall was empty. He recognizes me.

As Alcott's mind, alcohol-rinsed, just managed the act of recognition, a look of dismissal-in-advance followed across his face. It was a contemptuous and well-practiced twitch, a kind of accelerated sneer.

There were many things that Michael Alcott was never going to know. What he didn't know about himself would fill a small psychology library. He would never know, for instance, that his sneer that moment was an act that confirmed his doom. That look.

Beside him a moment later, the killer wore a small smile. No one is here. *Then the killer looked down, casually, over the atrium balustrade.* There is a knife. Get out the knife?

Alcott stood swaying a little in his particular atmosphere. Alcohol.

Now the killer, pointing over the ledge and down the atrium, suddenly spoke aloud, with oddly voiced enthusiasm equal on each syllable: "Isn't that Jacques Derrida? I think so! There was a rumor he'd be here. He's coming in the lobby door?"

And Alcott, first fan of the French deconstructionist who'd created so many American article-opportunities, leaned excitedly forward, trying to scan past the hanging vines that dangled from floor to floor.

Seeing nothing, Alcott turned his head upward and back, giving the killer an impatient look. It was his last.

"No, there! Back over there!" *the killer gestured, pointing emphati-* 103 *cally down and to the left. Alcott leaned out a little further, craning his neck.* No one can see.

With that, Professor Alcott found himself assisted forward as someone decisively pushed his shoulder blades and then yanked up his knees. Just as suddenly, thereafter, the hall of the tenth floor was very still. A low, hissing sound there was, only that, of breath between the teeth.

In the new clarity of the hallway, there were no scratches to be seen on the marble balcony ledge. No melodramatic handkerchief was fluttering to the carpet. There was no lost key or pen or any other trace of Alcott's objectionable person.

Quickly, then, the killer exited, using the south-side stairwell to drop down one floor. Coming out on the more populated ninth-floor hallway, the killer calmly and inconspicuously joined the small crowd waiting for the elevator up, then went in that direction for many floors.

☞ ☞

At lobby level on Wednesday afternoon, far below the tenth floor, shouting and commotion began. The uproar continued for quite some time. It was still echoing four hours later in the activity of the disgusted hotel maids and maintenance staff, who inherited the lobby after Malley and Hong had closed the Michael Alcott scene.

One of the Fairfax staff from Supplies, Alexandra Rostikoff, looking at the spatters spreading as far as the potted plants, spatters that promised unpleasant discoveries in other places here and there, declared stoutly that this kind of cleaning shouldn't be in their contract.

"Besides, laundry don't come 'til tomorrow and I don't know if we got enough paper towels."

There was an ensuing petty-cash dispute, then a delay for extra purchases, and some hard words between two or three staff people before the terrazzo floor subsided to its usual position in everyone's lives. For days, though, no one walked across that area except unknowingly.

104   Michael Alcott's death had taken place on Wednesday after-

noon, Susan Engleton's on Thursday morning. Now, Friday morning, Halleran, Hong, and Malley began again, in rotation, on the "Wellesley Four," as Malley had dubbed them. Boaz they left studying the Alcott reports.

"What the hell's he doing, anyway?" Malley grumbled. "We're doing all the work."

Halleran's narrowed eyes now were not a sign of amusement. "Is that right? Tell you what, Malley. First time you ever spend the night at the scene of an investigation, then I'll want to hear every little word you've got to say. But in the meantime" (Halleran's tone was pseudoavuncular), "why don't you just watch and learn a little bit, Malley?"

"Can I watch you, too, big Hal? Hong, you got a cigarette?" And the three went off together along their narrow personal edge.

As for taking Nancy Cook to the Alcott room, Halleran and Boaz had decided to postpone that until later that afternoon but not to drop Cook from the investigation yet.

"You've got to find out where she's coming from," Halleran insisted. "Every damned thing's got to get followed up, Bo, you know that. No way we take a luncher on this one." (By "luncher," Halleran meant a case that doesn't clear, that you end up eating, as it were, for lunch.)

And so, repeatedly interrupting the Wellesley interviewing schedule and making no apologies, the three detectives did not stop for Friday lunch. They kept the Wellesley people hungry, too, trying to make use of resulting resentments in order to ask unbalancing questions. Asking, nonstop, about problems with the difficult, imperious Susan Engleton. Asking about gardening, about pharmaceuticals. By one o'clock that afternoon, the Wellesley group felt as though they'd been taking GRE exams.

None of them had liked Susan; Susan wasn't likable. None of them except Muffie Murchison ever spent time outdoors. ("Outdoors, Officer, is where you put the car," as Lawrence Vaster said testily to Hong. "That's where the car lives." Hong just went on staring at him.) And Muffie Murchison's engagement with nature,   *105* it turned out, was confined mainly to ski slopes, places devoid of domestic shrubbery.

"*Could* you let us get on with our business, I wonder, Mr. Hong?" Herbert Gooch finally huffed. Wellesley still had its one job to fill and Gooch wanted to call a kind of huddle about it. Here it was almost 1:15 P.M. Annette Lisordi had agreed to see them later that day, but there were several other candidates backed up as well.

Gooch, remarkably limited in his scope of understanding (he was a specialist in James Joyce), would never realize that Hong's long questioning across that lunch hour would provide all the Wellesley committee with alibis very much needed.

Meanwhile, earlier that morning, Boaz sent off an assisting unit to check whether anyone on the Arizona committee happened to be acquainted with anyone on the Wellesley committee, particularly with Susan Engleton. Then, skeptically, he dropped into the kitchens, where he learned, with no surprise, that the berry hunting was proceeding without result.

Other cops that morning were turning pages back at the District One station on State Street. They were making phone calls, slogging through the identities of fired hotel staff, looking for motives, looking for a match with any known criminals.

Hour after hour, it was a mess. It was as belabored with verbiage and triviality as the panel discussions going on at the hotels. Unlike most panels, however, the police inquiries into their subject matter were based on sound reasoning and had an urgent point.

At 10:45 A.M., Boaz was back from the basement and scanning the lobby area. In front of him was a piano, seldom persecuted. Four Frenchified sofas perched inside the sunken octagon in the center, with upholsteries that looked both expensive and derivative. (They were nylon-blend approximations of Scalamandre and of Brunschwig et Fils designs.) Lobby lizards, male and female, were draped and distributed thereupon. Green and rose carpeting (an approximation of Stark) lay under more Frenchoid chairs and small side tables. In construction terms, this meant cheap deal furniture painted white with gold paint down the legs, the legs so cabrioled they looked bowlegged as anemic cowboys. Small groups of people tended to cluster near the octagon or in front of the "beaux-arts" mirrors that edged the walls of the wide atrium.

Christmas poinsettias stood in formidable installations near the octagon and beside the foyer doors. Another great pot of them flared upward on the TV console, lending it a tropical, Carmen Miranda look. Stolidly, however, the TV continued to flash its news that the Adams Room was located in the Hyatt Regency, not in the Fairfax; that "The Subcultural Signification of Gothic Rock Music: Ideology or Resistance?" had been rescheduled for 3:30 P.M. in the Ogden Room; and that the Child Care Center, open every morning at 7:00, accepted all major credit cards.

On the far side of the console, Nancy was standing, lost in thought. She hadn't noticed Boaz yet. A dark overcoat was draped in front of her over the hanger of her crossed arms.

She'd dressed more casually today, Boaz observed. A long, blue sweater, kind of rolled at the neck. (It was cadmium blue and fell below her hips.) Violet corduroy trousers tucked into blue cowboy boots. (They were blue leather boots, with pale blue suede inset patterning.) Accessories included a blue wooden bracelet and a short strand of chunky blue beads, and under her flaring hair were large earrings of round blue plastic: an effect cheerful and sophisticated, both.

If she were toying with the police, how would she have dressed this morning? Boaz wondered. Wouldn't she have worn a dress again, or a suit? Or not?

Well, she looked great, he admitted reluctantly. She also looked preoccupied. She greeted him almost routinely and didn't seem to notice him closely. He wondered if she were angry, but what Nancy was, was dismayed, almost demoralized. She'd been seriously asking herself whether she could stay in this profession at all. Her left hand, with a separate affection, was touching a red poinsettia leaf.

"Well, I went to a panel this morning. Mudge's. One of the *107* big events." She paused. "He's not usually so—well, Martian. He's been a camp follower of 'new historicism' for years, but he's usually pretty reasonable." She fell silent.

What Nancy had attended, though she didn't summarize it for Boaz, was the 9:30 A.M. lecture by the celebrated Sarton P. Mudge of U.C. San Diego, who'd directed a discussion after he'd read from portions of his latest collection, *Learning to Parse*. It was modeled, as were Mudge's outfits, on the work and attire of another scholar sometimes known as "The Father of New Historicism."

In his own briskly selling item, Mudge had eventually, in chapter 4, taken up his main topic of the *Malleus Maleficarum* (or, *The Hammer of Witches*), the 1486 tome which has never been out of print, and which, because it is a how-to manual for the identification and torture and trial of a witch, was consulted by credulous European magistrates for the better part of three hundred years.

Because the *Malleus* was of great interest to James I, during whose reign the terrible Dominican book was published and used repeatedly, it had aroused the interest, too, of the Renaissance scholar directing this morning's panel. First by way of several tabloid details describing slow, pigtail strangulations in nineteenth-century China, Mudge's work then excerpted two paragraphs from the *Malleus* and addressed them as the essence of the text.

That text was then seen to be in reality "a reasonable, even gentle work, long misconstrued." Since the literature of any given time is, as Mudge explained, a product of, as well as a rebellion against, the power structures of its time (a standing premise of new historicism), the *Malleus* should be understood to be actually a rebellion by its two Dominican authors against the existing power structure. Not only against the power structure of its Gutenberg time, but rebellion against the Jacobean era as well, rebellions that "the orthodoxy had consistently misused to sustain and propel itself."

The pale, epigonous Professor Mudge—late thirties, manicured, Italian-shoed, in a rumpled beige linen suit—was noticed by a few front-row people in his audience to become freshly animated while reading his description of child abuse by starvation in 1773. This incident, like the pigtail strangulations, had found its way into *Parse* in a manner most wonderful, evidently by free association of the professor's mind around the numinous nexus of blood.

Finishing up, wiping the palm of his right hand down his expensive suit, the new-historicism maven illustrated again, for the other wannabes before him, that gratuitous violence of any kind not only is an allowable element in academic work, but is outright sexy, exciting, and professionally hip.

Later, at the TV console, Nancy stood assessing the lobby occupants with her analytical look, and her straight dark eyebrows were a serious, almost-solid line.

"I can't talk about that panel right now," she said. "Let's just say I need to find a new role model. But how are *you?*" she asked then, with a smile that really took him in for the first time.

Boaz nodded. Nancy's fingers left the poinsettia and pushed back a wandering wad of hair. "The plants are in pretty good shape here," she noted, refocusing.

Plants. She likes outdoor gardening, Boaz remembered.

"You grow these things?" he asked. "Got a big garden of them?"

"Oh no, these are greenhouse plants, commercial stuff. They grow these on flats by the acre. I've just got a little perennial garden, out behind my apartment. It might look nice this spring, though; I put in some wild tulips. They're very tiny. . . ." And Nancy's long fingers measured in space a five-inch distance for the yellow inflorescence and stem of her *Tulipa sylvestris*.

"Got any evergreens around? Trees and stuff? Yews?"

Nancy looked at him curiously. Boaz noted the pause and wondered what it meant. The woman wasn't nervous, though, he saw.

"No yews," she told him. "Yews are kind of boring. Besides, there are some toddlers next door and I don't want them eating them. I've got a forsythia hedge over on one side. I was going to experiment with some cotoneaster under it, maybe. Oh, and there's a little Scotch pine in the corner. Why? What is it you're growing?"

"Oh, I dunno. I haven't decided yet."

Boaz was a troubled man. This woman was definitely aware of the wrong greenery. And smart enough to do anything she wanted with it.

"OK, what's next here?" he asked, to give her room to talk. "Any more orientation?"

Nancy looked at this strange man for a moment, then gave another mental shrug. "Well, something's going on right here," she told him, indicating the lobby arena and its circulating inhabitants. "Something I saw a lot of at the panel, too. A friend of mine, Ruth, calls it 'the MLA Swivel.'"

Discreetly pointing, Nancy said in a low voice, "Notice in particular Ashby Helks. He does it very well."

In front of a small group near the octagon was Cornell's Professor Helks, a prolix Marxist Trendy in his thirties. (The latest of his forty articles had addressed, across thirty-five pages, the cultural import of magazine advertisements for dish towels.)

Helks was wearing a bright mango sport coat, underscored by ski boots. Both were meant to indicate (as he explained later to a press interviewer) his "sarcastic send-up" of the polyester dress-habits in the academy. His shirt, tie, and trousers, meanwhile, were as haplessly ordinary as any other man's in the room.

It was not Helks's sartorial effort, though, that Nancy was referring to, but rather his facial and eye movements as he talked in the direction of three men around him.

To perform the MLA Swivel, Nancy explained, you must take up a conspicuous position in a cash bar or hotel lobby, somewhere you can be observed by many people coming by. Then you engage in talk with someone, preferably a group. Lots of bussing on cheeks and loud exclamations of welcome. But if your audience is what would be considered lower status, your tone of voice stays edged with condescension. If the other person is of equal or higher rank, you speak as familiarly as you can get away with.

Meanwhile, at frequent intervals, your head swivels left and right, to see, first of all, whether anyone is paying attention to you, and second, whether anyone else nearby is more important than the person you're speaking to. In which case, you abruptly terminate your chat and move off in the higher-status direction. Needless to say, men and women who enter the cash bars with name tags indicating the University of Idaho or an adjunct campus of the University of South Carolina do not find themselves engaged in conversation often or for long.

"The people who're really good at this," Nancy noted, "like Helks, don't even move their heads. They can look around just by shifting their weight a little and dropping one shoulder; then they just move their eyes."

The enormous mirrors in the lobby and ballrooms, Nancy added, are a great aid to the swivelers if used properly, with the right strategic positioning.

"Well, it's a good thing," Boaz noted evenly, "that these folks aren't out on the sidewalk. A woman on the street rubbernecking like that is maybe a pickpocket, but more'n likely she's a prostitute. You got a roomful of 'em here. And you see a guy lookin' around like that, then he's spotting for somebody or he's a mope gettin' ready to commit a crime himself."

Nancy had to laugh. "So is that what you're looking for, when you go by in the police car?"

"Among other things. Lately we look out for gym bags. Little guys with no muscles, but sweatsuits on and carrying gym bags. Those bags have got some tools in them to help the creep get into your house."

"Do you work on burglary cases, too, then?"

Questions. She's always asking questions.

"No," Boaz told her. "I'm workin' on murder. What else is there for me to know, Nancy?"

"Here? Well, there's the Book Exhibition I was going to show you," Nancy said, taken aback a little. This guy was a moody soul. When his face was hard, he didn't look so much like Hoagy Carmichael, she thought. A youngish Abe Lincoln, maybe.

They proceeded across the atrium. Around them, breezy bits of talk rose and wafted like effusions from fumaroles.

"Lacan's mirror stage again, but re-refracted, I'd say . . ."

"Commodification in the nonlinear modes . . ."

"Really a synecdoche for . . ."

"Well, but it's metonymy, really, not metaphor, wouldn't you say?"

And two young professors, female, assessed an absent third. "My God, she's bigger than ever! She's big as a house!"

"Oh, not really all *that* much more."

"Well, that's twice the Mary Beth that *I* remember."

But if some woman's voice scaled an octave while announcing, "Oh, the Preely talk was so *naive*—no critical depth at all, and absolutely hegemonic," or if some handsome man wearing a turtleneck (proclaiming him a member of a creative-writing contingent, therefore free from all regimentation and uniformity in dress), if that man continued to find reasons to cross and recross the lobby in front of various sofas and groups—Nancy did not really care. It was the MLA Swivel conducted with such rudeness in the panel rooms that had brought her to the end of her patience.

The Mudge panel had been interrupted several times by the door opening at the rear of the room. Some academic would peer in to see who was there and, he hoped, to get some notice for himself for a moment. Then would come the slamming of the door. At panels that were less prestigious, men or women in the audience would actually get up in midtalk, or turn around in their chairs to see who else was in the room, sometimes making comments audible across half the area. The success of the Swivel, when performed at a panel, depends on how clearly you get across the implication that you're too important to come into this room, or too important to stay for long.

("This is insane," Nancy had said at one point, low-voiced, to the unknown woman beside her in the Mudge room. "I mean, didn't these people get sufficiently breast-fed or something? They have to go on showing off forever in front of their mommies and daddies?" In stylish elderly dignity, then, Professor Emeritus Marj Machesny of Vassar had given Nancy a look of complicit appreciation.)

Now, up on the second floor, Nancy was leading Boaz into the

"Modern Language Association Exhibits." ("This will just be a quick stop.") These exhibits extended across the large Gold Coast Ballroom, opposite the Du Sable Ballroom and the Marxist bar. Here, under multiple dangling mirrored balls, a hundred or more booths and tables had been set up, displaying recently published academic books.

This exhibition had at times a fervid air of buried treasure. What was to be found was the most current and fame-making idea: pick it up and prosper. Each booth attempted to persuade the milling academics (idea-shoppers, many of them) that *these* published offerings were the map to that success. A variety of catalogs, one or more from each publisher, was available at the door.

Certain presses, Nancy explained as they moved down a few aisles, are known for certain topics, but nobody takes the risk of promoting just one fad. You might seek out Routledge for postmodernism, or stuff billing itself as "feminist science," or pontifications about "media and consumer culture"—by which was usually meant clothing or TV, and especially bodies hacked to pieces in relation to either of those. The Indiana University Press issued postmodernist controversies of several kinds, too, hoping that "feminist film criticism," for instance, would look tempting.

Cornell, Rutgers, Yale, and others hung out their bait in these troubled waters. Boaz and Nancy rounded an aisle where the University of Wisconsin attempted to capture attention for reader-response theories, Wisconsin hedging its bets, though, with highbrow titillation under the name of *Men's Thoughts in the Night*. These lay behind a bright white jacket with a dagger on it.

"Oh," said Boaz, with raised eyebrows, "tough guys." He shifted his shoulders in his blue suit jacket and moved on. A few moments later, he unbuttoned that jacket and surreptitiously rubbed a couple of his vertebrae. The belt clip of his short-barreled .357 Colt Python continued to scrape his back ribs and irritate him a little.

Halfway through the ballroom, they turned back toward the door. Boaz circled them around to 210A to pick up his overcoat and to notify Timmy that he and Nancy would meet him here 113 again after lunch. Halleran nodded with his usual moroseness. He'd been having trouble getting any more work out of McGuire, the hotel security officer. Cooperative noises, yes, but not much work, he griped.

(Old Donny McGuire was a retired cop who'd been a time-server on the force for the better part of two decades. Remarkable only for how little paperwork he'd left behind him in the files, McGuire's eighteen years on the force had produced important arrests that could be counted on the fingers of one hand. He was a patrolman who'd leave his siren blaring right up to the door of the destination address. That way, "the perp" was warned and could get away, saving McGuire the exercises of paperwork and court proceedings. Coffee-shop proprietors had absorbed the cost of his free meals and coffee with a philosophical shrug: just another street tax. But alert and gung-ho cops had found him demoralizing. McGuire had had a great many changes of partner.)

Having told McGuire to go down to the basement kitchens ("Maybe you can find a place to take a nap!"), and having left the Wellesley Four with Hong and Malley, Halleran was now looking over some other matters of detailed dullness; namely, the beige backgrounds of the grad students, all women, interviewing for the Wellesley job. Hadn't these people ever done anything but go to school? Halleran had privately decided he'd propose marriage to the first woman here who, above the age of twenty-one, might still ride a roller coaster.

When Boaz and Nancy left him, he was sitting in a mess of papers and objects, wide-kneed, his left fist scrunched into his left cheek in a pose reminiscent of Dürer's *Melancholia*.

The lobby was still populous. Boaz noticed (from the look of dismay on a swiveler who'd glanced at a man's lapel and found no identification there) that some people were not wearing the plastic name tags he'd been seeing in the Book Exhibition and everywhere for days.

The tag was a four-by-three-inch piece of white paper encased in plastic with a safety pin on the back. No professional ranking was typed on the paper, just the person's first name, last name, and school. On a strip of blue across the bottom, the observer was constantly informed (in case he or she were disoriented to place) that this was the MLA in Chicago.

To Boaz's inquiry, Nancy explained that the name tag is mailed to you in advance, in the summer or fall, after you pay your seventy-five-dollar registration fee. Ostensibly, you're required to wear a name tag in order to get into the Book Exhibition or any of the panels. But the tags are easy to forget or lose, so you can get a replacement "over there," Nancy said, pointing to the south side of the lobby where a folding table stood near the gift shop.

Boaz pointed out that anyone might wander around, then, and pass as an MLA member.

"Oh, people do get checked once in a while. You'd want to have a tag, just to avoid any hassle."

Boaz detoured them over to the table, identified himself, and asked to see the list—"Do you keep a list?"—of any people who'd requested new name tags during the convention so far.

Norma Walker, MLA official, handed him the neatly printed list of names she was maintaining on a yellow pad. Boaz looked it over. Not many folks were having trouble with this name tag thing. Requested new IDs under today's date included Cherkle, Todd, Russo, then Todd again—Professor Todd seemed to be a bit absentminded this morning—along with Kumble and Deppen-schmidt. Glunkmeier, Rames, Ditt, and Henderson on Wednesday, the day before.

"I'm going to ask the desk clerk to come over and make a copy of this list, ma'am," Boaz said. "I appreciate your help. I might come look at it tomorrow, too." Ms. Walker was pleased.

Then, the clerk having been told to get a copy of that list into the base room pronto, Boaz turned for the door.

Nancy looked quizzical.

"Just one of my little ways, Professor," Boaz remarked. "Just want to know how things work. Details. 'Makes wise use of time, books, and materials': that's what my old report cards used to say, Professor Nancy, every one."

Nancy liked this guy's bantering moods that came and went.

She tried to draw this one out. "Details. I suppose you know everything there is to know about the internal combustion engine, too, right? One of those guys with automotive DNA. Every make and model of car known to man. Am I right?"

"You left out tractors." (And, thought Boaz, you left out the machinery of poisoning and the machinery of the mind. I could spend a month of Sundays on those apparatuses, and with one of them, at least, be none the wiser.)

He was a little tired; it was time for food. It was time to get Nancy talking some more, get something resolved.

"How do you like having breakfast in the middle of the day?" Boaz asked her.

"Fine. I love breakfast. Any time."

"Well, it's a little far to go on up to the Busy Bee. But Lou Mitchell's, down here on Jackson—it's got the best breakfasts in the Loop. 'Course, that'll mean a little bit of time outside in this weather."

"Fresh air—that would be new. OK."

As they moved off toward the revolving doors, there was a sudden agitation in the lobby currents behind them. It was Joan Mellish, closely attended by her T-shirted male entourage, dramatically displacing a quantity of space and oxygen in the room. Professor Mellish tended to enter and exit any room almost explosively, with violence to the door hinges and then scraped chair legs.

Immediately the terms of the MLA Swivel became redefined. Prestige was now expressed exclusively in terms of the number of feet and inches one stood from this personage.

Mellish, whom Boaz had seen the day before in the Perfect Square, had, above her pink miniskirt, the scarfy, layered look of fat academic women. At second glance she resolved into a high, pear-shaped object not fat at all. Her beautiful face was that of a blue-eyed Scandinavian blonde, full-mouthed and pale, whose straight hair fell well below her shoulders.

But those narrow shoulders sloped, and as far to one side of the bell-shaped curve as Mellish's lovely face existed—some three or four standard deviations—equally far in the other direction was the peculiar distortion of her figure. Minimally breasted, long-waisted, her body abruptly flared at the pelvic girdle, out to proportions of a giantess much taller than Mellish's six feet.

When speaking, this woman's face would blush at unnerving, unexpected moments, but particularly when she'd been firmly challenged by an authority. At that point her motorlike drone of a voice would convert to a whine. With her straight hair parted in the old prep-school style, she had the air of the smart school-girl who, even at the age of thirty-five, still wishes to impress or shock her imagined elders at private school. Like many partly lovely, partly weird-shaped women, she was devoted to spectacle. Rattling with jewelry, she glanced at a nearby, tentatively-smiling woman from Bowdoin, looked her pointedly up and down, then turned to her companions with a *sotto voce* remark that made them laugh.

Nancy realized she was going to have to bring up and account for this woman. At this moment, though, the Mellish arrival was too much like another loudly banging door at the back of a panel room. Nancy looked away, saying nothing, and proceeded, blue woman with blue cop, out with Boaz.

8

Beyond the brass doors of the Fairfax, the Can-Do City was making it clear that what it intended to do now, and maybe from now on, was to be cold. The high of the day, eight degrees, had already been reached. Far across the sunken area of Grant Park, the choppy gray lake looked as paleozoic as the jagged skyscrapers near its edge. To the north, the visible portion of Harry Weese's Time-Life Building glittered like a tooth.

Under the rectangular shelving that served as the Fairfax awning, two uniformed doormen waved the cabs into the U-shaped driveway off North Columbus Drive. Or wanted to, at any rate. Ordinarily, a dozen fat cabs would have been available: orange and green and turquoise and yellow and white, clustered together in the horseshoe drive like so much winter fruit. But grad students had recently headed off in hordes for their 12:00 o'clock appointments in other hotels. There was not a cab to be had.

"The car's down around the corner," Boaz proffered. "That's about a block. Do you want to wait while I come around?"

"No, I'll walk," Nancy said gamely.

The two of them headed south, toward East Randolph Street. A light snow had been dusting the ice for an hour or more, lending added interest to uneven curbs and sidewalk cracks. The wind was Chicago standard.

"My God," Nancy gasped at the corner, "you can't get your breath." She turned sideways against the wind for a moment.

Boaz, reinvigorated, looked down at her with an innocently puzzled look. "You call this wind? I *have* heard it called wind. But

there's something more like what you might call *wind*, down in

Missouri. I don't suppose you've been there? Seen how the cabins there have those little crowbar holes? About three, four feet off the ground?"

Without a change of expression, Boaz was pulling out a set of keys for the unmarked white Chevy Caprice (marked, that is, only by ZA plates and a trunk antenna) at the curb.

"They put in crowbar holes so you can stick a crowbar out from inside the house," he went on, busy with the keys. "That way, you can test the wind when you hear it in the morning. You stick out the crowbar, and if it bends all the way over, flush with the logs of the house, then you know it's a little too windy to plow. You might stay indoors, do something else that morning."

He looked at her, totally deadpan, then opened the door. Nancy's laugh was explosive and incredulous: "Is that a fact?"

"Yes, ma'am—of a sort."

In a small lot at Jackson and Jefferson, they climbed out of the car—Boaz still automatically graceful, Nancy noticed. Eyeing the battered Jefferson pavement with suspicion, she took Boaz's arm and stepped over a patch of ice. That pressure on his arm, he noticed, was confident and steady. Just for a moment it made the man wonder about this woman's full repertory of touch.

But the case, as it were, of Nancy Cook really hadn't cleared. The thought was unlikely and distasteful, but Boaz reminded himself that this was a woman pretty enough to be a decoy, strong enough, if need be, to push a man over a balcony, certainly strong enough to have lifted the lid on a chrome coffee urn. He disengaged her arm without regret a moment later at Lou Mitchell's door.

Beyond the tiny, glass-encased vestibule, the place was turbulently busy, as usual. Boaz, raking his fingers through his hair, didn't bother to explain that this place was a traditional hangout for the law. Denizens tended to be lawyers and federal agents and cops in plain clothes; some uniforms; some clerks and secretaries from legal offices. Chuck Metek's small gang of toxicologists had long since come and gone. Conversations remained brusque and straightforward, reminders of the City That Hates Wimps.

No one besides Nancy glanced at or questioned the presence of two large aquarium tanks in the center of the room near the door, tanks empty of fish but full of tourmaline-colored water, on one of which a mysterious sign announced, "PURO Filtered Water." The tanks had always been there, always would be.

Lou's nephew, a slim, suited, middle-aged man, seated them at a small booth for two at the rear. Debonairly he presented a small box of Milk Duds to Nancy, as was his custom with all female customers.

Boaz ordered the renowned double-yolk eggs, sunny side up, which would arrive with potatoes and ham, real butter, and thick-sliced "Greek toast." Nancy decided on malted-milk waffles and stewed, clove-scented prunes. Coffee arrived with a six-inch pitcher of cream. Over at the long communal tables, customers were elbowing to dig into individual frying pans of breakfast specials that the waitresses slapped down on small wooden trivets.

"Now where were we?" Boaz opened. He looked a little fatigued, more hollow-cheeked under his brown eyes, but still sleek; in fact, almost elegant in his dark suit and small-knotted tie.

"Well—by the way, I'm not sure: Did you still want me to look at Michael Alcott's room today?"

Boaz nodded. "With Halleran, a little later on. You been thinkin' about this?"

Thinking he meant her orientation discussion, Nancy replied, "I didn't make any notes, no. But I did want to say that I'm aware the picture I've given you so far has been—well, from the perspective of the wet blanket."

In a random lull in the room's noise level, Nancy's voice had carried. An enormous Polish cop, ham-fisted and ham-faced, swiveled a little on his counter stool nearby and looked disgustedly over to see who was saying things like "perspective of the wet blanket." Brown-eyed and blonde-haired Nancy leaned toward him a little and gave him a beaming, conspiratorial smile. The cop, suddenly shy, returned to his walnut pancakes.

"To be fair," Nancy continued, "if you want to know the shape of things at MLA, my point of view maybe isn't the only one you should go by. I mean, there *are* people who think the profession's made advances lately. But still, it's not as if everyone at MLA wouldn't recognize what I've been talking about."

"So what would you do about it?" Boaz asked, his cup in midair.

"What I'd like to see in the academy? The ideal profession? Oh, I'd need my abracadabra powers now." Nancy playfully waved her palms in a circular motion over the table.

"Swami Nancy says: in the future, all tenured professors must endure a tenure review. Say, every ten years. If he or she has been unproductive or ineffectual, then that professor has to live with a lower salary or take early retirement.

"And the 'service' committees: they will be changed, changed utterly. Swami Nancy says that work will have to have something to do with the real world. Right now, the real world exists about once a year at Yale, when they have their United Way drive. It's the same at a lot of places. The March of Dimes is the most innovative thing the department chairs can think of."

What am I doing here? Boaz thought. There was nothing here to follow up on. Halleran was out of his mind.

Nancy was getting energized, occasionally tapping her delivered waffle with her fork. "But you know, you could set up something like, oh, some number of hours of literacy teaching could be required as eligibility for tenure. There's no reason why learning to teach literacy couldn't be part of graduate course requirements."

"Anything like that at Wellesley or Arizona?"

"Are you kidding? *Muy* dubious. But you know, it could be very simple. Universities could do things that businesses do. I know of a trash-burning plant in Dayton, Ohio, for God's sake, where the employees have a potluck lunch every Wednesday. Costs two dollars and fifty cents. All proceeds go to Operation Feed the Hungry. Well, Swami Nancy would have a service committee in charge of organizing things like that, right in the English-department building. Why not? Have the proceeds go to branch libraries *off campus*, or for equipment for poorly funded schools. Just open things out, you know? And attach some rewards, salary increases, to service work that's innovative in the community."

Nancy paused. "Good coffee. I wonder if it's made with water out of those tanks?" She was feeling much better. She'd just seen, under those rugged eyebrows across the table, Boaz's brown eyes regarding her for a moment with something like affection.

"Well, now you know, don't you, that I'm completely insane," she told Boaz summarily. "Completely out of it in my own professional world. You can imagine what I'd do with the Trendy personnel."

"Bump 'em off?"

"Oh, they'd never get on board," Nancy replied smoothly. "In The Academy According to Nancy, no grad student at MLA gets hired until he or she shows me some proof of outstanding teaching skills. They can put videotapes of their classroom teaching right in their dossiers. Or they can come to my school and teach a class, with the hiring committee sitting in the back of the room."

"So you see, at Cook University, I've gotten rid of the old tenured deadwood. And as for the Trendies—the ones who can't teach anything except Advanced Narcissism—well, they don't apply at my school. They go off and take jobs where they belong, in ad agencies."

Nancy laughed a warm, wide, square-mouthed laugh. "I love it. Yes, more coffee, please," to the deft waitress prowling the aisle of booths.

"You said something last night about 'money stuff,' " Boaz reminded her.

"Oh, that's right," Nancy said with a small groan. "Money, money, money. It's not what people think it is in the academy. You read about teachers being overpaid or underpaid: those same old stories in the Sunday supplement when there isn't any other news. No. Money is not doing what people think it's doing in the universities."

Nancy's propinquitous pen was out again now. "For instance," she said, "I suppose most people think equal pay scales for male and female teachers is something that must have been settled a long time ago. I mean, it was in the 1970s we started hearing about it, right? It's completely boring as a subject now. But real power, which means money, hasn't moved, not by an inch or an ounce."

"Power, huh?" He hated the way this word kept coming up.

"Yes. Power is *the* issue in the academy. In all kinds of ways. In this particular case—well, just because a university puts it in print that they're 'committed to equal opportunity' does not mean that their new women faculty are actually being paid what their new men are getting. It doesn't mean that the new women are going to get salary increases as high as the men will get, or that women will be offered high-paying administrative posts. More likely it just means the university has got a publicity department doing some good camouflage work.

"I've been looking into all this lately, along with my friend Jennifer. Because she's going on the market next year, too. I've got statistics by the pageful. Which I will spare you. But let me just tell you a story, a *narrative*: the true tale of Carolyn Beeman at Penn State. Jennifer knows her personally, and kept track of this.

"If you're a full professor at Penn State and you're a man, then your salary is about sixty-six thousand dollars, even if you've never written a book and even if the student evaluations of your teaching are all a cry for help.

"Meanwhile, if you're a full professor and a woman—and those *do* exist at Penn State, sort of: five women in a department of about sixty-five—well, as a woman, your salary is forty-six thousand dollars. Even if, like Carolyn Beeman, you've taught for twenty years, written six or seven books, and won a handful of prizes. Penn State is very high-profile in its 'equal opportunity' publicity, by the way."

"She file a grievance?" Boaz asked.

"Every year for the last seven or eight years. With the department chair, then with the dean of humanities. They smiled, they said they'd take it under advisement, then they'd say the school couldn't afford to bring her salary up.

"Now Carolyn was near retirement, so she didn't have a career to lose if she decided to fight. She's very feisty" (Boaz smiled a little at the southern word), "and she had the advantage of being   *123* well off. Her husband's also had a successful career in something—accounting, I think.

"Anyway, two years ago, Carolyn informed the dean that if her salary wasn't made equitable within six months, she'd retain an attorney. Six months later, her salary was still forty-six thousand dollars, and the dean was smiling and telling her that really she ought to discuss this again with the department chair.

"So Carolyn discussed it with an attorney, instead. Somebody with experience in this kind of litigation. And he told her this: that he'd like to represent her, but to prove a case like this, you have to show the court an example of *specific* discrimination that took place within a three-to-five-year period. But since discrimination against Carolyn had been steady and uniform for twenty years, there was no single incident that stood out. So she didn't have a case."

Boaz's "Hunnh!" was emphatic. "It does sound a bit like the justice system at work, all right."

"Well, there *is* a happy ending, sort of. Carolyn let it be known that she was considering going public about the whole thing—calling up the newspapers about it. Which is *not* done, believe me, in the academy. A younger woman who did that would alienate the administration. Her career would not exactly flourish after that. But after Carolyn made her threat, she came in one day and was told, by a pretty grumpy department chair, that her salary had been raised to equity level."

Nancy leaned back and sighed. "The other women's salaries at Penn State were *not* raised. And they won't be, not without an individual fight in every case. And academic women aren't usually fighters, you know. They're too genteel to make a fuss, and they think it's vulgar to talk about money. I really like women, but they drive me crazy sometimes. Some tenured women don't even *want* to see a lot of women joining their ranks. Being one of the chosen few makes them feel exceptional and powerful."

"Power again?"

"Sure. Absolutely."

"Is that the case at Wellesley? Arizona?"

"Oh, you know, I don't think I've got stats on them. Women's colleges tend to have a better record, though, as a rule."

"How about University of Illinois?"

"Your school?"

"Two years. But that was a while ago."

"Anything in particular you were studying?"

Boaz shook his head. "General studies." (*What am I doin' here?* he thought. *When's this woman gonna clear up?*)

"I've taken a bunch of night classes since then," he said. "Police work kinda stuff. 'The Psychology of Satanic Cults'—I did *real* well in that one."

"Oh, how interesting! I'd love to know about satanic cults."

Boaz looked over at this woman's satanic-cult eagerness and put a tiny check mark in another box of his mind. Not, though, with any conviction.

"What about U. of I.?"

"I don't know, offhand. I could find out. Well, sometimes you *can't* find out. Illinois might be one of those schools that are very sly. In their catalogs the faculty will be listed just by last name and first initial. It's a good trick: that way, you can't tell how many women they've hired lately. If any."

For Boaz, of course, affirmative-action issues had meant a different set of stresses, which he did not bring up. His own promotion, though, to Sergeant Dixon had been impossible for years and would continue to be, what with implicit racial and gender quotas in place in the Chicago PD.

And talk to a field training officer: any FTO in this town will tell you his rookie women are too hard-assed and they scare him to death: all of them Jane Waynes and Dirty Harriets. God help the John Q. that crosses them. The women think *you* don't think they're tough enough, and by God, they're gonna prove you wrong. So then they get in a tight situation and they turn on the force way too soon. They'll shoot before anybody else has even thought about it.

Good cops after a while, though, Boaz thought, when they get just a little more confident. A couple he knew of were top-notch at hostage negotiation, which is one easy way for a cop to die. It was Janice, in Vice, who'd showed him a memory trick to use with license plates, too.

Absently, he smoothed his brown hair back past his big right ear. He had a wrapup question or two.

"Nancy, something I don't understand now: you make it sound like women in these schools are somethin' rare as channel catfish. But I look around that hotel and what I see are hallways stuffed with women. Lot more women than men."

"Good point. But how old are they? Give me an average age."

"OK, they're young, youngish."

"They're young, they're not tenured, they're looking for jobs, and they're hoping the schools will keep faith with them and promote them at full salary one day. I hope they're right. But I suspect the schools know they can ignore the population pressure of all these women. Women disappear, and the administrations know it."

"Women disappear?"

"They fall away like leaves, Boaz. In grad school, first-year classes are packed with women—two or three women for every guy. By the time they're at MLA, it might not look like it, but thousands have disappeared. By the time they get to fourth-year review, which is pretenure review, their numbers will be a *lot* smaller."

Nancy concluded her summary of the deciduous nature of women with a datum discovered by Jennifer, who'd been following up about Penn State. A recent analysis, leaked to a local paper, had revealed that although ninety-four women had been hired in various departments at Penn State that year, another ninety-three faculty women had resigned.

"So where do they go?" Boaz demanded.

Nancy shrugged. "I don't know. Where do all the lost bobby pins go?"

"What's a bobby pin?"

Nancy smiled over at this charming man. "Bobby Pin is likely to be drinking very soon in a cash bar. Or maybe at that 'Square' place."

Memory of the Perfect Square brought with it the memory of the redoubtable Joan Mellish. Nancy wondered whether she could describe the Mellish phenomenon without embarrassment now in front of this man.

She regarded her dish of prunes thoughtfully. Then, with the kind of mental shrug common to good teachers—a willingness to lose, if need be, a little dignity—Nancy plunged ahead.

"That woman, tall woman, who came into the lobby? In the pink skirt? Had a turban with a jewel on it?"

"Mama duck with ducklings, that one?"

"I'm not sure," Nancy said with a short laugh, "that you ought to compare her that way. The Duck Protection League might object."

"How come?"

"Because that's Joan Mellish. This is more orientation about money, by the way. Because Joan Mellish is sort of the flip side of the coin about money in the academy.

"I guess I could safely say she's the Ultimate Trendy. If you want to understand the 'cultural criticism' group, you'll have to familiarize your mind as best you can with the Tall One. She's a phenomenon I personally think is—well, she couldn't have appeared if it weren't for all the turmoil in the academy right now."

Nancy stirred her prunes. "Mellish used to be married, some time ago. That's something she talks a lot about in her lectures. Says it was the formulating mistake of her life. She prefers to live now with one or another of the gay guys around her. At the moment, that's Jason Keggo. They go everywhere together.

"Of course, there'd be no reason for you to know this except that she deliberately tries to make her sexual life the same as her academic life. Which is what several 'cultural critics' are trying to do these days."

Boaz frowned. Where was this Nancy off to now?

Nancy took a breath. Here goes. "I've never met her, but everybody knows the shape of her career. She taught at Tulane for a while. That was where she got famous for a piece she wrote called 'Trailing Clouds of Glory: Freeing the Infant Within.' It has to do with her main assertion, which is that since the child is father of the man, we need to stop promoting our stale, culturally oppressive views of social growth and realize, instead, that regression back toward childhood is true progress in human life."

"What?"

(And at this moment back in the Fairfax, Professor Mellish was berating the hotel maid whom an intimidated clerk at the registration desk had dispatched to Mellish's room. "Well, what are you going to *do* about it?" Mellish was loudly demanding, arms akimbo on red-dressing-gowned hips. "Am I speaking too fast for you?" Unable to find a small piece of her luggage, Mellish had accused in turn every staff person she could accost of having stolen it. The hotel maid was pretty and sweet-natured, hopelessly at a disadvantage, then, and there were some terrible moments for her before she could get away. Half an hour later, when Mellish discovered the blue travel bag inside the armoire where she'd put it and forgotten it, she did not contact the staff. She unzipped the bag to make sure—and yes, the stack of Huggies and Chubbs Baby Wipes was intact.)

"OK, on the basis of that article," Nancy forged on, "U.C. Irvine invited Mellish to give a lecture to their English department. My friend Gwen was in the Kludd Room there. She told me later she'd just heard the kind of talk that guarantees success these days.

"Mellish's lecture there was called 'Bottoms Up: Diapering as Deconstruction.' It's listed, I gather, on the recommended-reading list she hands out in all her classes. It reveals, uh . . . what Shakespeare *really* wanted Titania to do with Bottom in *A Midsummer Night's Dream* and how so many great texts of the past, as she puts it, secretly yearn for 'our anal infantile potential.' Her conclusion, as usual, was a personal account of how getting in touch with these 'deeper realities' has freed up so much of her own creativity."

Thoroughly bepuzzled, Boaz had stopped eating.

"She read this in the Kludd Room. Gwen's take, which is probably right, is that Mellish is an exhibitionist and a masochist: that she knows how to manipulate an audience to get some kind of private excitement. If so, she's good at it; her talk was very well received. Some grad students, women, were actually praising Mellish for being 'so brave' about exposing herself.

"But you see," Nancy proffered, "academics almost never have any background in psychology. Gwen has some, and I have a little. But not many people in English could make a list of the symptoms of any mental illness: exhibitionism, or hysteria, or anything else. I imagine" (here Nancy cocked her head in an appraising way) "a police officer has more formal psychology training than professors do these days."

To Boaz's shifting of his blue-clad shoulders and his noncommittal "Hunnh," Nancy recounted more of the modern-day Scandinavian saga.

"After that big lecture, Irvine, being what it's famous for being, a complete slave of fashion—well, Irvine invited Mellish to give a whole *series* of talks and classes. Which she did.

"The same kind of stuff, I gather, makes up her classroom material. No works of literature, or very few. Some field trips to preschools and porno shops." (What Nancy did not yet know was that in press for *Diacritics* was Professor Mellish's latest foray into hermeneutics, "Threes, Threes, Threes, Diapasons of Diapering: The Cultural Significance of the Triform Fold.")

"What?"

"Oh, there's more. Things being what they are, Mellish became extremely influential. You can see Mellish clones nowadays at all kinds of conferences. Up at the Book Exhibition there was Melinda Frooney's book, *The Anal-Logical Philosophy of the Fag Hag.*"

"*What?*"

"And since my point is about money, now is probably the time to let you know that Joan Mellish is being paid a hundred and forty thousand dollars a year. What she's being paid to do, I don't know—to be herself, I guess. Certainly not to teach; I won't call it teaching.

"But Indiana University calls it that. And so did Tulane, and so did Irvine. Indiana bought her away from Irvine, in what's been thought of as a big coup. Irvine had bought her away from Tulane before that.

"This probably sounds as if I'm jealous of her success. I mean, I'll never make a third of her money. But I'm *not* jealous. As it happens"—Nancy's short chin was firm—"she appalls me."

Boaz stayed quiet. Nancy had moved some distance from her earlier, light-hearted Swami Nancy position. Her tone now was astringently ironic. She was regarding events she knew might indicate the devastation of a profession.

"It's so incongruous," she added. "Mellish calls herself a feminist. But of course, she dislikes women, really. I don't think she has any friends who can be identified with certainty as female. For about the last, oh, year or so, Jason Keggo has been her—well, nobody knows *what* exactly—her 'companion,' I guess. What they do, whether it's animal, vegetable, or mineral, no one has any idea.

"Personally, I suspect," said Nancy, "that Jason Keggo is just a cynical adventurer who knows where the smart money is. He's also at Bloomington now, with her. She refuses to give a lecture without him. Lately, along with another couple, they've been going on tours together."

"Along with the bearded lady? And the elephants?"

"It's ridiculous, isn't it? But team lectures are getting very big now. One of them that Mellish and Keggo just gave had something to do with Hitchcock's *Rear Window*—I can't think what."

Boaz blinked, incapable of remark.

"The two of them are going to give a very big-deal panel this Sunday, on 'Anal Re-Attention,'" Nancy concluded. "In the morning. The Grand Ballroom's been set aside for it. I'm not sure what Jason's going to do, but Mellish's part of the talk is something about overlooked anal allusions in Shelley's 'Mont Blanc.'"

Boaz's face was full of baffled irritation. He was also feeling a cop's aggravation at coming across a new variety of human failing in the world, one he hadn't known about.

(Like most people in police work, Boaz was generally convinced he knew all there was to know about corruption. Unlike most cops, though, he'd never believed that corruption was the most important knowledge to have. That assessment had kept him balanced. It had not saved his marriage, but it had kept him from burnout and from predictability.)

"I don't see why," he now interposed, "why some kid doesn't go home and tell his parents about all this, and get that woman fired before the week's out."

"Well, in high school, yes, that might happen. But after age eighteen—well, the student's parents pay thousands of dollars for her course, instead."

Nancy's laugh was rich. "It's demented, isn't it? And actually, I don't see why the gays aren't protesting outside her classrooms. The way she behaves, and her cronies: it just reinforces the old stereotypes about gays being trivial and sex-obsessed and, oh, sensationalistic. Mellish sees herself as a pioneer, but she's undermining the credibility of gay people who *are* serious in the academy.

"So." Nancy's long-fingered hands had come together in a soft, ironic clap. "The lesson we can learn from this is: a great deal of money *can* be made in the academy, if you can fill the role of Token Weirdo. There are English departments made up of almost nothing *but* weirdos now, and they're proud of it."

Nancy tilted her curly head back against the booth. "I can't believe it. I can't believe I'm planning to go to her panel. Maybe I won't."

She leaned forward again and continued doodling. Now she was reoutlining the letters *BCV,* and she was frowning seriously. There was a pause.

"A real Bastion of Civilized Values, huh?" Nancy concluded. There was detectable pain in her voice that she was being offhand about.

"A real Bastard what?"

Boaz was challenging her to be personal and specific about all this, and Nancy knew it.

"A real Bastard of Civilized Values. You're right. And you know, *131* from what I saw in grad school—I think there aren't that many people who wouldn't admit that that's the case. I even think everybody has a kind of heartache about it."

There was a suggestion of defiance in Nancy's look across the booth. She was challenging him not to jeer, and Boaz knew it.

His nod was very slight and the moment that followed was quiet before he raised his hand to signal the peripatetic waitress.

More coffee was poured, the homemade apple pie was declined, and Boaz stirred the mahogany brew. He'd learned his overview here, but it was time to get back with Halleran. Nancy Cook had told him all he could use.

"Well, we should be getting back, I guess?" Nancy said. "I hope the investigation's going—well, never mind. It's just, it seems as if . . . something about this nightmare in the hotel just seems inevitable. Not surprising. There's just something about MLA, I think. Everybody goes into a kind of bizarre state. It brings out the worst in people."

"Could it bring out murder?"

A little startled, Nancy's look was questioning under the pressuring stare of the man opposite. She was startled further by what his tone and look must mean. She suddenly realized that this cop had actually suspected her of murder.

Professor Cook was astounded. This guy she'd been talking to! Then she felt annoyed. Disappointed as well, but for the moment, annoyed. Sternly, she told herself that her reading of the text of the last eighteen hours had been deficient, to say the least.

Firmly, Professor Cook put down the lunch check she'd picked up intending to pay. And she looked at this cop with a sarcastic, citizen's challenge that the professional Boaz found interesting, but that nonprofessional Boaz wished he had not provoked.

"Well, you know, there *is* a person I would just love to see done away with," she told him crisply. "Why, I've wanted her removed from the scene for years. A feminist, too." Nancy leaned forward, her eyes wide in mock alarm. "Maybe she's in *great danger* right this minute. It's a certain 'Sharon.' You might want to make a note

of that.

"And the reason I'm almost sure to do her in"—Nancy was looking straight at Boaz—"has to do with the conniving she did to get her son hired at Boston, over a much more qualified woman, my friend Ruth, who'd already been *promised* the job by the Boston chair. Sharon even called up Ruth's advisor and got him to phone Boston on behalf of *Sharon's son*. A real shaft job, feminist to feminist."

Nancy saw Boaz's face move into an uncertain frown, something approaching chagrin.

"Now I was with Ruth last year when she ran into this Sharon jerk," she went on. "And Sharon *was* a little embarrassed when she remembered what she'd done. But then she said to Ruth the same thing that men have been saying to women ever since women started applying for jobs: 'Well, my son really *needed* that job, you know. He'd just gotten married.'

"You know," Nancy concluded, "you really might want to look her up at the hotel and see if she's all right: Sharon Plu . . ."

But suddenly Boaz's pager went off in his jacket, and Sharon's last name had to remain undisclosed. Boaz rose to take over the phone in the vestibule, where he spoke briefly.

Back at the booth, Nancy was gathering her things together. She'd been wasting her time trying to help this Boaz Dixon, she told herself. And she hadn't come to this convention to spend her time like this. Time to get back to the world she was familiar with. She looked around Lou Mitchell's critically. Why didn't some of these guys go on diets? They looked like cops. Hell, they probably *were* cops.

Nancy couldn't help wondering, however (across the room, Boaz's back was to her inside the glass vestibule), whether a different man would come back to the booth, as had happened at Slade's.

It *was* a different man. He wasn't thinking of her at all.

"Let's go," Boaz told her curtly. "Somebody's been shot at the hotel."

9

"Someone's been *shot?*' Nancy repeated blankly, wide-eyed. Then a superstitious horror arrived. "Oh, my God, who is it? It's not *Sharon*, is it?"

"Woman named Foster. Come on, let's go."

It was a quarter to two when Boaz—Nancy all but forgotten beside him, the usually hidden siren out on the dashboard—swung fast around the corner of East South Water Street and into the horseshoe drive of the Fairfax. A squad car with its strobe still on and one of its doors open stood parked in front of a narrow alley between the Fairfax and the Amoco Building to the south. The squadrol wagon had also pulled up. The mouth of the alley was busy with uniformed cops, the morgue photographer adjusting his lens equipment, and the few hardy curiosity seekers who could tolerate the wind.

Telling Nancy to go back to her hotel room until he contacted her, Boaz nodded to the beat cop at the cordon and stepped into the crime scene.

"Get a cordon up across the other end of the alley, too," Halleran had told that same beat cop twenty minutes ago. But one or two John Q.'s had kept trying to move around the improvised line (strung up between little crabapple trees at both sides of the alley), and Pat Flanagan had stayed put to keep them out. He left the other cops to take care of the Michigan Avenue end. Halleran, talking to De Bartolo and to Pete Montenegro kneeling beside him, was paying no attention at the moment to the exit behind him.

A City of Chicago sanitation truck had stopped about halfway down the alley. Boaz could see, just this side of the truck where the investigation was clustered, a row of four dumpsters lining the north side of the wall. Beyond them, Malley was shooting pictures at the far end of the passage.

Also in the alley were three sanitation collection personnel. They were rugged, laconic, square-headed men, the kind who disdain all superfluities—who have all-but-undetectable necks, for instance—and who, with secretly proud indifference, wear gloves with holes in them in subzero weather.

One of them, the driver Andrei, leaned by the truck cab with his arms hugging his chest. His coworkers, Jerzy and Tadeusz, had been the ones to come upon the bloody body of a woman fallen between the second and third dumpsters. Yelling up at the driver, Jerzy had run to call the police. He'd found a lot of bodies and knew what to do. Tadeusz didn't. He'd only found one body, a baby, about a month before.

The ETs, amazed to be back at the Fairfax again ("Jesus Christ, Blood City"), had a body bag unzipped and ready to put on a stretcher to carry to the squadrol. The photographer was recording the woman's face, and details of the dumpsters and alley were being scrutinized for trace evidence. A week later Halleran would still be able to tell you that the old, worn-out "Fuck You" on the bricks had been scrawled about four feet up, in green paint.

The chief medical examiner was on his knees in the snow beside the body. De Bartolo had slowly pulled the woman from between the dumpsters, examined all the areas of her back, then carefully turned her over. Now he was checking her ears and throat, feeling through his surgical gloves for other wounds. Ordinarily, for a shooting incident, he might have postponed his on-scene arrival, but he'd had a lot of autopsy work out of this hotel lately, and he needed to deliver all findings immediately. He and his overworked staff of three had been sedulously producing the necessary jars and labels and reports. Now he abandoned all hope of getting caught up before the city's weekend rush.

What Boaz most wanted to know at this juncture was Russ's estimate of the time of death. "Oh, only about an hour ago, I'd 135 say. Blood's still real fresh. And she's not very hard, even in this cold. Coat's not even that cold in the lining. Skin's not much dried out. Say 1:00 o'clock. These guys probably drove in and found her just a few minutes after she died."

One o'clock. He and Nancy had been in Lou Mitchell's at one o'clock. Good. Now, unless this woman's death was independent of the others, or unless Nancy had an accomplice Duffy hadn't noticed, both of which were unlikely, the Nancy Cook case had cleared.

The dead woman, in a brown wool coat, looked to be in her early forties. Brown hair, loosely curled; large metal-frame glasses. Simple face. No makeup other than lipstick. Gray wool gloves and sturdy L. L. Bean duck boots on her feet.

She had been shot between her shoulder blades, through her coat, which displayed evident powder and burn marks. Exiting her chest, the single bullet had dented one of the dumpsters and was easily found. Forensics would later confirm that it came from a .32 caliber revolver fired at point-blank range.

The woman's name tag, still optimistically pinned to the lapel of her coat, said "Irene Foster, The University of South Dakota." Her brown handbag, firmly full of maps and address books and medications and keys, as well as a modest wallet, was found wedged beneath her body, its contents intact. She'd been lying so humbly and harmlessly face down between the dumpsters that the collection men hadn't even spotted her at first in the grime.

Now one of them, Tadeusz, was shuffling around the alley in distressed indecision. Boaz saw him cross himself several times. The man looked close to tears: "It's a woman. It's not right." The man couldn't seem to stop moving. Boaz went over to him and began to talk quietly, his hand on the man's shoulder, then took out his notebook and made some notes.

Hong, Boaz noticed, was looking west down the alley. Malley had waved once, perfunctorily, to Boaz from that far end, where he was up to something. This time Malley had taken only two shots of the bystanders and gawkers at the cordon. Now, his back flat against the filthy south wall, Malley was aiming his Nikon repeatedly at the snow-dusted ice at that end. He waved now to Hong, who nudged Halleran.

"What the hell's he doing?" Halleran said. Squeezing Tadeusz firmly on the arm, Boaz went to see, following Malley's waved direction for him to stay close to the south wall.

Doglike, Malley's camera was pointing at a series of boot prints in the snow. There were no other prints down this half of the alley. The tracks led clearly down the length of the alley from the dumpsters (where police, milling around, had mashed the ice crust to a smear), then turned right where the alley debouched onto Michigan in the direction of Lake Street.

The tracks were considerably smaller than his own heavy shoes, Boaz noted. Telling Malley to get shots of every track and get the prints blown up as soon as possible, Boaz took off on the trail.

"They don't go anywhere, Bo," Malley called out. But the distance between the tracks got shorter, Boaz noticed, and they veered to the right before being lost on the sidewalk. There Boaz found himself about twenty feet from the secondary entrance of the Fairfax.

Shop owners in that entry area were questioned rapidly from their doorways. Had they had seen anyone unusual coming in the door at about one o'clock? Anybody who looked in a hurry or looked frightened? Somebody shorter than himself? The shop owners looked at Boaz's lanky six feet and said no. Although the Michigan entrance was never as busy as the front lobby, it did open and reopen dozens of times a day, and lunchtimes were busy. No one coming in had been unusual.

Boaz worked his way back through the corridor to the concourse and main lobby. From a dismayed registration clerk ("What's going on, anyway? It's so weird around here!"), Boaz demanded a key for Irene Foster's room, 3417, and jotted down her home and departmental phone numbers in South Dakota.

His expectations about Professor Foster's room were not rewarded. One look at the pristine chamber, with its duplicate maps of the shuttle bus route, its book on the bedside table (*The Iliad*, Alexander Pope's translation), its stacks of clean handkerchiefs in the dresser drawer—the edges of the hankies all perfectly aligned—and Boaz had the sinking hunch that this was yet another academic event that did not make any sense.

He rummaged carefully through her brown suitcase, through her few toiletries. Nothing. The ETs showed up to take slides and dustings. Pete Montenegro frowned around the room and shook his head, and the detectives eventually taped the door.

Back in 210A, then, Boaz, Halleran, and Hong distributed assignments quickly. Brief, combustible remarks from Lieutenant Mulcahy had been endured, and Mulcahy was now calling a press conference in order to temporize again. For at least another day, Mulcahy would emphasize that although this latest event had taken place *near* the Fairfax, it was not necessarily connected *to* the Fairfax, that the CPD was making use of its every resource, et cetera. But the next editions, especially the *Sun-Times*, were going to be splashy. Meanwhile, new units of plainclothes cops showed up to patrol the halls, conference rooms, lobby areas, all the hotel messuages.

The three detectives agreed to emphasize the following inquiries: Who knew Irene Foster and what was the South Dakota story? Any connections between the three schools? What was each member of the Wellesley and Arizona committees doing at 1:00? Where was Annette Lisordi, and where was that busboy, Firtch, the one who'd delivered the Wellesley coffee? Had there been any deviation in the hotel staff's work schedules or performance in the last twenty-four hours?

But the Wellesley Four, as Hong pointed out, had been under his scrutiny for more than two hours just before the Foster shooting. It was quickly established, too, that Annette Lisordi had treated herself to a well-attended lunch at the Greek Taverna across the street in the Illinois Center.

As for the University of Arizona people: to make up for lost time, they'd been conducting interviews on an onerous, nonstop schedule all morning, and no one had left the suite. A half-hour lunch had been taken, also in the suite, attended by all members.

This was confirmed by room service, the busboy noting grumpily that nobody ordered coffee, either, and the tip was lousy from those people.

Halleran, assisted by beat cops and Donny McGuire, started sorting the schedule stacks for hotel staff who'd worked all three shifts coinciding with the hotel deaths.

Boaz had no confidence in a lead in that direction. Given the range and depth of conflicts he'd learned about, Boaz was more and more convinced that, alibis notwithstanding, the killer or killers lay among the academics.

In 311, meanwhile, Nancy had been waiting for Boaz's call. She'd tried to reach Annette Lisordi, only to find her being questioned by the police again. ("Nancy, will you call me later? *Please* call?" was all the dismayed Annette could say.)

Two panels at the Hyatt Nancy had considered going to that afternoon ("*Auto*eroticism or *Car*nal Knowledge: Steven Spielberg and the Vehicles of Desire" and "Rapping/Raping in the Eighteenth Century"), Nancy dismissed now with little sense of loss. Of course, not being able to talk closely about those would put her at a disadvantage in the Yale English hallways next week, but she'd wing it.

Meanwhile, Nancy was telling herself to calm down. She'd caught a glimpse of a body in the alley and had given up her attempts to put it out of her mind. Instead, she was doing some deliberate thinking about it.

Michael Alcott's death was probably a murder, Nancy grimly decided. It just seemed contextually right. If three academics are dead at a hotel, two of them murdered, why assume the third to be an accident? Three, then, since Wednesday afternoon, with MLA slated to continue for two more days. The prospect was definitely, as her friend Jennifer might say, "creepiness-laden." Little sounds were making her jump. And poor Professor Foster!

On a yellow legal pad, Nancy began to jot some notes under the headings M.A., S.E., and now a woman named Foster. Who *were* these people?

Eventually her phone rang. It was Annette, who wanted nothing so much as "out of this place! I mean, Nancy, what is *happening*? I feel like I'm in a Pinter play! Or Strindberg?"

Nancy commiserated with some quick phrases but apologetically added, "Sweetie, I can't tie up my phone right now." The two made plans to get away from the hotel that night, to take a cab over to Joe Segal's Jazz Showcase in the Blackstone Hotel, then maybe drink their way over to George's on Kinzie Street.

"And Annette? Be careful 'til then, will you? I mean it."

"Oh, I look left and right before I even cross my room now," Annette said. "You be careful, too. 'Bye, Nance."

When Nancy's phone rang again, it was Boaz, saying they could use her input on a couple of things, if she had the time. She agreed to come down to the headquarters room right away. Boaz made a mental note to check whether Jimmy Duffy was keeping an eye on Nancy the way he was supposed to.

It was 4:50 P.M. when Nancy appeared at 210A. Duffy, the cop tailing her, a man whom she'd noticed but wasn't sure was a cop (he dressed so much like the department chair at Yale), eased into the room a moment or two later.

The atmosphere, Nancy noted at once, was sternly businesslike. Several cops were there she hadn't seen before, two of them women, both in uniform. She took a seat on one of the folding chairs, put her note pad on the table, and looked at Boaz a little warily. Oh, surely these people weren't going to *interrogate* her?

Boaz noticed with a distant part of his mind that Nancy had found time to do something with her hair since being in Lou Mitchell's. A blue bandanna was in it somehow, and her lipstick was fresh.

Halleran, an earth-colored heap in a far folding chair, spoke up. "Nancy, this Irene Foster: did you know her, know anything about her?"

"No, I didn't," Nancy replied, and she turned slightly, so as to speak very firmly to Boaz.

"I didn't know Michael Alcott or Susan Engleton, either. I've never had *any* contact with *any* of them."

Boaz nodded and cleared up that little matter. "I know you didn't. We all know that, Nancy." Boaz, like most cops, wasted little time on explanations, apologies, or sentimental gestures.

"OK, then," Nancy said firmly.

"OK," Boaz said, equally firmly. "Now what we'd like you to do, Nancy, is sit here for a while and listen and let me know, or let Timmy know, if anything comes to your mind about what you hear, no matter how little it is. Then I want you to look at the rooms.

"Of course," he added, "you don't *have* to do any of this at all, if you don't care to. I don't mean to be confiscatin' a citizen off the hallways. But we can use any information we can get at this point."

"No, that's fine, I want to help," Nancy told him. "What's been happening is just terrible." The seriousness of the attention in this room made her brown eyes very alert and her short chin a little nervous.

"All right, then, to start off with," Boaz went on, "I want to know what's the situation at—what is it? The University of South Dakota. 'Trendies' and all like that, are they out there?"

"South *Dakota*? Is that where she was from? Well, it's pretty much an invisible school. I don't think I've heard of anybody associated with it. I couldn't even tell you where it *is*, exactly. Is their committee here?"

"No. I've checked the bulletin board down there. Only this one person, Irene Foster, is listed for the University of South Dakota."

"So South Dakota's not hiring this year," Nancy said. "Maybe she came here to give a paper? Just a second."

Nancy wiggled the November *PMLA* program issue free from her capacious blue leather shoulder bag. No Irene Foster was listed under "Program Participants."

"Well, then, she must have come here just to go to some panels or maybe to look for another job," she said.

Boaz asked whether MLA prepared any list of the people looking for jobs.

"No. It would be too many people to keep track of," Nancy replied. "Besides, a lot of people want to look for a new job without their departments knowing about it. If Irene Foster was on the market, that would have been a secret known just by the schools waiting to talk with her."

"Hunnh." Boaz sent Hong down to the registration desk. It was TV time again, more Fairfax "Tales from the Crypt," Boaz thought. This time the message added to the lobby console would request any person having information on Irene Foster, including knowledge of interviews or panels she'd attended, to contact the authorities in Room 210A immediately. The same message, in Hong's handwritten and xeroxed announcement, appeared in the lobby shops and restaurants within the hour.

Boaz then put a call through to Vermillion, South Dakota. The English department chair, Hans Lauffersweiler, whose intelligence that afternoon had been directed to the problem of getting his old Volvo out from under a nine-foot snowdrift, had his attention diverted.

"Reenie? Reenie Foster's been shot? She's dead? Reenie's dead? Why? Was there a robbery?"

"No sir, there was no sign of robbery. Her purse was found with her and there was still money inside it."

"Then why was she shot? That's crazy! There's no reason for anybody to kill Reenie Foster, that's ridiculous! What's the *matter* with you people up there?"

It was a while before Boaz could complete his inquiry. Professor Lauffersweiler did finally confirm that Foster, an associate professor, was the sole representative of USD at the MLA this year. She'd come, as she always did, to hear some lectures being given. On myths. Attending the MLA had been something of a hobby for her, an annual big outing and vacation. As for her personality and habits, this larger picture gradually emerged:

Irene Foster ("Reenie" to her collegiate peers, who heaped her with committee assignments requiring detail work and little imagination) was a woman innocuous by nature, gray to colorless by impact, except when being something of a complainer. Mousy, she was the very picture of the spinster lady teacher in the provinces, except for the fact that in her twenties she'd been divorced three times.

Aside from her marital history (about which she'd retained a certain vanity), what most distinguished Professor Foster were her traits as a worrywart and as a constant talker about problems that struck other people as less than significant. She was the kind of woman who loses sleep the night before a plane flight because she can't decide whether to carry her one piece of luggage on the plane or to check it through instead. She'd consulted the chair about this matter the day before leaving for Chicago. (And she'd shared the tale of this dilemma to her longsuffering seatmate on the shuttle bus from O'Hare.)

At the suggestion that Irene Foster had been interviewing at MLA for another job, Hans Lauffersweiler snorted. Reenie had been a USD fixture for many years, he pointed out. She'd seemed well content, and in any event would have had little in the way of publications to display to another school. In her little house at the edge of Vermillion, she'd devoted herself to her classwork and to the care and promulgation of her pedigreed cat.

That was her main conversational topic, added the chair, who could hardly believe he'd never hear another word from her about Woojums. Foster was by no means impecunious, but it was Lauffersweiler's impression that she'd put much of her cash into sumptuous furnishings and toys for that animal, including gourmet cat food and first-class travel arrangements to cat shows.

(Irene Foster, in fact, was survived only by that one splendid grand champion bronze-and-cream Maine Coon. A muscular but languid animal, it was one she'd carried into cat-fancy competitions as if on a royal litter. Even in that setting, however, Foster had blended invisibly into her milieu: cat fanciers are likely to be either one of the hapless Fosters of this world, or else some wild-eyed oddball in cowboy boots. Both types eventually evolve into elderly humans in triumphant wheelchairs who block the narrow aisles of the show—people who glance up, perhaps, but without apology, as they go on ministering, hierophantic, to the needs of the Perfected Cat.)

Throughout Boaz's call to Vermillion, Nancy had jotted questions on her note pad and slid it toward him. But the information he then gleaned as to Professor Foster's salary, field, and committee work looked unremarkable. Especially her field, which had been the extremely unfashionable one of myth criticism.

Boaz was just concluding his conversation with the USD chair, requesting that Lauffersweiler be available for more questioning and telling him to expect to be contacted by a Chicago funeral home when the morgue completed its autopsy, when there was a racket across the room. The 210A door jumped open noisily. It was Malley, toothy and swaggering, fit for a cat show, and in his hand were the enlarged photos of the footprints in the snow.

10

If Malley expected applause, and he did, his expectation ran aground on the bulk of Halleran. "It's too goddam bad we can't get more shots or get some molds made, Malley," Halleran said, with more asperity even than usual. Boaz gave Nancy a quick look.

Excusing herself tactfully, Nancy said she wanted to ask around among her colleagues about the status of USD. "Maybe I can find out something. Then I'll be in my room."

"OK, Nancy, that'd be fine," Boaz said. A moment later, Duffy moved out of the base room door behind her.

Halleran was still glaring at Malley. He had more to say about the fact that just moments after Boaz had run into the back entrance of the Fairfax, a delivery truck had turned off Michigan into the west end of the alley and had obliterated the boot prints. Malley had had to flatten himself like a ferret against the alley wall to avoid getting squashed. No cordon had been put up to protect that end of the crime scene.

Boaz kept a disgusted silence, but this was the kind of thing that drove Halleran to a baleful fury.

"I have heard one of our colleagues from the Ozarks say there are some people that couldn't pour piss out of a boot, even with printed directions on the heel. You wouldn't happen to know anybody that matches that description, would you, Malley? How about you, Hong?" Neither of the younger detectives replied.

The beat cop at the east cordon had already heard Halleran attach the epithet of "Tomato-brain!" to his identity. The schooling Halleran had given him Halleran now repeated: "Cordon the area, seal off the scene, the *entire* scene—that's the second rule of an investigation. The first rule is to get your head screwed on straight!"

"Let's see these photos," Boaz said, with a sigh.

Malley pointed out how clear the blow-ups were. He fanned them out on the table and selected two that came close to life-size.

The boots that had pushed these prints through the ice crust and into the snow were ten inches long, almost three and half inches at the widest spread. A corrugated pattern of small S-shapes ran down the length of the sole, with three concentric circles patterned at the ball of the foot. A narrow toe, somewhat rounded, the heel only two and a half inches wide. The tread pattern was quite clear in some prints, indicating very little wear.

"Brand new boots here," said Boaz. "And not very big." He ran a knobby hand over his square chin. "Chicago, you buy your new boots in the summertime, or in the fall. And the tread on your boots is worn down by now. So are these some Christmas-present boots? Or maybe if what you're doing is going to a convention in Chicago, you go get yourself some new boots for the occasion. Especially if you're a woman. These look like those nylon boots a lot of women wear: short-tops."

"Yeah, or a short guy might wear them," said Halleran. "Little, lightweight jerk."

At their widest distance, about twenty feet from the dumpsters, the tracks lay thirty inches apart, with smeared and deeper impressions at the toe and ball of the foot. "On the run," Halleran said. "Then, see, they get close together at the end of the alley—killer was slowing down to take the turn."

"If we had all the time in the world," Boaz pointed out, "and also had some molds of these things, we could get a height-and-weight profile and the brand of the shoe. All we can go on here is that this runner isn't real tall and isn't real heavy, either. Wears something like a seven or eight shoe."

Hong put in a reminder that this shooting really might have been unrelated to the hotel. Irene Foster might have come up against some random violence: wrong place at the wrong time. Then for some reason the mugger got scared off before he could get her purse. Boaz noted patiently that Hong's own experience with muggings could not have generated very many crime scenes like the one in this alley: "A shot in the back being inefficient if what you want is the purse."

Halleran agreed. "It looks like the body was just given a quick push after the shot, then the guy takes off." The killer could feel pretty confident that Foster was dead, shot point blank between the shoulder blades. "And the point," Halleran insisted, "was to kill this woman."

Boaz got up to pace a little. "There's a long-shot chance that there were two people with Foster. One shoots her, then they run out of the alley in opposite directions. But now, there was a delivery truck, stopped in traffic over on Water Street for a few minutes. Driver could see the front of the hotel and the whole sidewalk down Columbus Drive. And he didn't see anybody run east out of that alley. It's not totally impossible that another person was involved, but I'm going to rule it out.

"It makes sense," he added, "that these tracks turn toward the Fairfax at the end of the alley. This killer didn't have a lot of time. He or she, whoever it was, had to get out of that alley and get safe. The killer headed for familiar territory, home base, the way that killers do. This person's living in the hotel; I'll put money on it."

"But nobody spotted anybody coming in?" Hong asked.

"No. This is somebody that walks right past you in broad daylight, and you do not see and do not remember this person. We're not looking for a real colorful personality," Boaz concluded.

Halleran took the phone call that came in then from the station. It was Sergeant Kelly, routinely forwarding the news that after further extensive searches by several Area One cops, no red berries or greenish-black seeds had been found in any nook or cranny of the many kitchen rooms. Lab reports on Irene Foster would be available tomorrow. So far there was no reason to expect more than the finding that the cause of death was a projectile bullet.

Lieutenant Mulcahy then came on the line. The press was very hotted up about the Fairfax, "and I'm getting a hot little ulcer," he informed his big detective. Mulcahy had denied and denied and finally persuaded the reporters not to print the rumors about the "Fairfax Curse" and a "black hand of death" being found on some of the hotel walls.

"And other crap, too," Mulcahy said. "I can't hold them back much longer, though. The Outfit popped some guy over on the West Side yesterday, and that gives them something they can play with for a while. But it's a slow news season and they're sick of writing about Santa Claus. They want blood, Halleran, and the Fairfax has got it. They're going to do a front-page splash if something doesn't come down about this damned thing, and soon.

"You can tell Boaz, too, that the Man on Five" (Mulcahy meant the mayor, whose office is on fifth floor of City Hall)—"the Man on Five gets the blue nasties if a convention gets screwed up in Chicago. I've already gotten two calls out of that office, and I don't want any more of them. I need to clear this thing."

"Nothing," said Halleran afterwards, to Boaz's questioning eyebrows. "More nothing."

The detectives then spent some time assembling the known information. Their preliminary conclusions were as follows:

a. This is not the work of several killers. Given the hotel crowds, a witness would have probably spotted someone by now if there were more than one player. This is a single killer, someone comfortably familiar with these academics, the kinds of things they do and the places they go.

b. This killer is smart and resourceful, able to take advantage of opportunities quickly. Which suggests a killer whose pathology is still contained, still rational. The poisoning alone suggests careful thought and deliberation. Not for nothing are poisoners an elite among murder criminals. ("But not after they get into prison," Hong put in, adding, "This guy won't live long there. Poisoners never do: you got to eat in the same room with them and they can't be trusted.")

c. The killer isn't through. There are two, maybe three different MOs so far, and no way to predict the next, no way to know what to monitor or who to try to protect.

d. Random killing cannot be ruled out. And if the player's here to kill randomly, the advantage stays on the killer's side.

"Grudge," Halleran stated.

"Well, let's talk motive," Boaz nodded. "Sex, revenge, money. That's about it in the human repertory. I do think that Irene Foster makes sexual jealousy look like the least likely of the three. And revenge doesn't much fit with her case, either, Timmy."

"If it's money," Boaz added wryly, "well, just about every woman under this roof has grounds for murder if money and equity are enough for murder."

"Yeah, but I'm talking about staff, Bo," Halleran insisted. It was his contention that a psychopath on the hotel staff was operating, somebody with a grudge that wouldn't make sense to anybody else.

"Those guys have an invisible profile. Nobody would notice him in the halls. He could just come and go."

"Not so invisible now," Boaz objected. "If I'm that guy, I've got me a problem. When I'm off duty, it's mighty risky for me to come back to this hotel to make another hit. I can weasel past these English teachers, yeah, but the staff's keeping a lookout now. Anybody on the staff sees me, they know I'm not supposed to be here. And they're nervous, they're gonna run right over to the cops. I'm gonna have to work my homicide habit right into my work schedule in the kitchen or the maintenance rooms.

"So I think if this killer's on the payroll," Boaz concluded, "it's somebody on duty at the time of the deaths. Now who does that amount to? Can we narrow some names out of these schedules now?" Halleran made a call for some beat cops to come to the base room.

Boaz, meanwhile, decided to pay closer attention to the implications of there being a single killer not on the staff. That person, then, would have to have checked into the hotel no later than about Wednesday noon, probably earlier—although, as he noted, "if it's a local guy, he could just walk in and out of the hotel any time."

The desk clerk groaned to hear Boaz's telephoned request. Duplicate lists, he'd told the young man, were to be brought to him of all the hotel registrants for the last couple of weeks.

"I want everybody who checked in or out. Make it the last three weeks. And where they're from. Yeah, I *know* you've got seven hundred rooms here. I'm not telling you to memorize the list to recite in church. I'm telling you to get it to me. You got a problem with that? 'Cause if you've got a problem with that, I'll just impound the original and you won't do business of any kind until I'm through with it."

The next voice on the phone was Ms. Carstairs-Norton, who was subdued and had been ever since the dreadful news of the third death. The copier machine behind the front desk was put into service immediately.

Then Nancy Cook, who'd just returned to her room, got another call. It was time to try the long shot of having her look at some more rooms. She arrived at the base door soon after.

"I wish I could tell you some revelation about South Dakota," she said. "But all I got was people shaking their heads. USD's been a quiet university for local students for more years than anyone can even remember. If there's a scandal, it's buried. Not the best choice of word; sorry."

Halleran narrowed his eyes appreciatively at this earnest woman. She was OK. Heaving to his feet with a grunt he tried to suppress, he smoothed down his hopelessly wrinkled suit jacket and went through his pockets for the three grudgingly provided passkeys to the victims' rooms.

"Let's do Alcott's room first," Boaz suggested. "1012."

Halleran set a couple of beat cops from the kitchen search party to the task of sifting again for common staff names in all departments at the times of the hotel deaths. Soon, dozens of sheets of names and hours had spread across the card tables and floated down onto the folding chairs like leaves. Eventually they would sort out fourteen names, six of them men. One by one they'd be located and rigorously questioned.

Meanwhile, out in the second-floor hallway, Boaz, Halleran,

and Nancy moved between the few people who were ambulating, in various forms of self-conscious cool, toward the Marxist cash bar that had just opened for business. Boaz looked in for a moment. This bar was, after all, near 210A. Was anyone in there keeping an eye out on the police?

Nancy mentioned that the "Marxist Literary Group Cash Bar" was known for a few things: weak drinks, hopeful young Trendies, "and, supposedly, the best-looking men. It's usually packed with people."

Boaz took another look. Tonight—well, either the grad students were not receiving invitations from schools to meet in this bar, or, if they'd been invited, they weren't responding. The Crystal Room was so empty there was a slight echo. Only one small group of young professors was proceeding with the usual behaviors. With many gestures, Jeff Frech from SUNY Buffalo was enthusiastically trying to be included—one of the guys—in the conversation of young Professors Pepecito and Lopez. The gringo's effort was being indulged ironically, but with cruel pauses and private looks.

All these folks depend on crowds so as to stand out at all, Boaz thought. Now they better find some crowds to huddle in. Put all this space around them, they're as foolish as bantams—and as easily picked off by a predator.

Up on the tenth floor, Boaz and Halleran waited inside near the door as Nancy moved slowly around Alcott's single room. Odd how it was not much different, she thought, from being in the room of a businessman or a technician. Her assignment, as she knew, was to provide the academic angle. But what she saw—the inadvertent emotional starkness in the world of Alcott's possessions (his studied purchases from the Sharper Image, including Porsche Design Collection sunglasses, a Braun quartz travel alarm clock, everything pathetically expensive)—made her feel sorry for this colleague. She was grateful for the feeling; she hadn't liked being unable to feel the slightest loss regarding the man.

No work of literature was in the room. Michael Alcott had often remarked that he hated to read and only wanted to *know* things. 151

He advised his graduate students "not to waste time" reading anything but current criticism. "Read literature only to meet a course requirement and just take notes on what has to be known about it," was one of his recommendations.

Atop the dresser were two copies of *The Tremulous Physique*, his book, along with reprints of his two articles in *Representations*. In Alcott's suitcase, which he'd left open, was Peter Goon's *Bolts and Nuts: The Machinery of Flesh*.

Nancy said nothing but remembered overhearing one of Alcott's Marxist confrères who'd been talking about Alcott just before the Mudge panel. "Yes, poor Michael. Still, you know, his body right there on the floor was quite an advertisement for his stuff. I mean, from any angle, he looked just like those mutilation photos in his *Representations* pieces. And let's face it, his book's going to sell like crazy now. I could almost think he planned it that way."

Nancy noted aloud, musingly, that Alcott's subject matter was always about dismemberment, body distortion, deformity, and the ways those connect with the limits of language—always something about the public presentation of the body. The two cops looked blank but patient with her.

Actually, she thought, it *is* odd in a way that he would die like that; the irony of it.

Walking into Irene Foster's room on the thirty-fourth floor felt very different, more like violating a very private space. The bed looked as though it had been tightly remade by its occupant to meet some personal specifications. Two pairs of shoes stood side by side primly on the floor of the closet, from the rack of which Professor Foster's simple clothing hung with the buttons all facing the same direction. A few hapless details, though, showed the woman's indulgence in a little flair: a small bottle of Opium perfume—"Not cologne, but perfume," Nancy noted—stood alongside some toothpaste on a glass shelf in the bathroom, a shelf otherwise bare.

"The bottle's full," Nancy noticed with a pang. "She probably bought it just for this trip."

Framed on a bedside table was a snapshot of an enormous cat, back arched and tail plumed, under the eyes of an admiring judge. On that same end table, it was the old, long-out-of-print British edition of Pope's *Iliad*, its faded green leather the size of a psalter, that was an intolerable rebuke. Whatever else Reenie Foster was or did, she had located and cherished something very fine.

It was unbearable, the little book. Tears were in Nancy's eyes and her voice was angry when she turned to Boaz. "You have got to—you've got to take care of this! This is terrible! This woman was an English teacher, in South Dakota, for God's sake! This was her cat! You can't just let this happen!"

For a moment, Halleran's sad-looking face was more than just an illusion made by flesh. Boaz said, "I know, I don't like it, either, Nancy. Let's go on out."

The door retaped, Halleran again took the fast route down by service elevator, leaving Boaz to escort Nancy to her third-floor room. During the wait for the elevator, Nancy stood close to Boaz and then took his hand in silence. Her mouth was closed and serious, and she was looking straight ahead. She was not girlishly seeking protection, but womanly acknowledging that there really isn't protection. He closed his hand firmly around hers. A moment later the elevator arrived and they stepped in.

It was crowded with dinner-seeking people. A woman in the rear was finishing up a set of remarks. "If that makes any sense?" she concluded, her voice scaling upward. The man beside her, manipulated into a corner in more ways than one, had a reassuring "Oh, yes" extracted from him. "Mary nodded, pa-rump-a-pump-pump," contributed the speaker over his head.

"Well, Becky, what it shows, of course, is that you don't go walking into big-city alleys. Doesn't everybody know that?"

This was Professor Larry Schlaggdorf of Barnard, addressing his same-time-next-year companion, Professor Phlee. "It" was evidently a reference to the murder of Irene Foster. "It" had provided Schlaggdorf, a native of New York City, with a chance to display his urban know-how. Phlee did not reply. She longed for the oblivious circumscription of the College of Marin.

153

Stopping on the seventh floor, the elevator took aboard Jeremy Tone, grad student from Berkeley. The crowded car gave Mr. Tone an opportunity to be overheard by everyone while pretending to talk only to the other grad student he saw therein.

"God, I'm so tired," Tone said, languidly. "Just had my ninth interview. And five more to go! How many have you got?" The crestfallen other candidate was forced to admit in public, then, to having "only four." Such moments are felt (by the hottest marketable commodities such as Tone) to be, in and of themselves, worth all the years of graduate school.

Out on the third-floor hallway, Nancy Cook, who'd hit her limit in that elevator, announced, "I am going to go wash my hair. Something about MLA today just makes that seem like a good idea. Then I'm going to go hear some music."

"Where are you going, Nancy?"

"Annette and I are going to the Blackstone."

"Annette Lisordi? OK, but I want you to be *real* careful, Nance." Boaz scratched down the phone number of 210A on a sheet from his little notebook. "That's the second-floor room. You can get in touch with me all night long. And there's gonna be a cop real close to you the whole time you're out."

With a movement of his head, Boaz indicated Jimmy Duffy, the plainclothes cop down the corridor, a man who appeared to be trying to figure out the intrahotel telephone on the wall. "That same guy you've probably already spotted."

"All right, Bo," Nancy agreed, in a voice implying a serious pact with him, or at least the serious potential of such a pact. At her door, she looked at him without smiling. They did not embrace. Boaz was feeling something odd and difficult; namely, that he owed this woman something. He wanted to show her some indication of his usability, some recompense for Irene Foster.

Nancy's door closed, and Boaz headed toward the cop to give him firm directions and make sure Duffy had a working pager.

What Boaz had not wanted to elaborate on to Nancy was that if you don't have a smoking gun (there's the guy standing over the body with a gun in his hand), and if you don't have a known-but-flown (you know who did it, but he wasn't present during the first questioning), then what you have to do is wait for the killer to strike again. Hope for a witness, hope for a slip-up, hope for some pattern to show. In the meantime, all you can do is keep looking and looking at what's in front of you.

He spent the next couple of hours interviewing several wide-eyed and adamant staff people, including the still-irate Alexandra Rostikoff from Supplies, all of whom had apparently good alibis. He then did some manipulations with room numbers and names. Somebody nice in the kitchens sent him a meal on the house. Eleven-thirty found him out in the halls again. Halleran had gone home for the night, but Boaz, restless, went on prowling and thinking.

Nobody was socializing late any more. Down the all-but-empty hallways, the flat, speckled-maroon, airport-lobby carpeting, with its big "F" emblems at the elevator doors, looked vulnerable and pathetic in its pretentions. Something about the hotel's forlorn anonymity suggested luridness and sadness, both. Somebody is here, Boaz thought, whose mind day and night is a lot like this.

Five o'clock Saturday morning found Boaz back at his apartment for another cleanup and change. It was at 8:00 A.M., blue-suited again but with a checked blue shirt and yellow-moduled silk tie, that Boaz stopped off at the State Street station to confer with the growling Mulcahy. A bottle of Pepto Bismol stood in pink obviousness on the lieutenant's desk. Under it was a folded paper towel.

"In case you're wondering, Dixon: that's *not* something on loan from the art museum," Mulcahy said. "It's what's keeping me going lately." A set of expatiating complaints followed.

Shortly after 9:00 Boaz was back at the hotel. The base room was quiet. The other detectives there were looking at statements. Duffy had left a message that both women were OK, the evening had been uneventful, and Nancy and Annette Lisordi were now at a 9:00 o'clock panel in the Alpine Room.

Boaz had brought from the station the latest lab report. Its few pages addressed Irene Foster, whose autopsy and toxicology workup indicated that if a close-range missile had not stopped her heart and splintered an edge of her sternum, she would have been healthy enough to have served as chief councilor to many, many generations of cats.

On the headquarters table, too, was the delivered list of names and home addresses of everyone who'd checked in and out of the Fairfax as far back as the first of December. The stack was a thick one. Boaz riffled its pages with his thumb and began. He'd managed to look over all the morning registrations on the day of Alcott's death, as well as registrants on the two days before, when the phone rang. It was 11:05 A.M.

The agitated voice on the line was that of the security officer. McGuire's news was that the maid had just found a body in the bathroom of room 3800. Boaz and Halleran were out the door at a run, leaving Hong to dial 911—the alternative phone number for the Fairfax these days. Malley went flying to alert the cops at the Fairfax entrances. Hong directed the desk that no one was to check out of the hotel without police notification on the spot.

The single room on the thirty-eighth floor had been registered under the name of Professor Malcolm Gett of Johns Hopkins University. At first, from the door, the room looked like the tidy domicile of Irene Foster. The bed showed itself made up in advance of the maid's arrival. Objects in the room were neatly placed. Only a few reddish stains here and there on the carpet at the left indicated something out of the ordinary. You had to step into the room before the red-spattered base of the bathroom door, which opened inward, displayed itself like a small drip painting on white wood.

"Shit, here we go," said Halleran, who'd once had the experience of brains dripping from a ceiling onto his shoulder at a crime scene he'd walked into.

Bleeding to death very quickly, Malcolm Gett had slumped into fetal position in the bathroom, his back against the tub and his knees drawn up beside the toilet, the lid of which was down. The right side of his head, brown-haired with a balding crown, lay in an asymmetrical puddle spread under him like a nimbus. His thin brown beard and mustache were both smeared; his left eye was open and expressionless. Fresh blood, hardly viscous, had splotched surfaces everywhere in the room and had flowed to the molding under the sink. Over that sink, across the six-foot width of the mirror, the word FREEDOM was written in black print a foot high. An emphatic line had been drawn savagely beneath it.

The arriving examiners made no wisecracks. Gingerly they took turns in the room, De Bartolo, Montenegro, the photographer, the detectives.

The victim was fully clothed, "probably getting ready to go to lunch," Montenegro ventured. A bullet, moving downward out of its victim, had ricocheted off the high edge of the porcelain tub, nicking it. Montenegro and De Bartolo agreed the shot had been at close range, almost certainly while Gett was in a seated position on the lid of the toilet. It looked like another medium-caliber wound, De Bartolo said, and came across a shell in the saturated carpet by the wall.

Boaz pointed out a small letter *F* that had been almost rubbed out on the left side of the mirror, as if the writer had begun again, the second time with much larger letters. "Probably one of those dry-erase markers that write on glass," Boaz said. No writing implement of the kind was found in the suite.

The drawer of the bedside table disclosed a half-written note, a letter to "Jesse," drafted in Gett's small block-print lettering. The man did not ordinarily write large.

The smudges on the carpeting, lighter toward the main door, suggested the killer's shoes had come into contact with the bloody results of Gett's dying.

"Looks like the killer waited just inside the bathroom door while the guy died," Halleran opined. "Picked up some blood and walked away."

"There was lot of spurting when this guy was shot," De Bartolo noted. "The bullet went through the jugular, so the blood would arc for several feet at first. That's how you get the spatters on the door jamb. The killer would have been hit by some of that blood if the killer was standing by the door. The faucets haven't been turned on, though; sink's dry. So's the tub. The killer went off and got cleaned up somewhere else." Fiber samples were collected from every smear on the carpet.

"Not dead long at all," De Bartolo said. "Within the hour. Blood's still wet on his beard. Well," he added resignedly, "at least we're getting closer and closer to the time it happens, Halleran. The way things are going, I guess we'll just keep coming back 'til we catch the perp right in the act."

De Bartolo was tired. His pessimistic wife had canceled their vacation hotel reservations in Miami—if he'd ever get away from this hotel to take a vacation at all.

Boaz got on the phone to the State Street people, then set himself the task of trying to contain hysteria in the hotel. People in adjacent rooms having been interviewed, he braced the service elevator open and got the hallway cleared. But the big-boned, sagging body of notorious Malcolm Gett was not easy to extract from his final circumstances.

He'd been a man in his thirties, ordinarily psittacine of complexion, and though not fat exactly, he was bodily sloppy in a way that reminded one of fatness. What with loose lips and trousers a bit too tight across the thighs, he'd always given the impression of being clumsy even while sitting down. Now, too, he did not go into his body bag without difficulty.

For all Boaz's efforts, the efficient police cordons and rapid, white-sheeted deployments that moved Malcolm Gett out of the Michigan Avenue entrance could not fail to attract attention among the MLA conventioneers in the concourse. It was only moments before a rich new set of rumors took flight through the hotel.

And the rumors ("Gett's gay lover shot him, shot him four times, then killed himself," or the alternative rumor that Gett's lover was "prowling the hallways now") were soon known to everyone. By 2:30 P.M., panic-stricken individuals were packing up and checking out with, in many cases, a descent from rationality as rapid as Michael Alcott's downward trajectory three days before.

Something about the rate of behavior, in fact, appeared to be almost formulaic, and analogous possibly to the great electromagnetic and gravitational formulae of the physical world. But in the MLA equation, the terms were $D = (I)\ R_1R_2/T^2$, where R_1 is the first Rumor, R_2 the second Rumor, their product divided by T (for Time) squared, all multiplied by the constant I, which is the Intensity of the desire to appear important, yielding the force of D, the Descent from rationality. Suddenly, dismayed airlines personnel heard dozens of demands for rescheduled flight plans. All the colorful cabs had their services vociferously shouted for. Physical bodies were turning from the registration desk, turning to lift luggage, and turning into the back seats of vehicles, as if to show that a Theory of Everything might one day include human particles spinning in their emotional fields as well.

However, the majority of conventioneers did *not* check out, enjoying as they did being at the hub of things for a change. All afternoon, there was a run on souvenir Fairfax coffee mugs in the gift shop—something to put in the office back at school, placed with an eye to its noticeability. ("Oh yes, I was there; I talked to the police about it.") The gift shop was unable to keep enough Chicago newspapers in stock and began with the evening editions to sell them at even higher prices.

What's more, when the Marxist cash bar opened on the second floor that day, a large game table was in evidence, with Clue Master Detective laid out for play. The sign-up list remained enthusiastically long. The game rooms had been relabeled with various ballroom names and suites, including, cold-bloodedly, Wellesley, Arizona, South Dakota, and Hopkins. Revolver and poison weapons, of course, were most frequently guessed about, but all the pieces were moved with relish.

"Fear death by coffee," quipped a complacent winner, Professor Rorie Crider from Bennington. But none of his gamemates, alas, shared the field of modernism, so although they all nodded, his allusion was lost.

Lieutenant Mulcahy, issuing another directive that was probably unnecessary, ordered his detectives to make all background checks and Hopkins inquiries in double time, and to accept no excuses because of the weekend. Chicago reporters in private were already referring to the place as the Fairfucked, Mulcahy added; the press conference for this was going to be a doozie.

Overworked was the condition of everyone on the case now. Although a police officer usually handles several cases at a time, on a big case like this an investigator is expected to work around the clock for several days, with just a few hours off during the "dog shift" at night. As tac officers, Boaz and Halleran had done many seventy-two-hour stretches and longer. For them this case, though, had frustrational components that were particularly wearing. The investigation, no matter what point they took up, immediately became as blank and featureless as the hotel walls and generic décor.

The TV announcements in the lobby still had generated nothing. Curiosity seekers might peer into the little headquarters room for a wide-eyed moment, but no one had come forward with usable information. Continued interviews with the fourteen on-duty staff people continued to lead nowhere. Meanwhile—it was a cop's nightmare case—there were sure to be black and Spanish and Asian families getting burgled and shot and beaten up, and not enough cops were out on those cases, so many had been shuffled over to the Fairfax. It was just a matter of time before the press accused the department of giving preferential treatment to a few white professionals over the continuing needs of minority communities.

Boaz himself was starting to look a little haggard. He was irritable with worry. "This thing's drivin' me straight up the nearest wall," he griped to Halleran.

He felt sure there'd be another attempted murder. Maybe a single victim again, maybe not. Were the folks in an elevator going to be eliminated in some gruesome way? Was a homemade bomb being put together with sugar and weedkiller brought from home? Would somebody stuff the laundry chute with a small professor? Stand up at a panel and blow the speaker away? Was Nancy in any danger? Who wasn't?

The evidence technicians had left frazzled. Donny McGuire, looking hunted, was going around with his mouth hanging open. Halleran, Hong, and Malley, too: they weren't talking much about it, but they all had the tenseness and quick head movements (the Cop's Swivel when in a room of people) of men who knew the situation was bad.

It was just past 2:00 P.M. Saturday when the detectives congregated in the base room to discuss the Gett scene and preliminary findings. McGuire came in, balancing half a dozen cups of coffee from Slade's. He'd been trying hard to be the gofer since Halleran had taken him aside and bellowed at him.

Boaz was back from another all-but-useless interrogation, this time with the three people left on the Hopkins hiring committee, all of whom were frightened and stunned. Patrolmen were still cross-checking their statements.

None of the Hopkins group (Professors Gary Goby, Ray Burba, and Allan Hislop) had any knowledge of the people from the other victimized schools. None of them knew of any problems in Gett's personal life. His professional life had been controversial in the extreme, but no threats had been made that the three men had heard about. Malcolm Gett was not known to have long-lasting interludes with the young men, usually grad students, he attracted. Again, insurance, inheritance, and salary did not seem to be issues. The "Jesse" in Gett's unfinished note proved to be a half-brother in Toronto, well-alibi'd.

Meanwhile, as Hong determined, the Wellesley Four, eager to leave town, had decided that morning to make an offer to a candidate at the convention. Their modernism line had been accepted by Trixie Stern, the glamorous Marxist grad student from NYU. (She'd hoped for better and was already laying plans to move further east in Massachusetts as soon as possible.) The five of them had gone to Chez Toi for an early, celebratory lunch. Again, their numbers were well-alibi'd. So were the interview activities of Arizona, the committee members having decided to stick together night and day.

As for Annette Lisordi, she'd been in an interview with the University of Virginia when her life was interrupted again with questions about a Fairfax death. She hardly knew whether to laugh or cry. After her stammering statement to Malley, she'd made the mistake of trying to ease tension by saying to the UVA gentlemen that she seemed to be "associated with everything going on in this benighted hotel."

The UVA men (there being only three tenured women on the UVA faculty, none of them on the hiring committee) concluded, of course, that this woman was hopelessly *infra dig* and inappropriate. A real lady would have no such sordid experiences. Besides, although Miss Lisordi came with stellar recommendations, was the Tidewater really constrained to add to its numbers a somewhat swarthy Italian?

("It was not a Strindberg play, Nancy," Annette would later tell her friend. "It was Ionesco, pure Ionesco, the whole time I was there.")

"OK, what have we really got here?" Boaz began, putting down his coffee cup in the base room at 2:15 P.M. His tone was curt and no-nonsense. "The pattern's kind of thin. We got four victims. One death per day. Two women, two men, but the deaths don't alternate by sex. Everybody dead was a tenured professor. Everything's done in or around the Fairfax.

"But we've got four different MOs. Maybe three if Alcott fell by himself, which he didn't. The victims didn't know each other. The names of the victims don't stack up in alphabetical order, and the names don't anagram in any way, unless the names of Gett and Hopkins make a pattern—which I doubt. The killings happen at different times of the day that don't lay out in a sequence. So far there hasn't been a pattern with the room numbers or the floor numbers.

"Now with this guy, Gett," Boaz continued, "there was no ransacking his room. His wallet's in his jacket on the chair, there's about forty dollars in cash right on top of the chest of drawers. Undisturbed room: looks like a stranger. This wasn't a killer looking for a personal memento to take back, something that had meaning for both of them."

After more discussion, it was agreed that this was possibly a killer obsessed with power and control, maybe into revenge, but not a "serial killer" per se. There'd been no attempt to disguise the identity of the victims, as a serial killer would do, at least one with an organized personality. On the other hand, these were killings that showed intelligence, precision, and quick execution, unlike the methods of killers with disorganized personalities.

"Well, Gett was gay," Halleran put in. "That might be a lead. Maybe this was one of Gett's pick-ups—one of those mopes that hang around the hotels a lot. But jumped-up, a duster maybe" (someone high on PCP), "rough trade. They're messing around in the bathroom, then the trade shoots him. Did Russ find any sexual evidence?"

"No, nothin', " Boaz said. "If Gett had a date, it hadn't gotten very far. Besides, trade on PCP would shoot him more than once, and probably in the balls."

"Yeah, well, that's right," Halleran admitted, and put aside some professional memories of a scene in Wrigleyville that neither he nor Boaz ever cared to recall.

"Besides," Boaz pointed out, "a guy like that probably would have been noticed running in from the alley.

"Now that handwriting on the mirror's not going to help much," Boaz added, considering the penmanship he'd seen on the statements. "Might not be Gett's handwriting. Could be, but lots of these professors print when they write, and they print little-bitty. Handwriting analysis would take a week or more, and we don't have that kind of time. This killer's gonna hit again."

Halleran impatiently scraped his folding chair, which was invisible behind and under him. He knew Boaz was right and that time was short.

"There are some other signs," Halleran said, "that whoever did it didn't know Gett personally. For one thing, the body wasn't covered up with towels or the shower curtain. You get a covered-up victim, you can start thinking you've got a personal relationship to look for, you've got a killer that wants to hide the body away and make the whole thing history. Maybe you can even figure on some remorse in the killer.

"But this is flagrant," Halleran went on. "You've got a scene here that's wide open. The body was left right where it fell. And the bathroom door: it's open. No attempt to close it even part way. This is somebody that doesn't care about shocking the person that comes in and finds this guy. All that's impersonal. Angry, but not personal.

"*But*," Halleran emphasized, "there's a facial assault here. And that's the most personal assault there is. Indicates the killer *did* know the guy and was mad as hell at him."

Boaz noted that the killer had gotten Gett in the neck, not exactly the face. High up on the neck, but still the neck. "The killer could have shot him right in the face, but didn't," Boaz said. "Maybe the barrel wobbled down a little, but I don't think so. This was real close range. The killer could choose where to shoot. You know, this killer's standing and facing this guy. Gett's sitting on the toilet, probably begging or crying. The killer wants to shut him up, but then doesn't shoot him in the mouth that's doing the talking. That looks to me kinda personal and impersonal, both."

Halleran agreed that the bathroom signs pointed to a killer who knew Gett but in some ways didn't care personally about him at all.

"And that's weird," Halleran said, "especially with that 'freedom' thing. Real angry. This is one angry dude."

"Or one angry woman," Boaz said. "But a woman would have been more likely to close the bathroom door."

"I think it's a guy," Halleran said. "A little guy. Wears cute little nylon boots out in the snow. He just forgets to close the bathroom door after he's done his business. Resents Engleton, she's a woman. Picks off Foster when he gets a chance. Resents Alcott, too, for some reason, maybe sexual, maybe professional."

To Boaz in particular, Halleran added, "Looks to me now like Alcott probably *was* offed." Boaz nodded.

"But," Halleran concluded, "good luck trying to find every guy here that's—uh—'in touch with the feminine side of himself.'" Halleran's tone was weary.

"Maybe it was a nightcrawler," Hong put in, "working day shift? A lot of doors here." (Hong was referring to a hooker in a hotel who specializes in trying hotel room doors and stealing wallets from the rooms she can get into. Now and then the crawlers get surprised by the occupant coming in, and the occupant doesn't live long.)

"Yeah, or maybe a ballknocker," Malley put in, meaning a woman or a two-woman team who follow a man into a hotel elevator, grab him violently in the groin, hurt him, rifle his pockets, then jump out at the next floor.

"In *these* elevators?" Halleran expostulated. "You been on an elevator in this hotel yet, Malley?" Malley did not reply, which at this point wasn't a good sign.

"So where do we go from here?" Boaz demanded. "Things are pointing in too many different directions."

Donny McGuire at the door now produced another delivery from Slade's, this time cheeseburgers and mushroom burgers in take-out plastic, with wads of french fries in grease-splotched wrappings.

Halleran regarded the pool of cooling grease at the bottom of his styrofoam with an air of martyrdom. But it was the limp, salty, canned mushrooms under the bun that tortured him into speech. To the world in general he pointed out, "It's not hard to find fresh mushrooms, God damn it. It's not even hard to grow them. I could grow them in the trunk of a squad." He scowled. "It's also not real, *real* hard to go to the store and buy them. Dumb fucks."

"You into mushrooms, Halleran, is that it?" Malley jeered. "A big deal excitement for you, Halleran? Can't get enough of them?" 165

Halleran moved his head slowly. His weight was a sedimented slab in the room. "No doubt mushrooms are nothing to you, jerko. I've heard you grow them between your toes." Hong snickered, only to find Halleran glaring at him, too.

Halleran had eaten garbage for three straight days. He hadn't slept very well. He was near, and he knew Boaz was near, they were both right next to something, but they couldn't get the smallest grip. To make matters worse, Irene Foster had sort of curly hair. If Malley got in his way or just popped off now, Halleran was ready to fall on him like an avalanche.

Malley, however, had a sense of the friable edge of things, and kept his mouth shut.

Next at the base-room door was Nancy. She had on her blue boots again, but now under a long brown washed-denim skirt and patterned camel sweater, with a very narrow, blue-plaid scarf tied complexly at her throat. It was more of a schoolteacherish look, and under the circumstances more vulnerable-looking. Boaz's worries went up a notch at the sight of her.

Nancy had heard the news of Malcolm Gett's death from passersby in the halls late that morning. Her plainclothes *doppelgänger* had been able to answer her questions with only a sketchy description of the Gett discovery. She knew the man had been found shot in the bathroom, but little more than that. Having attended the Gett panel at 9:00 that morning, she was astounded but also somehow not surprised at all.

"What do you know about this guy Malcolm Gett, Nancy?" Boaz asked. "Famous, a big Trendy at Hopkins, is that right?"

"Yes. Very big. Annette and I went to his panel this morning. He came to Hopkins several years ago from—I think it was Dartmouth. And he's very 'in,' very important to be seen with lately— or used to be. Oh God, this is awful! I can't say he was a likeable guy. Not any more than Michael Alcott was. Gett was more controversial than anybody except maybe Joan Mellish. I suppose he could have had a lot of enemies."

"Well, it wasn't a friend that offed him," Halleran put in. "Did
you ever hear anything about his boyfriends?"

Nancy took a seat beside him. "Everybody knew Malcolm Gett was gay. He was flamboyant about it sometimes, very aggressive. But I never heard any talk about anyone in particular with him."

"Well," said Boaz, "maybe one of Gett's partners will get scared and want to tell us something. That TV announcement's gonna get kind of crowded, but I suppose we ought to add Gett's name to the list of people we'd like some information about."

Halleran moved his chair back in preparation for the effort of rising. "I still don't want to rule out that we've got a couple of nuts to look for. I know the staff's got alibis, but somebody in this hotel is working on a grudge. He's somebody that figured something out about poisons. But the other guy is somebody borderline: a schizo that got excited when he saw Alcott dead. Made him feel like a big guy. Got more excited when he heard about Engleton. Goes off on a spree with Foster and Gett."

Boaz replied, "We got a lot of ways we could divide up the possible sets of killings. Some of the victims, it looks like it didn't make any difference who they were."

Boaz was just about ready to contact Jay Grandy, Chicago's FBI-trained expert at profile development of serial and multiple murderers. But Grandy was still tight with the FBI, and when you call the Sisters into a case in any way, you get turf problems with the lieutenant. Grandy had thrown his weight around with Mulcahy enough to provoke another purchase of a pink bottle for the loo.

"I want to look at Malley's shots again," Halleran said. "The lobby shots, right after Alcott landed. See if there's anybody in nylon-type boots."

Malley shuffled through some papers under a chair and produced the five snapshots he'd taken on Wednesday. None of the academic onlookers in the atrium lobby had been wearing anything but wing-tips, Reeboks, or stacked pumps.

"Damn it," said Halleran.

"These are a waste of time, Timmy," Boaz said, "and we've got to get going."

Halleran now looked over at Boaz with skeptical irritation. *167*

"You've thought of some place we can go? Like where?"

Boaz, elbow on the table, was rubbing his forehead. He shook his head briefly. "No, I haven't. This whole thing's got a little bit different tempo now, though. It's just about openly crazy. If it's one killer, then it looks like the guy's getting more and more into it but also is losing control. Has to write something magic on the mirror to keep control.

"But it's the scenes all together that just don't add up," Boaz complained. "How come some crazy guy would write 'freedom' on the mirror? I mean, is this guy into slave games? He gets untied, comes back the next morning and shoots his sex partner, and then what? He goes off and waters his yews? He's got a thing against little quiet ladies in brown coats? His mama's got a brown coat hangin' in her closet?"

Halleran shrugged. "We've had weirder stuff."

Nancy's pen had stopped over her note pad. Her head was tilted to one side and she was frowning.

"'Freedom' was written on the mirror?" she asked slowly.

Halleran nodded. "Yeah."

"Just that?"

Halleran nodded again.

"What I don't get," Boaz said, still rubbing his forehead, "is all the different weapons. Why bother with all the MOs? You wanta kill these folks, why not just pick them off with your .32? You could get a lot more of them that way. Right now, we don't know what's next. We gonna walk out this door and there's a noose hanging down the atrium, and guess what's at the end of it?"

Boaz shifted his shoulders inside his suit. "I tell you, this thing just don't signify."

There was a movement to his left. Nancy, he noticed, was sitting bolt upright on her folding chair. She was staring at him.

"What did you say, please?" she said.

"Oh, somethin' my cousin Haskell says: 'It don't signify.' He's just another dummy in the family."

But Nancy had a hesitant, assessing look of amazement on her face, as if she'd just thought of the principle of natural selection, or even an alternative ending for *Moby-Dick*.

"That's it!" she said. "*Could* that be it? Oh my God! Oh, I don't believe it! Boaz, Timmy, listen, *it doesn't signify!*"

"You sound like Haskell."

But Nancy was shifting back and forth on her chair. "Listen to me! *The signifier does not necessarily indicate the signified.* But the whole thing *might* signify, provided you can read the discourse of the community. Oh my God! The whole thing's a set-up! The clues are false, Boaz, all of them! No, not false; I mean, they *seem* to be false because they're *meant* to look that way. I *think* so. Maybe I've lost my mind in this place."

The cops were staring at her.

Now Nancy was rushing headlong, thinking furiously. She pushed back a wad of hair. "Because, see, they're *literary* killings. Nancy, Nancy, slow down, get a grip. How can I explain this? The mirror: I need to make sure about that mirror."

She was on her feet. "The mirror says it's a killing about words. And so were the other deaths, I *think*. Listen, I need to see that room! Are you sure there weren't any *other* words?"

"OK, OK. Slow down," Boaz said.

"Boaz, I want to see Malcolm Gett's room. Right now! Please."

Boaz and Halleran exchanged a look of what-is-there-to-lose and got up. Halleran still had the 3800 key.

Nancy, talking almost to herself, went on. "What I've also got to do is double-check about the publications. What they *all* wrote. I'm going to call Jennifer, I think she could help."

"Who's Jennifer?" Boaz asked.

"That friend of mine at Yale and a really good RA." Nancy was already at the door.

"A what?"

"A research assis . . . oh, Boaz, never *mind* right now!"

11

Outside the door to 3800, Nancy steeled herself. The human vulnerability implied by bathrooms could be unnerving at times, and this was going to be awful. Boaz, behind and near her, pushed the door open with two fingers. She felt his hand for a moment on her upper arm.

"I'm all right," she said.

Boaz told her Gett's body had been taken to the morgue. "But there's a lot of blood in the bathroom, on the floor and all. You don't faint at the sight of blood?"

"I've never fainted in my life. And I *give* blood at the Red Cross."

"That blood's in a clean little bag. But OK. You just let me know . . ."

"Don't touch anything except the carpet you're standing on," Halleran told her, with emphasis. "You got any sores or cuts on your hands? *Don't* get any blood on you. Just move slow. Look in from the bathroom door, but don't go in."

Boaz stepped into the bedroom while Halleran waited, now and then checking the hall.

For Nancy, after the first shock of the blood, it was the bright fluorescent lighting that made the bathroom so grotesque. That and all the ordinary hotel details. The "Honey & Almond Bath Gel" with matching shampoo and cream rinse on the shower shelf. And the tiny Quasar TV, the size of a big index card, mounted on a metal post left of the sink, its image doubled in the magnifying mirror on the opposite side.

There was blood on the toilet handle, on the phone, on the

bathroom scale, and on a small hair dryer that had been knocked to the floor. One hand towel was still vividly white, the "F" insignia on it so white compared to the other towels that it was frightening.

The word FREEDOM stood above all this in something like demented triumph. The black letters sloped slightly upward. No other words appeared on the walls. Nancy checked carefully, though, from the door, holding in her skirt and squatting on her ankles to look up under the sink. Nothing.

Then, steely-voiced, she said, "I should make sure there aren't any other words in the room. Like inside the closet, maybe?"

She looked over the inner closet door and walls, then the areas behind the draperies and over the lintels, even into the interiors of the deal chest of drawers. The room recorded no other excursion into rhetoric.

"OK. It's *freedom*. Now let me call Jennifer to do some research for me, Bo."

She started off, but Boaz touched her arm. "I'm not real sure what you're up to, Nancy, and I know you're in a hurry, but now listen to me. Write down the phone calls you make, every number. And every name you talk to. Go on the record. So somebody else could read your notes. And be careful, Nance. You're gonna have your cop at the door. But you *call me* in the base room, you don't leave your room to come downstairs."

Aside to Jimmy Duffy, Boaz added, "You see thing one from now on and your gun's out, you got that? I don't want any chances taken. Not even somethin' so little you could put it in a pea pod. You get tired, you call me. I'll get you some relief."

"Sure, Bo." Duffy unbuttoned his jacket and left it open so he could reach his holster quickly. Boaz's and Halleran's jackets had been unbuttoned since that morning.

The two detectives dropped back to 210A, Boaz to spend another hour with anagram experiments and numerological fiddlings just to make sure "Malcolm Gett" and "Hopkins" and "3800" didn't pattern out in some way. They did not. Then he 171 doubled up with Halleran to reinterview, this time in the base room and one by one, the three Hopkins professors.

Nancy organized her notes and finally got a hotel operator. Hoping her friend would not be, as she usually was, in the rare-books library, Nancy dialed New Haven. Jennifer Starke, age twenty-seven, her sleek carrot-colored hair in a sling cut, sun-glasses in place, was down-jacketed in red and about to leave her apartment. She stopped to answer her phone.

"Nancy? Nancy! Are you OK? You're sure? I tried to call you this morning, but the hotel lines were busy. The operator said I ought to wait 'til tonight. What is going *on*? When are you getting out of there?"

"Oh, don't worry about me, Jen. I have police protection, be-lieve me. I'm going to stay 'til Monday."

"Well, I don't know. The news makes it sound like Madame Tussaud's has moved to Chicago. My vote would go for the first plane out of there. But you're always stubborn.

"And by the way," Jennifer added, "here's my new item, XIII.t. in the files." She quoted, then, her latest entry, a squib from George Carl Lichtenberg: 'A book is a mirror: if an ass peers into it, you can't expect an apostle to look out.'

"Not bad, huh?"

Nancy was not surprised. Even Jennifer's newest acquaintances received these deliveries. An aficionado of brilliant footnotes, Jennifer had recently begun databasing her personal collection, kept in notebooks for years, of *bons mots*. Not for nothing had she attended the University of Chicago and absorbed the influence of the great Kate Turabian. Now in her fifth year of graduate study at Yale, she was a stickler for beautiful details in all writing.

Jennifer had not, of course, been assigned as Nancy's research assistant. Temporary faculty such as Nancy Cook have to proceed with their teaching and book writing without help in grading or research. Jennifer Starke had begun as an ally among the graduate women and then had become a good friend.

A pretty and acerbic gamine, with blue eyes, freckles, and a very pointed chin, Ms. Starke had made several frankly savage assessments of the department's book productions. Despite those breaches of discretion, she'd remained highly valued as a research assistant. By now, having RA'd for several professors, she could cite chapter and verse of Vico, Benjamin—and de Man and Bakhtin, of course, since this was Yale—as well as (for her own work) the middle period of Freud.

"Want me to repeat it? Have we got a bad connection here?"

"No, Jen, that's fine. Actually, I've even met somebody here who knows what a jackass is. But listen: I know you've got research to do, but I have to ask you to do me a favor. I've *got* to get some bibliography by tonight. I could try to do it here, but I don't know the university holdings. And besides, I don't have time to travel around. Yale's got everything and you know how to get it.

"What is it there, 4:30 now?" Nancy went on. "OK, the library might be understaffed in the periodical rooms. But if you need access to any sections, you can call me, *please*, collect, right from the library desk. I can get a police order from Chicago to keep the library open."

"You're kidding."

"No, I'm not. I'll probably never say this again in my whole life, Jennifer. But this really *is* a matter of life and death. I'll explain about it later, though. You have a pen?"

"Do *I*, Jennifer Starke, have a pen? What is it you need?"

"I want full bibliography—articles, books, publication dates— for four people. If you have to make some long-distance calls to libraries or faculty, that's fine. Just keep an account and I'll write you a check. Jen, don't even eat dinner. It's that important."

"OK, what's the fax number there?" Jennifer demanded, crisply organizing her yellow pads and post-its. "In case I can't get through on the phone."

Fifteen minutes later Jennifer Starke was out the door. Within an hour and a half, the red call-waiting button on Nancy's phone was glowing. Lying across her bed with a legal pad, Nancy took Jennifer's dictation.

"Hope this helps," Jennifer concluded. "And by the way, Nancy, there's a new sign in the restroom in the library. Nancy Reagan's drug message has been modified. The poster now reads, 'Just Say No—to Theory.' An interesting development, don't you think? Novelty-laden. And also by the way: I *am* still worried about you."

"We'll have dinner next week, Jen; my treat. The Hungarian restaurant. I will tell all at that time. Keep your fingers crossed that this works, Jen. And *thanks*."

Nancy then distributed all her notes on the bedspread, one stack per name, and did some thinking.

It was 6:55 P.M. when she phoned the base room. "I think I've got something, Timmy. Please tell Boaz and please come up." The two detectives knocked at her door soon after, Boaz having scooped up Malley's bootprint photos on the way out. Whatever Nancy had, it had to mesh with what they had.

"First of all," Nancy said to the two cops in her room, "you need to know something about Malcolm Gett's panel this morning. It was called"—she glanced at her underlined *PMLA* program issue—"'The Postmodernist Necessity: The Violation of Genre/Gender Limits.' Doesn't sound thrilling, but actually it was very provocative. There was almost a fight about it afterwards.

"Gett was repeating all kinds of assertions he'd made in his book. That book's been very controversial for about a year. It's called *Final Freedoms: Violation as Value.* What it's about—well, his position is, or was, that the ultimate human freedom resides in the act of murder. *Freedom* was his buzz word, in a way."

"What do you mean, 'murder'?" Boaz demanded.

"Well, no one could tell just how serious he really was about all this theorizing. It was very sensationalistic, deliberately so."

Nancy was sitting on the edge of her bed, her pen tapping the stack of notes under the rubric "Malcolm Gett." She was thinking hard, talking sometimes as if to herself.

"Gett's trendy location was Derridean rather than Marxist-materialist, but he was also very much into the power implications he perceived in Foucault. Basically, he was another of the young Turks: very smart, very verbal, very fashionable, and—" (Nancy looked up at the detectives) "frankly, very much an insect, emotionally.

"Anyway, his book: it was published by Berkeley. I'm sure it was there at the Book Exhibition, Boaz, I don't know if you saw it: it had a bright red cover with a smeared design. Not too subtle. And what you could read in it was the claim that without murder 'the human psyche remains crippled and unfulfilled.' Murder frees the soul. We all know this at some level, according to Gett. But we choose not to be free by denying it."

Boaz and Halleran exchanged a look that spoke volumes.

"Something else Gett did in his book: he collected various horrible remarks from serial killers that supposedly supported his position—something about how free they all felt after their crimes—and he put those remarks in here and there, as chapter headings. Just for shock value.

"He liked to say—it's part of the conclusion of his book, and it's what he said at his talk, too—that the attentive audience has already committed a killing in his or her imagination by now. If you're not a hypocrite, you'll admit that you feel more free from the burdens of society as a result of imagining that act.

"But that wasn't enough, according to Gett," Nancy went on. "Complete, *real* freedom comes only . . ." (Nancy consulted the notes she'd taken at the Gett talk) "'by making the morally confirmational act for the self that only deliberate death-making can eventuate.'"

"What a jerk," Halleran said levelly.

"Well, yes," Nancy agreed. "But you need to realize that his argument can appear to be well thought out. It was based on the idea that since language can't signify an objective, 'real' exterior world, no moral rules can be said to exist in anything but a temporary kind of way. Nobody could figure out whether he was actually serious or just striking a pose. He liked to avoid answering questions about that, to keep people guessing."

Nancy went on to say that Gett had shown up at the panel wearing a white T-shirt proclaiming, "Cain: The First Free Man."

This was in keeping with his usual, self-advertising habit. More of those T-shirts had been for sale at the Book Exhibition and at the Hopkins campus, too, Nancy had heard. (What she didn't know was that the T-shirts had sold out hours earlier at the Book Exhibition, as souvenirs.)

"Well, some people in the audience this morning got really furious," she went on. "Somebody at Berkeley, of all places, stood up at the end of Gett's talk and said something like . . ." (Nancy read again from her notes) " 'Aren't you being just a little bit cavalier to present such a set of ideas, given the fact that real human beings have been really dying at this convention, something that even an asshole like yourself might have perceived?' "

There was a twitch at Halleran's mouth and his eyes narrowed, an expression corroborated in Boaz's nodding features.

"There was some shouting after that from a couple of guys in the audience. Finally the session chairman went up to the lectern and made a plea for 'multiculturalism' and 'tolerance of all views in the academy,' and then he declared the discussion to be over. Gett didn't really reply or do any shouting. In fact, he left right away."

"Who was the Berkeley guy?" Halleran asked.

"I can find out," Nancy said. "Annette would know. But I think—let me just tell you about these other things first." She looked at her note pads.

"Remember, Boaz," she said, "you were talking about there not being much of a pattern? That some of the killings look as if it didn't matter who died? And remember how I told you that in English departments nowadays, you are what you write? OK, what have we really got here? For one thing, what did they all write?

"First, Michael Alcott. His book, very influential, was called *The Tremulous Physique*. And on every tenth page or so in that book, he describes another deformity or mutilation and how that's related to language and cultural assumptions and what not.

"Then Michael Alcott ends up deformed, even mutilated. He ends up being an example of what he wrote about. So did Malcolm Gett. I don't think that's an accident. The killer is someone very aware of what these people published. Now there's a problem with that thesis; namely, the other two people, but let me go on . . ."

Halleran, to help himself think, took a seat at the desk. Boaz slipped out his dogeared notebook from his inside coat pocket and let Nancy talk uninterrupted.

"Let me skip to Irene Foster. And here, I think that logical thinking won't help us very much. This is nonlinear. It's not a thing that goes from point A straight over to point B and then to C. We have to float."

"Float?" said Halleran, skeptically—though in water it was something he could do very well.

"Yes. Think nonlinearly, associatively. I want to let some facts about Irene Foster and Susan Engleton just sort of float in the air for a minute. Because for one thing, the killer probably isn't always thinking logically. And also because the killings are *meant* to appear illogical.

"I've found out," Nancy said, "that about fifteen years ago, Irene Foster published a book, then later two articles, all in the field of myth criticism. Which is just about the farthest possible distance away from trendy subject matter. Jennifer tells me that Foster's book is very plodding and dull.

"One striking thing about her work, though, is a fondness she has for the word *irenic*. Which means, oh, 'peaceful' or 'conciliatory.' All three of her works have *irenic* in the title."

Nancy consulted her stacked sheets labeled "Foster." " 'The Irenic Aspects of Poseidon.' And 'Hera, the Irenic: Making Peace on Mount Olympus'—those were her articles. Her book was *Development of the Irenic in Hellenistic Greece.*

"It's way out, I know, but I think maybe the killer made a connection between the name Irene and *irenic* and *ironic*—the kind of punning that's going on in trendy writing these days. For instance, there was a panel on Thursday called 'Rapping/Raping in the Eighteenth Century.' That's pretty standard these days in academic papers: making wild puns and juxtapositions of words that sound alike. It's a way of being what's known as 'postmodernist.' The killer, I think, saw Irene Foster's name somewhere, maybe on her name tag, and that set off some connections in the killer's mind.

"You have to assume," Nancy said, still as if thinking aloud, "that this killer is a little or a lot psychotic. But a psychotic academic. Someone who's seen Irene Foster's work, at least her titles, and is familiar with postmodernist projects. And I think you have to assume the killer has an investment in making all sorts of ironies happen."

Halleran's jowls had lifted an inch or more, not in a smile, but in tight-mouthed disbelief. "That's nuts, Nancy."

"Wait a minute!" she insisted. "Irene Foster actually isn't the problem here. It's Susan Engleton. She's the one who doesn't seem to fit, because she didn't write anything. They almost never *do*, at Wellesley, the old guard."

Nancy explained that long ago, early in Engleton's career, she had published one article, "Forms of Rhetorical Address in Beowulfian Narrative." Her rise to the department chairmanship without firm scholarly credentials would have been a scandal anywhere else. Engleton's only other work, though, which she'd still been revising, was her unpublished dissertation, "The Iconography of the Heroic in Beowulf."

(If generations of Wellesley students had found the doom and glitter of *Beowulf* like nothing so much as dray horse sledge-hauling competitions, with themselves in harness, it had to do with the fact that Engleton taught her classes on the basis of her own texts.)

"Now here's where we float over to your idea, Boaz: that some of the killings look as if it didn't matter who died. Well, what if that's exactly the case? That it didn't matter, specifically, who died every time? What if Engleton were killed simply because she offered an opportunity? I know a lot of MLA people weren't checked in yet on Thursday morning. But still, this is a huge hotel. There must have been a lot of coffee carts standing out in the hallways for some length of time.

"Maybe the killer wasn't looking for Susan Engleton. Maybe

the killer was just looking for a coffee service. To make a victim happen somewhere, anywhere. To set up a pattern.

"But a *certain kind* of pattern," Nancy insisted. "A pattern that's a postmodernist nonpattern: one with randomness and contingency in it. A pattern created in part by the victim, in the way that literature is created equally by the reader who is reading—that Jack London stuff we were talking about, Boaz.

"Now if what we've got is creative irony here—I mean, if the killer is deliberately creating a kind of *text*—then Susan Engleton died a postmodernist death which she helped to make happen because of her responses."

"Her responses?" Boaz asked.

"By ordering that coffee when she did and where she did. But let me go on, please.

"You see, if the whole set of killings is read as a contemporary text" (Nancy was looking toward her beige-draped window as if to force, by squinting, the stupid opacity of things to break into its specific truthfulness, its prismatic spectrum), "then the underlying pressure would be irony, the text would be self-reflexive. It would deliberately disrupt its own patterning; it would subvert some parts of itself. It would have connections that are overdetermined.

"I imagine," she said to the detectives, "that you've been looking for repeated patterns that make for closure. But what if the killer is setting up a text that's indeterminate? Then there wouldn't be closure, there would be, oh, radical ambiguities, weird juxtapositions, things that are startling."

"Hunnh. Well, I dunno, Nance," Boaz said, rubbing his chin. "There'd still have to be a motive for all of this. These killings are mean and these killings are smart. There's somethin' real throwaway about them, and I don't just mean that poor bastard, Alcott. I mean when the killer put the poison in that coffee pot, that killer right then was feeling fine about doing away with everybody in the whole Wellesley group. More than just Susan Engleton could've died if they'd just drunk a little more, you know. You gotta have a motive for all that."

"Grudge," Halleran put in.

"Exactly," Nancy agreed. "And now what would you need to arrange if you came here with that kind of agenda?" Nancy began ticking off items on her long fingers.

"You'd need access to the hotel; you'd need to be checked in to a room so you could get around quickly. And you know, there'd be no way you could know what everyone's schedules would be. Alcott, Engleton, all of them: people go to different panels at different times, and people's schedules change all of a sudden. So if the killer decides on one of these people, like Malcolm Gett, then the killer would have to follow that person around for a while—don't you think?—looking for a chance to strike. So who could that person be?

"Some groups can be ruled out," Nancy asserted. "The killer can't be somebody who's on a hiring committee. Even after the interviewing's over for the day, a committee member has other work to do. You have to go see people at parties or the cash bars, you have to discuss the candidates with people on the committee: it's an all-day project. You can't just take off a couple of hours at noon and go shoot someone in an alley.

"Grad students can probably also be ruled out. Irene Foster's school wasn't interviewing anyone. So there's no reason for hunting her down because of a hiring problem. That leaves, then, the people like Irene Foster who come to hear the panels, and the few people who are outside MLA.

"Assuming the killer's not on the job market, assuming the killer's here freestyle, for revenge: well, if I'm right about this ironic patterning, then only one of the four victims was the actual target. I mean, these were wildly different people. They don't fall into the same categories, except Alcott and Gett, who were both trendy theorists.

"So suppose you're here to do this," Nancy proposed. "Would it be Malcolm Gett, your real target? Would you wait 'til Saturday to make a move on your main target? I don't think so. All that blood makes a spectacular emphasis, but it appears so late in the series that maybe it's diversionary, a kind of overdetermined motif.

"Irene Foster you already know my hunch about. That the killer made an ironic association off her name and writings. Well, then: Susan Engleton? But that second killing was so sloppy in a way, wasn't it? Just as you said, Boaz, anybody might have died in the Wellesley group, not necessarily Susan. And the killer couldn't be sure that anyone would die at all. So I don't think the killer came here to get her.

"It's the first killing that would be the one you really wanted to commit. Because you'd have to take into consideration that there might be a slipup later in your plans. You might be seen and get caught at some point.

"So you'd want to strike first where you most wanted to strike. The others to a certain extent would be just your diversionary setup. Of course, when you arrange for bodies to become an ironic text, that's so enraged an act that it falls within the category of revenge, too."

"Why Alcott?" Halleran demanded.

Nancy, with a rueful movement of her shoulders, replied, "It's not hard for me to believe that Michael Alcott would become a target. I've heard stories about his cruelties, breathtaking stuff. I know he said once, at a party at Georgia, he said something like, 'Yes, I've looked over these new grad students and, frankly, I don't think there's one who can last a year. Where *are* these people coming from?' Alcott was a loathed individual, even though he was courted by people who didn't feel comfortable with him."

Boaz, moving around the room, was frowning. "Why not just leave the hotel, then, after getting him? Why bother with this 'ironic pattern' you're talkin' about?"

"Because . . . because the killer is infuriated about something. Because the killer's making a statement. Is the killer angry about Trendies, about postmodernist stuff, and so sets up a kind of parody of all that? Am I losing my mind? Do these killings say, 'OK, you want ironic texts, you want subversion, you want postmodernism, I'll give you exactly that'?

"Also," Nancy went on, "I've been thinking about something

else. There haven't been any witnesses. With a *lot* of people here. Either this person's very lucky, which is possible, or it's somebody very inconspicuous. That's some indication, maybe, that it's a woman."

"Shit, this is beyond *me*," Halleran griped, but he picked up the boot-print photographs and tossed them to Nancy. "Take a look at these. They're shots from Friday, out in the snow. Taken by that famous artist, Malley-in-the-Alley."

"These came from the alley where Irene Foster was shot? Oh, my God. Oh, you see those kinds of boot prints all the time. Women wear these, you know? Those little all-weather boots. I have a pair myself."

"Are you tellin' me that you've got a pair of boots with this print on the sole?" Boaz demanded, with fatigued incredulousness.

"No, no," Nancy said, with a little laugh. "My boots have stripes on the bottom and they're back in New Haven. But these pictures could be more evidence it's a woman."

"Not evidence," Boaz said. "There isn't any evidence, Nance. It's another arrow in the direction of, that's all.

"I dunno that I'm convinced of all this," Boaz continued. (Halleran grunted.) "It's kinda wild, Nance. But if I go on down that road with you, I think it'd mean that this killer *might* fling in another random body next time, to keep the pattern unpredictable. But more'n likely not, since time's runnin' out. Now according to you, what the killer particularly can't abide are the Alcotts and Getts of this world. Well, who does that mean exactly here? Who else is big that way?"

"You mean scheduled for the panels? I wonder who's coming up."

Once again, Nancy dug out her *PMLA*. "There *are* a couple more trendy critics scheduled. There's Kip Prates from Indiana, and Daniel Salmon from Cornell, both on tonight at the Hyatt. In about, oh, an hour and ten minutes from now. Nine o'clock and ten o'clock. And of course, there's Joan Mellish and Jason Keggo here on Sunday morning. Tomorrow."

She glanced at Boaz and their eyes held.

"Mighty slim, mighty far-fetched, Nancy. But I think you're on to something about the first death bein' the main one."

Nancy's tone was decisive. "I want to talk to the Arizona committee, Boaz. Will you come with me? Or Timmy? I have some questions for them in light of all this. Departmental questions."

"OK—what do you think, Timmy? I think we can't take the chance of not warning some of these people. Nancy, give him those names again, will you?"

Halleran remained a skeptical man, but he took Nancy's note and reached for the phone. He arranged through Hong for some beat cops to notify Prates, Salmon, Mellish, "and that skinny guy with her all the time," to take extra precautions, that there was some reason to think they might be in particular danger. Cops were to stay in their vicinity from now on.

Annette Lisordi having provided Nancy with the names of the expostulating Berkeley audience at Gett's panel, and beat cops having been dispatched to bring those three men to the base room, Halleran, Boaz, and Nancy then headed for the Arizona suite on the fifteenth floor.

Down on the eleventh floor, it was "Jump" McCafferty, from Area One, who intercepted the Tall One, Joan Mellish, at the door of 1123 just as she'd exploded out of her room to go to dinner. Jason Keggo was behind her. At the appearance of the cop, the two looked suddenly abashed and uneasy, as if caught at something.

"Me?" she whined, after McCafferty's warning. "Me?" Her blue-eyed, flaxen-surrounded face seemed unable to process information from the world beyond herself.

Jason blanched. After a few more minutes, he declined to stay with Mellish any longer. He decided to take a cab and hide out in some of the grungier Chicago bars he'd been meaning to get to anyway.

McCafferty looked on, nonplussed, as the pear-shaped woman pursued Jason a short distance down the hall. Her five ankle bracelets jangled over her fishnet stockings. Pleading with Jason not to leave her, she then screamed, "You cocksucker!" at the departing

Keggo back. Skittering in an unfruitlike manner back to her room, she then began haranguing McCafferty for more protection.

"Somebody will be in this hallway soon, ma'am," said McCafferty, determined that it would not be himself.

"That's not good enough!" shrilled the Bloomington professor. Her vocabulary, ordinarily Latinate, migrated again to the Anglo-Saxon regions of the language. At that point, McCafferty excused himself with a controlled, dignified voice and beat a retreat.

Inside her locked room, Mellish then called the Perfect Square. Her voice was a breathy melodrama as she described her situation to her cliquers and claquers there. She demanded they come to her room to keep her company. There was a long, awkward pause down in the bar, then a brush-off. Mellish's Anglo-Saxon resources were all but fully deployed before an excuse was found to hang up on her.

Professor Mellish then phoned and rephoned the MLA organizers, first canceling, then rescheduling, then canceling again her panel for the next day. Obtaining the number of the police room from the desk, she called 210A to ask whether they advised her giving her talk on Sunday: "Well? What the hell are you going to *do* for me?"

Before Hong could get off the line, he found himself longing for the good old days of gang wars and drug busts. Wearily he told Mellish to stay in her room.

Meanwhile, up in the Arizona suite, room 1515, Nancy had moved the desk chair in the main room to sit facing the sofa. On that sofa three associate professors (Ethan Blackwell, Lewis Esposito, and Annie Pogue) were lined up, equidistant as sparrows on a wire. Jerry Sprague, the head of the department, had claimed an easy chair for himself. Halleran half sat on the arm of an empty easy chair on the other side of Sprague. Boaz deliberately remained standing.

Nancy proceeded to ask some close departmental questions regarding Michael Alcott's activities among other faculty members. Who were Alcott's graduate advisees? Was Alcott on the dean's

committee or executive committee or tenure-review committee—
any powerful structures responsible for decisions in the department?

Boaz noticed that Pogue had looked uneasy at the words *tenure
committee* and that Pogue had glanced quickly at Esposito and then
at Sprague.

But the department chair temporized, it being a bureaucratic
habit to downplay anything that might place the department in an
uncomplimentary light. Boaz interrupted him.

"I'm particularly interested in the tenure committee," he said
firmly.

Sprague acknowledged that Michael Alcott had been a member
of the tenure-review committee for the last two years.

"Did he have a great deal of influence on that committee?"
pursued Nancy.

"All members of the tenure committee have an equal say,"
Sprague answered defensively.

"Whom did he get fired?" Nancy asked.

"Really, I doubt that Arizona's experience in this regard differs
from that of other universities," Sprague stated.

"Let's find out about tenure decisions at the other schools,"
Nancy said to the detectives. "That should be easy to check and
I think we need to know this. May I use your phone here—
thank you."

She placed two brief calls, first to Wellesley's Muffie Murchison,
then to Allan Hislop in the Hopkins suite. It emerged that Wellesley had not turned down a tenure aspirant on their faculty since
before the Cretaceous period. As for Hopkins, all tenure candidates had also been promoted for the last several years. ("For, oh,
at least four years," said Hislop, "although this next group coming
up does not look uniformly appealing. They'll probably all pass,
though.")

Hanging up, Nancy resumed her seat and crossed her arms
over her camel sweater. "Did Michael Alcott represent a powerful
lobbying influence on the tenure committee?"

"Yes, he did," Sprague admitted reluctantly.

"Was anyone dismissed while he was on that committee?" Nancy pursued.

"Well, percentage-wise, not a great number of faculty have left the department," Sprague answered. "There's been some attention in the last few years to—uh—to an effort to upgrade the department. And some of our younger people have been no longer retained, yes."

"Why didn't you bring this up on Wednesday?" Halleran demanded, his voice loud and all but reverberant in the suite.

"Goddam good question," Boaz added, his voice also loud and disgusted. He was biting off his syllables, one by one: "You have not been fully cooperative, Sprague. Or any of you. You have not been forthcoming during a murder investigation. *Four* murder investigations. Now I'm gonna ask all of you just one more time for the whole story here. And if I don't get it, pronto, I'm takin' all of you to the station."

"You don't seem to realize to whom you're speaking, Officer," Sprague began.

"Shut up," Halleran told him. "And check this out, asshole. There happens to be a certain holding tank. Not very far from here. A long time before your lawyer can get you out of there, you're going to have some experiences that you'll never get over. Know what I'm getting at?"

To some extent, this was a tactic—the loud voices, the epithets, the implied horrors at the station. Boaz and Halleran had employed these together on other occasions when a citizen needed instruction in the virtue of candor. They understood one another's moves in this way. The anger that fed the tactic, though, was real.

Sprague and his committee sat wide-eyed.

"But Michael wasn't murdered, was he?" Annie Pogue asked in a small voice. "*Was* he?"

"We think he was," Boaz told her. "And I think maybe there's no reason why Michael Alcott's death couldn't be followed up with some more dead people from Arizona. You better tell me what's been goin' on."

Gradually, from Pogue and Esposito, a picture emerged. Led by Michael Alcott, a group of half a dozen faculty at U. of A. had persuaded the chair to perform what were still known as the April Massacres.

For two years, younger staff coming up for pretenure review—those whose work was not "alert to new developments in critical theory," as Alcott put it—had been informed that their professional work did not "merit advancement." "I cannot bear the professionally inert," Alcott had sneered at one of them.

"Who *was* that?" Esposito tried to recall, turning to Pogue. "Was that Neiderthal or Rames?"

"What are the names of everyone who was fired?" Nancy demanded.

Sprague's low-voiced answer was that two people had passed their pretenure review in the last two years, whereas five faculty had been fired in that period: Buck Nickens, Aaron Botomer, James Diltz, Deborah Rames, and Pierce Neiderthal. The last-named three had been dismissed just last April.

Jotting the five names in his notebook, Boaz stopped and looked at what he'd written. He then looked up and off toward the rosy print of the *Family of Saltimbanques* on the wall. He was not seeing it. He was remembering something.

Boaz then put in a call to the base room, where Malley answered. "Malley, up on the wall, there's a list. Got a pushpin through it. Says 'Name Tags.' Get it down, quick, I want you to check somethin'."

Malley did so. It was the list of conventioneers who'd been issued replacement name tags on Wednesday and Thursday. The list had not been brought up to date beyond then, a detail that had nagged at Boaz from time to time.

"Malley, I'm gonna read you five names. Look them up on that list." Malley's blunt, freckled finger moved slowly down and over the list in turn. Under the entries for Wednesday night, he located one of the five: Deborah Rames.

"Thought so. Don't leave the base room, Malley. You're gonna hear from me in about a minute."

"Who we got?" Halleran said. He was on his feet and his voice was rock.

"Rames, maybe." Boaz was dialing the desk. To the answering clerk, he said, "I want the room number and the registration date for Deborah Rames, R-A-M-E-S. Now."

The clerk's reply drew a low "Sweet Jesus" from Boaz. Then, "I'm sendin' a cop down for that room key, right now. Have it ready."

As Boaz called the base room again, he said over his shoulder to Halleran, "Rames checked in on the *twenty-first,* a week ago Friday."

Halleran stepped to the door of the suite and yelled down the hall. "Duffy!" Nancy's waiting, tag-along cop loped over to the door. Halleran indicated for him to listen and wait.

Boaz was speaking to the base room. "Malley: get Hong and every cop on this. Deborah Rames, wanted for questioning. Description as follows." Boaz's long left arm jabbed in Sprague's direction with a pointing finger. "How old is she? How tall is she? What color's her hair? Come on!"

Sprague stammered out a lengthy and redundant description of a Caucasian woman in her midthirties, medium height and weight, brown hair of medium length, no distinguishing features other than glasses, dressed typically in skirts and blouses.

"And she wears those—uh—sandal things a lot, what do you call them?" Sprague added.

"Birkenstocks," put in Annie Pogue.

Boaz forwarded the description to Malley, adding, "Suspect armed, extremely dangerous. Nobody leaves this hotel 'til we find her. Malley, I'm tellin' you to lock this hotel *down.* Get on it!"

"Come on with me," Boaz said to Halleran. "Nancy, you want to stay here now. We're gonna be comin' come back here if this doesn't pan out."

His eyes swept the Arizona members with something less than full respect. "Nobody comes in or leaves this room for any reason 'til you hear otherwise from a police officer."

Sprague, rising from his chair, began to protest but was cut off by a voice as lithic as Halleran's. "I have indicated what's going to be happenin' here. Did I use some words too big for you? Sit down."

Closing the Arizona door behind them, Boaz tossed the service elevator key to Duffy with a terse order that Duffy get himself down to the lobby desk and pick up the key to 3108. "I want that key in my hand right here in one minute, Jimmy; move!"

Big Jimmy Duffy turned and accelerated like a train down the east wing of the fifteenth floor. When he pushed past the shoulder of Assistant Professor Kimberly Traphagan from U.C. Riverside, he didn't even say excuse me. Traphagan sucked in her cheeks with contempt. "I'm pretty sure that's a cop," she said icily to Assistant Professor Tree Swallow (from Evergreen State College, Washington), adding a remark about limits needing to be placed on police aggression.

Moments later, in the lobby near the desk, Ms. Carstairs-Norton saw the approach of a charging cop. "What, what is it?" and she pushed past the honeymooning couple from the thirty-third floor without even saying excuse me. The clerk, leaning over the front desk, was holding out a key in his extended hand. Duffy grabbed it like a mail train hooking a sack. Circling the MLA bulletin board like a roundhouse, he charged back to the service elevator. Ms. Carstairs-Norton pressed two manicured fingers to her left temple and took a deep breath.

Outside the service elevator on the fifteenth floor, waiting for Duffy, Boaz was conferring with Halleran about how to proceed.

"You know, we can't just grab one of these professors and slam her against the wall," Boaz said. "The kind of evidence we're goin' on, we better not even mess up her hairdo. We'll get charged with excessive force and false arrest. Professionals like these, they've all got three or four brothers and sisters and they're all attorneys.

"If she's in her room, Timmy," Boaz concluded, "I want to confront her first. Ah! That's Duffy!" The service elevator door opened.

"Confront her? What do you mean, confront? We got bodies waist high, Boaz. We can make an arrest. We get problems, Mulcahy deals with them."

"Come on and cover me, Timmy. I'm gonna talk to her."

"Shit. Stay on with us, Duffy. Boaz thinks he wants to hold a little panel all his own. Shit. I hope this babe's in the lobby and Hong's already busted her chops."

Duffy checked his piece, a Ruger .38. Halleran, as usual, was more comfortable with his Smith and Wesson 9mm automatic, fourteen rounds in the clip and another in the chamber. Boaz rubbed his back ribs under his belt clip.

At the end of the thirty-first floor east wing, the service elevator opened quietly. At the far end of the wing, about a dozen conventioneers had gathered, waiting at the regular elevator bank. Between that group and the suited trio now on the floor was Room 3108, three doors away from the MLA professors.

Duffy joined the waiting crowd and stood facing the elevator. Some of these teachers were going to get pushed real hard real soon, maybe. He made a mental note to shoot high. Halleran took up a position further down the hall, facing the conventioneers, but a few feet back from the 3108 door.

His ear to the Rames door, Boaz heard a noise like a drawer being slammed shut, then the click of the door lock being turned from the inside. He gestured to Halleran and stepped quickly to the edge of the waiting crowd.

Deborah Rames emerged, an inconspicuous brown bird in the human aviary, but with an ample black purse in her hand. Her tweed skirt and jacket fitted her loosely, her figure invisible. On her simple face, her large tortoiseshell glasses were the only ornament other than a bit of lipstick in a quiet shade. Despite the eccentricity of wool socks and Birkenstocks under her suit, she was a woman who would blend in anywhere at the convention, who could roam at will, forgettable.

When she joined the back of the elevator crowd, Boaz edged over and stood at her right. Halleran ambled up directly behind her, his right hand on his belt.

With the opening elevator door, there was the usual brief turbulence as people getting off pushed between the people getting on. Then the waiting group began to move forward in an orderly way.

Staying side by side at the right of Deborah Rames, his left shoulder brushing her right, Boaz waited as long as he could. Then suddenly, close to the door frame, he pivoted between her and the man stepping on the elevator in front of her. Pivoting another ninety degrees, he stood in front of Rames, his craggy face not a foot from her blank features. When she instinctively moved a little to her right, her dominant side, Boaz, expecting such a move, shifted half a foot to stay exactly in her way. The last flow of people moved around them, as his body kept blocking hers from the closing elevator doors.

Boaz did not speak. He continued to hold the eyes of Deborah Rames for two beats, three beats, four. And he watched the readable sequence of her thoughts: seeing him first as just an object in the way, then wondering what this man was doing, then her first blinking annoyance, but not yet alarm. Still not taking his eyes from her face, Boaz said very clearly one word to her: "Freedom."

And he noted the emotions that moved across her face in rapid, predictable sequence: confusion, then realization, then panic, then determination, and then a new confusion. She was still readable, therefore not totally mad. He proceeded on that basis.

"Both hands up! Drop the bag!" The woman said nothing, but in her confusion, paused. Halleran, behind her, shoved her elbows up as Boaz knocked the handbag from her right hand. It landed on the speckled maroon carpet with an audible thump.

"You're under arrest," Boaz told her. "You have the right to remain silent, you have the right . . ."

But Deborah Rames made no remark as the litany was recited and the handcuffs snapped behind her back. She walked in silence as the two men, hands tight around her upper arms, moved her down the hall.

A search of Rames's room began immediately, turning up evidence so extensive that Malley shook his head. "Don't fuckin' believe it! Look at all this stuff!" He and Hong had to come back the next morning to complete the inventory.

Traveling down in the service elevator, this time with four aboard, Boaz pressed the big "15" button and let Duffy out for the Arizona suite.

"Tell Nancy I'll get in touch with her later," Boaz said. "Rest of that Arizona group: tell 'em they can go do whatever mischief they can think up now. Then tell those others in the base room they can go."

Rames, still handcuffed behind her back, stood beside him in eye-glazed silence.

That an arrest had been made at the Fairfax was news that transmitted itself with something like laser rapidity in all directions: to the district station, to the concierge, to the various committees, and eventually even to Joan Mellish, who'd moved most of the large pieces of furniture in her room against the door.

"How can I be sure?" she whined aggressively to the cop at her slightly opened door. "Maybe you don't know what you're talking about!"

Within a couple of hours, though, she was triumphantly holding court again. Grandly she rescheduled her panel for Sunday morning. And during that panel (Mellish beside the forgiven and reinstated Jason Keggo), a new booming expansiveness, for all the world like real confidence, was heard in her Grand Ballroom remarks. Later on Sunday, blonde Mellish fulminations and scarfy gestures were reflected in the baroque mirrors in the lobby. More of the same appeared in the airport waiting lounge. She and Keggo presented their boarding passes for Indianapolis and burst into the coach section with many calls and cries.

All of Sunday, the conference rooms and hotel areas were vivid with delivery and embellishment of the news. Professor Gurgana of Rice found a way to make two shots be fired during *his* story of the arrest, while Professors Swayze, Watson, Flimmer, and Cly, all from Baylor, were certain that Deborah Rames had an accomplice still on the loose. Flimmer began outlining a book to expose the Rames Conspiracy, which involved the CIA and Cuban refugees.

And so, by Sunday, the quotidian life of the hotel was settling back into place, like long-jostled water resettling in a barrel. Even the weather was returning to routine. The ambient temperature, having risen to a sultry thirty-five degrees for two hours on Saturday, dropped again on Sunday as a light snow began. Hong and Malley finally quit the Fairfax premises for good on Sunday— glad, both of them, to trade the professional and hotel worlds for areas of town dirty in different ways, but more familiar.

Professor Rames, after her first questioning in the lockup at the district station, remained in the lockup Saturday and Sunday nights. When bound over for trial, she'd be moved into Cook County Jail at 22nd and California. Separate true bills for each murder charge were being made out, to be signed by a judge, thus changing the charges into indictments. Bail would be set at one million dollars, cash.

For much of Sunday Boaz was at the station, filling out paper-work, debriefing the lieutenant (who was eager now to talk with the press), and interviewing (ahead of Halleran, as they had ar-ranged) the floor-staring Deborah Rames.

During an afternoon break on Sunday, Boaz had phoned the Fairfax concierge. This was to let Ms. Carstairs-Norton know that Boaz had written a note that he'd send over, a note commending her for her assistance throughout the investigation.

"That might help smooth things over a little bit over there." He could not see, of course, the concierge's blink of astonishment. But the thank-you he heard was level-voiced and sincere.

In an earlier break that morning, he'd gotten in touch with Nancy. Postponing all her eager questions, Boaz said he'd like to tell her all about what happened, maybe over dinner that evening if she had the time? Professor Cook accepted with alacrity. Since she intended to do some serious investigations at Krause's Music Store in Lincoln Park, as well as rifling some jazz specialty shops, the two arranged to meet at Anna Maria's Pasteria on Broadway at 6:00. It was a place that carried a firm recommendation by Halleran.

"They don't have a wine-and-beer license," Halleran had told him. "That's the one bad thing. But you can go to Sam's Liquors first," he told Boaz, "over on Sheffield. Get a good red. Just a minute, I can give you a couple of names."

(Halleran was cheerful. He'd dined the night before at a Thai place near Winnemac Park that he would reveal to no one, and his first interviews with Rames had gone well.)

"Tell the waiter—that's Federico—tell him you've brought a bottle. You might ask him if they've still got the rigatoni al forno. Get that if they do. And don't wear a tie that's radioactive."

Halleran jotted down four vintages he knew to be in stock at Sam's. In that warehouse later, Boaz decided that "Library Reserve," a term on the discreet label of the Joseph Phelps 1981 Cabernet Sauvignon, would be the most appropriate for a beautiful professor. He bought one bottle. It was a move he never regretted, even when the credit card statement arrived.

12

The grubbiness of North Broadway is long-standing and, block after block, the same. The dilapidated, depainted, one-story shops have a just-hanging-on quality. By contrast, a few big new businesses, mostly video malls, have the garish, outsized, loudmouth character of the *nouveau-vide*. The narrow street looks too tired and worn out to be dangerous, even though a car stereo here would not remain in its original metal nest for long. It is a street for transactions, in or out of the law.

In this dolorous surround, Anna Maria's is not always easy to find. Tucked under an awning, the painted snowflakes and green and red neon script on its small front window ("Pasta & Pastry") are so incongruously cheerful that the eye at first overlooks them.

Inside, a small single room continues the assertive optimism. "Pasteria" appears again, in orange and green neon, across the south wall. Two red ceiling fans turn above white walls and a gray tiled floor. Tables, a remarkable number of them, perhaps a Guinness record, are squeezed in front of a deli case. White paper place mats upon red plastic tablecloths are set for two or four. The accordion music from the speakers is so preposterous the ear overlooks it.

Here, at 6:10 P.M., Nancy put down her packages at a table by the south wall, where Boaz helped her out of her coat. (Lord, she's good-lookin', Boaz thought.)

The dress before him was one of Nancy's finds from the late 1940s, forest-green gabardine fitted at the waist. Its matching jacket offered a whimsical, multicolored string tie at the throat. Across the bodice was a cutout area, about six inches square, created evidently by giant pinking shears. The ensemble made you think of Ginger Rogers. Above her red bakelite dangling earrings, Nancy's complicated hair was swept up on one side. The skin under her dark eyebrows looked like satin.

"You look great, Nancy. Real nice."

Pleased, and still energized by the charge of great Chicago shopping, Nancy took her seat hoping the faintly glowing neon script on this wall would not play tricks on her complexion.

Boaz, scanning the room, routinely turned his chair slightly so as to sit with his back more to the wall. Discarding his battered overcoat, he revealed, with a small private pride, his best suit, a chunk of double-breasted chocolate: wool flannel, soft-shouldered, and wide-lapeled, with a beige, grain-lined dress shirt. This was fronted, like an elegant hood ornament, by a 1950s tie from his collection. Sporting an extremely energetic, twelve-toned, asymmetrical pattern, it had faded from its original blowzy tackiness and was now simply beautiful. It was very wide, but tied in a tight, tiny knot. Above it, Boaz's face was shaved to the bone. His features had the look of rain-scrubbed rocks and pebbles at Blue Shoals Beach.

Nancy was in high spirits. And why not? She and Annette had ignored the Mellish-Keggo panel and had taken various cabs north of the Loop, eventually to the Jazz Record Mart. There Nancy had located, *inter alia,* an original 78 rpm of Ellington's 1928 "The Mooche," plus an aircheck tape of Peggy Lee's first recording (Benny Goodman and Orchestra, 1942), "Why Don't You Do Right, Like Some Other Men Do?"

Associating from the song title to Mark Reese, Nancy had mentioned then that a Nancy-Boaz date was pending later that evening.

"*That* guy?" And Annette smiled knowledgeably at her friend. "You always want to do something a little *outré,* Nancy. Something your mother wouldn't do."

"Guess so," Nancy amiably agreed.

"Well, he *is* cute," Annette hastened to add. She wanted Nancy to have a terrific time with some new guy, and soon. She, too, knew Mark Reese, a man who made for dismayed sighs, slumped shoulders, and eye-rollings when his name came up among Nancy's female friends.

"Do you think he's cute? *I* think he's cute," Nancy had smiled.

And now she was in the company of this extremely interesting specimen of an extremely interesting gender. She liked his rough, slightly gray-touched eyebrows, she decided: very dressy.

"Nice tie," she said. "Nice suit, too. Did you find out everything?"

Boaz nodded, feeling that the week was wrapping up rather well. Nobody ever noticed this tie.

Federico, the lone waiter, wiggled between the tiny tables with a swivel-hipped dexterity that made the discovery of his being a former tennis pro unsurprising. The menus he distributed in a perfunctory way: people who knew this place at all knew to order from the handwritten list of daily specials tacked up on two walls.

Federico's interest grew, however, when his nearsightedness brought Nancy into clearer focus and when the '81 Phelps was handed into his care.

"Perhaps just eight minutes to breathe before the first tasting?" he suggested, cradling it in his arm.

"That'd be fine," Boaz said.

"Now," said Nancy, as the waiter stepped away, "you found out everything?"

"Pretty near everything," Boaz said. "And I have heard happier stories in my day—*narratives*, I mean. Sorry. *Narratives*." Nancy registered the mood and moment with an appreciative smile.

"Tell you the truth, though," Boaz said, "if what you want is entertainment value, what I ought to tell you about is my nephew Tandy's dog. A singing dog, it was."

An open, brown-eyed look of innocence was on Boaz's face. "Really just a puppy when it took up its career. And where it all started was on the courthouse steps in Jane . . ."

"I realize," Nancy interrupted, "that you are trying to drive me mad. But it's not going to work. I am going to order my dinner from that waiter. He looks as if he'd like to help me. Do you think he's Italian? Then I suppose I could try to call Timmy Halleran. Surely he would tell me what I've been patiently, patiently waiting to know all day."

"All right, Professor Cook. The high C hit by that Redbone hound will have to remain a mystery. And I will save you a night of huntin' around. Lord knows how many restaurants you'd have to go through to find Timmy Halleran tonight."

"Boaz, what about Deborah Rames?"

But Federico had swiveled back to their table. Following his staccato descriptions, Nancy ordered the porcini ravioli with aurora sauce, Boaz the rigatoni al forno.

"When I left Deborah Rames," he began, "she was asleep again." She'd fallen asleep a couple of times between interrogations.

Boaz shifted slightly on the white-painted folding chair. That belt clip was going to have to be replaced.

"That's a point of some interest, by the way—falling asleep," Boaz noted. In custody, a guilty person frequently does fall asleep, right in the holding tank or interview room. He or she feels relieved; the suspense of waiting is over at last.

"But you get an innocent person in jail, that guy gets frantic. Longer he has to wait, the louder he gets. Sleep isn't somethin' he gets a lot of."

Boaz went on to explain that late Saturday night at the station, Deborah Rames had made an impassive, careless confession but would not respond to detailed questioning.

Then, Sunday midmorning, sag-faced Halleran had come into the First District headquarters, eventually seating himself opposite Rames in the interview room. Moving at a pace no more rapid than mud on an incline, he'd first looked around for napkins and mugs. It was a routine that Boaz recognized.

In easy, low tones, the big cop had said, "I'm Timmy Halleran, Professor Rames. I'm an investigator. And I have to talk to you about some things. But I think we could have something to eat first. Boaz, we've got some extra cups around here, don't

we? Fresh coffee?" And Halleran casually laid out the fresh-baked mandelbrot and ginger snaps he'd picked up on the way in from the Swedish Bakery on North Clark Street.

And after a while, to his slow, deep-voiced questions, Deborah Rames had bleakly begun to talk.

What emerged across several interrogations (and what would be highlighted later throughout the defense attorney's case), was that Deborah Rames was a woman who'd struggled at great cost, both financially and emotionally, to create a career for herself in teaching. Her father had died when she was small, and she had no siblings. Attending Reed College in Oregon, she'd then put herself doggedly through graduate school at the University of Minnesota.

A long-standing marital engagement had not survived her move to the Midwest. Then, what with her mother's illness, it had taken her eight years to complete a five-year graduate program. Her mother had died during that period, of bone cancer, though Deborah had done everything conceivable to stave off that loss. She'd even made a file folder of "Hints from Heloise," which she showed her mother sometimes so as to let her mother know she was trying to be completely responsible. Her teaching of composition courses at that time, and later her classes in myth and the American novel, were notable for their same assiduous attention to detail.

To produce, and quickly, a publishable book replete with the latest literary jargon, particularly for a field outside the usual purview of critical attention, was no small requirement for this woman. She'd been hired by the University of Arizona along with three other people, a cohort of average size, but she had not been anyone's first or even second choice. For the hiring committee that year (having made the decision to become a department *au fait* with the latest theoretical trends), the Rames candidacy did not appeal. But the school had needed so badly to fill its Americanist line that, reluctantly, Rames had been hired. She had continued to be perceived as a necessary but regrettably retrograde addition to the faculty.

No detail of this was lost on Professor Rames in the U. of A. hallways and faculty dining room. In her second and third years, as her pretenure review approached and she became more nervous about her position, she grew prone to depressive episodes. As if in compensation, the developing of highly praised and well-attended courses became something of an obsession for her.

"Now here's where Alcott comes in," Boaz proceeded, as the first quantities were tasted and then poured of a red velvet wine.

Michael Alcott had been hired with tenure a year after Rames's arrival. He immediately became a powerful, shaping force in departmental hiring decisions. He hadn't been assigned to the hiring committee this year for the first time in three years, but that was only to make it appear that a single individual did not dictate unilaterally the U. of A. hiring decisions. Nevertheless, his behind-the-scenes impact on this year's committee had already been considerable and would have been more so.

In the matter of tenure decisions, Alcott's influence had been equally emphatic. Last April, when Deborah Rames submitted her dossier to the tenure-review committee, her book, on the subsidence of the Oedipus myth in eighteenth-century American literature compared to the recrudescence of that mythic structure in works of the nineteenth century, had not been accepted for publication by any university press.

It was in the faculty dining room before the meeting of the tenure committee that Deborah Rames had heard her work publicly dismissed by Michael Alcott as "negligible, even if published, which is" (turning to Rames in the room), "as you must realize, a dubious enterprise in your case." The sneer on his face was memorable.

"I'm not sure what all happened in that tenure meeting that afternoon," Boaz told Nancy. "Rames wasn't there, and Sprague says as little about it as he can. But I think you could safely assume that Alcott was meaner than a yalla dog about the whole thing."

"You're probably right," Nancy said. She touched her swept-up side of hair impatiently. She pointed out that Deborah Rames might have become an excellent, if not a fashionable, scholar, one of those indispensable workhorses of academic life who compile excellent documents—volumes of letters, for instance—that other scholars gratefully use forever after.

"Did she stay on and teach last fall at U. of A.?" she asked.

"No, she left right away after the review. Finished up that semester, but that was all."

Boaz was flipping up pages in his crowded little notebook. "I knew," he said, with a mock grumpiness, "you were gonna ask me every last little thing, so I regarded the entire interview as a kind of classroom I better take notes in."

"Oh, good," said Nancy, and refurbished their half-empty glasses.

"Yes. OK, here it is: Rames finished out that spring semester, but instead of going back that fall to teach for her last year, which I guess she could have done if she'd wanted to, she left the school. All that summer and fall, she lived real quiet in Tucson. Didn't see much of anybody. Broke off all her school connections except for this one guy, a chemistry professor she'd been going out with. She went on seeing him now and then 'til late November. I'm gonna put him off 'til a little later, though," Boaz said.

"So now here she is," he described, "most of the time all alone in her house, for months on end. I think by summertime Rames had made up her mind to get even with Alcott at the convention. She could probably take it for granted that he'd be there and that she could find him.

"Around about that same time, she concocted this plan to make a whole set of confusing killings, so as to get even in a big way. When she called the hotel in September, she reserved a room for Friday, December 21—real early. That gave her a whole weekend before the convention started so she could set up some stuff in Chicago.

"But more about that in a minute, too," Boaz, said, looking over his delivered salad and homemade rolls. Nancy pronounced the vinaigrette dressing excellent, and would have smiled more had she not had an Arizona summer on her mind.

"So Deborah Rames had finally become enraged," Nancy said.

"Well, enraged and *still* quiet," Boaz amended. "She's quiet right now, too. By the way, she *did* say the word *postmodernist* one time when I was askin' her about the plans she made. I can't say it exactly the way she did, but I can tell you it was pretty spooky. She's definitely quite a ways around the bend.

"That's not what got in her way, though," Boaz remarked. As he explained, Deborah Rames's disadvantage had been her inexperience as a criminal. She didn't have, as even the youngest street tough will have, ready access to fake identification sources: phony credit cards, buyable social security numbers, renovated birth certificates, all the paperwork of crime.

What's more, she could not feel certain, when laying her plans to be at MLA, whether she could safely register as a faculty member of the University of Arizona. She probably could have, but a certain timidity overcame her. She could assume that if someone at Arizona noticed her name on the MLA bulletin board or saw her in the halls, that person would simply think she was there to interview for another job. Still, she wanted to avoid all listings that might include her in the Arizona group. She'd reserved a room, then, outside MLA, at regular hotel rates, and had arrived midday on the twenty-first.

"It's a detail," Boaz emphasized, "but a crucial one, that Rames had to use her own name on her credit card for hotel registration and car rental. That was the one serious risk she had to run."

On the afternoon of the twenty-first, Rames had rented a car on a ten-day plan, to be returned on the Monday following the convention. As the days went by, it was simplicity itself for her to find names on the bulletin board and get room numbers from the harried staff at the registration desk.

Boaz and Nancy had made some headway through their salads as well as their cabernet. Nancy waited through a couple more bites.

"Did she tell you about meeting Michael Alcott at the hotel?"

"Sort of. She's still got a bucket of angry feelin's in her, and the name of Alcott—well, kind of tips it over. But yes, she said some stuff."

Boaz's tone was reluctant. "Lot of this isn't real pretty now, Nancy."

In the case of Alcott, the actual MO was partially opportunistic. Rames had stalked Alcott on Wednesday morning, watched him come out of the Chez Toi with Dennis Doog, then had followed him up to the tenth floor on the next elevator.

"What happened there is known only to Rames," Boaz said. "What I can tell you for sure is that Rames carried a good-sized knife in her purse, one of those jagged, serrated things. We found another one in her luggage. Probably she had a knife with her, *and* the gun, most of the time."

Boaz added that he was unsure to what length Deborah Rames was prepared to go to make Alcott resemble the kinds of things he'd written about. "But she had her mind made up, that's for sure," he said. "Stalking him around the hotel. Being the Invisible Woman. She must have done some real quick thinking when she got off that elevator and saw him there in the hall."

But then that old inexperience came to bear again. After a crime, a killer likes to feel comfortable right away, Boaz explained, sure that he or she isn't isolated in some way that makes for notice-ability. That Wednesday night, Deborah Rames decided to get a name tag so that she wouldn't come to anyone's attention at some inadvertent moment.

"That was her second mistake," Boaz asserted, "after checking in under her own name." When Rames went up to the name-tag-replacement table in the lobby and claimed to have lost her Arizona tag, she was bluffing, but it was a good bluff. The MLA assistants there, eager to be helpful, were not concerned about proof that this woman was on the Arizona faculty. She looked like a teacher, her old U. of A. faculty ID card was in her hand along with a hotel room key—and they gave her a name tag.

"No problem," said Boaz, "except that put her name on a list, a short list, of people who did that on Wednesday night."

"You are amazing," Nancy told him.

"Thank you. I should tell you that I also have an amazin' effect when it comes to tables and chairs. As you can see." And he demonstrated, with a brown-suited elbow and a mock disgust, another of the wobbly tables that followed him everywhere.

"This has been happenin' to me all my life," Boaz noted. "I had to put all of Hong's matches under that table in the base room. I can't sit down anyplace but what the table turns into a support-impaired appliance. I think we'd better have a little more wine so we can keep up with this table here," he concluded cheerfully, his knobby hand lightly touching the neck of the cabernet.

Federico now appeared, dinners in hand. The pasta had finished drying just two hours before and had been cooked to order on the spot.

"This Rames stuff is a little bit peculiar subject to go into at dinnertime, Nancy," Boaz noted, after a few moments spent addressing his plate.

"Oh, I don't mind a bit. Here, try this; this aurora sauce is fantastic," she said, placing a discreet fragment on Boaz's plate. "What about Susan Engleton? Did Deborah Rames talk about her?"

"Yes; and of the four of them, that one's pretty clear." In Engleton's case, he explained, the MO was entirely opportunistic. It was an accident, as Nancy had surmised, that the Wellesley contingent had been poisoned, though not accidental that *some* committee would encounter the physiology of yews. Rames had set up the poisoning to introduce confusion into the investigation of Alcott's death.

"What Rames had to have on Thursday," Boaz said, "was another body, and quick. And she'd thought out just what she was gonna do."

Out in her rented car the weekend before the convention, "Deborah Rames went berry pickin'." Off Irving Park Road, she'd harvested yew berries in Graceland Cemetery from the shrubs around a few of the vaults, then had driven north to the Chicago Botanic Garden in Glencoe. On Sunday, she'd harvested the shrubby residential streets in the western neighborhood of Oak Park.

"Around all those Frank Lloyd Wright houses?"

"Evidently."

On Monday, then, back in her room, Rames had methodically rubbed away the red fruit from many dozens of berries and crushed the hard seeds with a mortar and pestle brought from home. In two cups of purchased coffee, she'd steeped the seed mash for three days in an empty Skippy peanut butter jar—a wide-mouthed item also brought from home.

The alkaloid fluid was very potent by Thursday morning, when she'd poured in the liquid sweetener. A little before 7:00 A.M. that day, Rames, dressed in a gray sweatsuit so as to resemble the athletic individuals headed for the top floor spa, placed the jar of fluid in a gym bag over her shoulder, and began to roam the halls above the thirty-first floor.

She was looking for a coffee service. Just two floors up from her own, she'd come across the cart delivered to the Wellesley suite. Using one of the napkins on the cart to pick up the tureen lid, Rames had quickly decanted the poison, and with it a small quantity of seeds. To replace the coffee lid, put the jar in her gym bag, and exit by the stairwell down to her own floor, had taken only a few unobserved moments.

Shortly thereafter, Rames's activity provided new business for the hotel dry cleaners and many nearby restaurants, for the police and medical examiners, and eventually, two weeks later, for the Rushings Funeral Home in Wheeling, West Virginia—a family origin that Susan Engleton had been at great pains to disguise for thirty years.

Boaz's narrative was interrupted now by Federico's arriving to ask, in the declarative Chicago mode, about the status of the food. The waiter knew, of course, that it was excellent. People had been looking at other people at adjacent tables with expressions that said, "Can you believe this? Don't tell anybody!" Boaz maneuvered more rigatoni with his fork.

"So you found all this equipment, a mortar and a pestle and a jar and everything, right in her hotel room?" Nancy asked.

"That's right. And a lot of other stuff. The Skippy jar was right in the closet. And there was a pair of boots in there with that pattern on the sole—plus some bloody clothes. And there was a list of room numbers for all sorts of folks."

"Who?"

"Well, Mellish and Keggo were number one on the list. And there was Harold Snaff. Gerald Merk. That guy Helks. Salmon—a bunch of people. She just stuck that list up on the inside of the closet door. If she'd gone on and gotten just a little more careless, the maid might have spotted something.

"You know, a lot of killers don't care very much about hiding the evidence," Boaz remarked. "Some of them think they're too special to get caught. They live off in a world of their own. The rules don't apply to them, they think.

"But now with Rames . . . she seems to be a little different. I think she really didn't care if she got caught or not. You talk to her, she gives you answers. Or most of the time she does. But she acts like somebody whose life is over. Well—more like somebody whose life's been over for a long time."

Nancy was very quiet at that. She nodded when Boaz lifted the Phelps inquiringly.

"How did she know about yew berries?" Nancy asked. "That's odd. I know a little horticulture, but that's because I had some summer jobs in a greenhouse. People in English usually don't know much outside their fields—except maybe movies."

"Well, I asked Rames at one point if she had a garden. She'd been real quiet for a while and that sort of woke her up. Turns out gardening was something she used to do a lot of, ever since she was little. She and her mother had a garden together for years in Oregon. I gather that was something she remembered as real important. But she didn't put in a garden this last spring—didn't plant a thing. Just didn't feel like it any more, I guess. Anyway, it might not take a whole lot of time with plants before you'd come across information about poison ones."

"That's true," Nancy admitted. "Especially if you've got a cat, since they eat everything. I bought a book on poisonous house-plants because of that—after I found out my cat was really a pig in a fur coat. Did Deborah Rames have any cats?"

"Dunno. Sorry."

"Well, Irene Foster had a cat. Oh, I almost don't want to know about her. But how did Rames get involved with her?"

"Right now, looks like Irene Foster got killed in place of

Malcolm Gett. If Gett had gotten killed on Friday when Rames meant for him to, then Irene Foster might still be alive. We know that Rames stalked Malcolm Gett all Thursday afternoon and Friday morning, but Gett always had people around him or somebody with him in his room.

"Now at that point—Friday—Rames is still needin' more bodies. Somebody else to die after Engleton so that the 'pattern' would be extra-confusing. And she's not less angry, she's more angry the farther she goes with all this. I'm not sure how she latched onto Irene Foster. This is the one of all the four of them that she won't talk much about. She might have seen Foster's name on the registration board, or just come across her in the lobby on Friday.

"From things Rames says here and there, you get the idea that she got to talking with Foster in the lobby, or maybe right outside the hotel. Somethin' about how hard it was to find a cab at noon time. I don't know where Foster was headin', but Rames led her to believe they could get their cabs faster on the Michigan side of the hotel. Then after she got Foster to take a shortcut with her through the alley, it took Rames about a half a minute to do her work out there and then run back into the hotel. 'Course, she blended right in and nobody noticed her.

"So now it's Friday afternoon," Boaz continued. "Rames thinks she's got things just the way she wants. A set of killings, nobody can figure 'em out, she's gotten away with murder in broad daylight. From here on out she can pick and choose—carefully, of course—to get rid of some more of the people that really aggravate her. She makes up her mind she's definitely gonna get this guy Gett: he's one of these high-falutin' Trendies and he makes her sick."

"Wait a second, please," Nancy interrupted. "You make it sound as though Deborah Rames would have shot anyone available on Friday noon."

"I gather you don't think that's the right answer?"

"No," said Nancy, "I don't. I think something else was going on. Deborah Rames felt betrayed, she felt shot in the back, as it were. And she hates herself, too. Then she comes across a per- 207 son, a woman, who's like herself in exactly the ways that Michael Alcott sneered at. Irene Foster is inconspicuous, she's just an old-fashioned schoolmarm type. She's in a field that isn't glamorous, a field that overlaps Rames's own myth criticism. I think Deborah Rames saw some parts of herself in that poor Foster woman. She might have felt driven to reenact the destruction of herself."

"Could be," Boaz agreed, with a lift of his shaggy eyebrows. "Rames gets real quiet when you bring up Foster too often. Starts looking down at the floor again. I do think there are gonna be some things we're never gonna know about, because Rames can't tell us about them. But it *has* been my experience that you tend to know what you're talking about, so I'd take your word for it about that."

"Well, thank you," Nancy said. He'd managed to surprise her with his compliment, and Boaz enjoyed that. Then he remembered the final murder.

"Well, now we're getting up to Malcolm Gett," he said, "and things get real nasty."

Rames, as he explained, was determined after Friday to go on with the hunt for Gett. But the man's constant socializing—the furtive visitors exiting his hotel room quickly and sauntering down the halls as nonchalantly as possible—these things made him difficult to pick off.

Boaz said, "I think it's safe to imagine that Rames has what's called the 'killer's exhilaration' by this point: all these revenges goin' off without a hitch. Probably had the swollen-up feeling that she could do whatever she wanted. You can also pretty much be sure that she was disgusted about Gett's panel on Saturday morning. When she went out of that meetin' room, she took along an idea that that guy was gonna be a dead guy real soon."

Nancy was startled. "You think she was there at the Gett panel? There in the room?"

Boaz gave her a steady-eyed, thoughtful nod. "Pretty sure, yeah, from what she says."

"Oh, Lord. Wait 'til I tell Annette. She won't believe it. Actually, though, maybe I won't even tell her for a while. She's already saying that somebody back in Italy put a curse on her."

Nancy traveled the edge of her wine glass with a long index finger. "OK, what happened in Malcolm Gett's room, then?"

What had happened was that after Gett had scurried away from the argumentative premises of the Alpine Room, Deborah Rames, a trench coat over her left arm and a black purse in her hand, had knocked on his 3800 door. In her right hand was a copy of *Final Freedoms*.

Having asked Gett to autograph her copy, Rames followed him into the room. When he'd fumbled at his shirt pocket for a pen, Rames had told him, "Use this," and had tossed a large, dry-erase marker on the table top.

Confused, Malcolm Gett had picked it up. The theorist was more confused when he saw the gun now in her hand. "Use it in there," she said, indicating the bathroom with a movement of her head. Her .32 still aimed at his midsection, Rames had ordered him to write FREEDOM across the mirror. Dissatisfied with his small first start, she'd told him to rub it out and begin again. "And underline it." A moment after obeying her next order, that he sit down on the toilet lid, Professor Gett was free from all orders in this world.

Rames had remained with Gett long enough to make sure he was dead, a matter of just a few minutes. She'd donned her trench coat, then, buttoning it over the stains on her skirt, put the marker in her pocket, picked up the book, and returned to her room.

"She was crazier by now, of course," Boaz noted. "Killers on a jag do get more and more escalated in their feelings. That *freedom* word was a kind of defiance. She was defiant in her statements whenever she talked about him. And of course, like you said, it was a deliberate kind of joke about his book, the freedom thing."

Rames's copy of Gett's book, Boaz added, was never signed. It had been found where Rames had tossed it—into the hotel wastebasket in her room.

"That was quite some roomful," Boaz remarked. Fibers and blood were on another pair of Birkenstock sandals. She'd made no effort to remove the blood on her gray skirt. ("Just changed into a 209 nice fresh outfit and proceeded with her business.") The shoe and skirt stains were being tested at the lab, but were no doubt blood from Malcolm Gett.

"Lord knows what all she had in mind," Boaz said. "But now that gun thing: you look into that and what you find again is a dedicated killer, but then really not a killer at all."

What Rames had carried and used was a nickel-plated, snub-nosed, .32-caliber Smith and Wesson revolver, the source of which was a certain Winfield Hanby, from the U. of A. chemistry department.

From inquiries by Malley, it was learned that Rames had dated this older, divorced colleague for a month before and several months after her dismissal in the spring. When contacted, Professor Hanby proved to be a very worried man, uneasy among other things about Deborah Rames, whom he hadn't heard anything from for quite a while, not since after Thanksgiving.

Moreover, Hanby's .32 handgun was missing. He'd reported this to the Tucson police a week or two ago without hearing more about it. How long it had been missing, he didn't know: he almost never thought about the thing and had discovered its absence in his closet only by accident.

"My hunch," Boaz speculated, "is that Rames went on seeing Hanby just to get his gun. She'd probably learned about his revolver early on. Then it came to mind again when she started putting together her MLA plans. I don't believe romance was much on her mind. I suppose she hoped that Hanby wouldn't notice the gun was gone for a long, long time.

"Which is not, you know," Boaz went on, "what your usual Murder One premeditation involves. Tell you the truth, I think Rames was only planning out her life up to the MLA. But not past that point. The missing gun was sure to be noticed sooner or later and connected up with her. But she didn't care, or just couldn't plan past this one convention. A lot of despair in this woman."

"Do you think there would have been another killing, then, after Malcolm Gett?" Nancy asked.

Boaz's eyebrows shrugged. "There *was* another day left at the convention. And there was no end of folks that she was riled up at. She was on her way to the Prates panel when we picked her up. And she'd put a circle around Mellish's name right in her schedule book, that same book you're always carrying around in your purse. It looks like Rames intended to show up at Mellish's talk. Or maybe go to her hotel room. She definitely was gonna do somethin'. She came here to stir up hell with a long spoon, and there was no reason for her to quit."

"What will happen to her?"

"She'll be looking at four counts of Murder One. That'll amount to quite a while over at Dwight."

"Dwight?"

"The women's prison in Illinois."

"Could she get the death penalty?"

"Well, Illinois's not much for executing women. It's not a problem they've had to pay a lot of attention to, up 'til recently. If you're a woman, you gotta be pretty flabbergastin' to get yourself onto death row. But there is one on there now."

Boaz now oriented Nancy to the fact that only about 12 percent of all homicide and manslaughter arrests in the United States are of women.

"And in Illinois, there was only one execution of a woman this whole century, back in the 1940s. Before that, you gotta go back to 1845, if I remember right: Elizabeth Reed. I read up on her. She took a notion to put arsenic in her husband's tea—that was Leonard—and the state took a notion to hang her."

"Hanging? Illinois still hangs people?" Nancy looked appalled.

"No, not now. It's lethal injection now. But I wouldn't worry about Deborah Rames. I think she's way too far around the bend to have that happen to her."

Now Boaz leaned a little over the little aluminum table, which immediately responded with a wobble under his elbow. He ignored it.

"I think it's about time that I said outright what a help you were, Nancy. I believe Deborah Rames could've done in just about everybody at the Fairfax corral if you hadn't done some real good thinkin'. That's a thank-you that comes from Timmy, too, but I especially . . . well, I appreciate it."

"Oh, you're welcome, Bo," said Nancy, very pleased. She finished the last of her wine.

There was a pause of a beat or two. Then Boaz, slightly lifting his knobby right index finger as if to ask a question in class, said, "There's one other little thing I'd like to know about. Just for my orientation."

But Federico, noticing the raised finger, was now beside the table with recommendations for dessert. Homemade pastry included *tiramisù* (or "pick-me-ups"): creamy mascarpone cheese over fresh ladyfingers soaked in marsala and espresso. They ordered two, with coffee.

Now Boaz persisted. "You see, I *have* wondered from time to time why you go on doin' what you're doin'. I did not see a lot of Pure-D happiness over in that hotel. And you have the mind to do what you want. So now seriously, why don't you do somethin' else?"

Nancy observed that her MLA interviews next year just might make doing something else a requirement for her. Truth to tell, she said with a smile, she was "hopelessly curious" about the outcome of that next convention. "Just a glutton for punishment, I guess.

"Of course, I do have an Alternative Plan B," she confided. "As all mothers say to their daughters, 'A girl needs something she can fall back on.' I thought maybe the wonderful world of Motel Six. They're looking for managers all the time. I know it for a fact. I think Jennifer told me. I thought the Motel Six in Dead Pig, Georgia, might be right."

"Georgia? I cannot comprehend why you would go to Georgia—why anybody would go to Georgia. Not when there happens to be Dead Pig Hollow, just right around the ridge from my own second cousin. That's Edwin. And not all that far from Rolla—in Missouri.

"You might like him, too," Boaz continued informatively. "He makes bottle-cap sculptures. Mostly lamps: different-sized lamps made outa bottle caps. He's got a heart he made, too, out of pine, I think it is, right out in his front yard. It's about as tall as you are, and stuck all over with bottle caps. I imagine he could use the material from your coke machines at the motel. Remind me to give you his address."

"Oh, do. I'd like to meet all your family." Nancy's two sentences had begun teasingly and then moved to affection. They addressed their delivered *tiramisù*.

"What I'm going to do in the meantime," Nancy began again, "is some traveling in Europe this summer." Explaining that an interest in early swing and small-group jazz had gradually grown over her life "like moss, wild moss," Nancy showed him her purchases of the day and outlined her plan to hunt for recordings next June, mostly in Sweden.

There was a pause at that point as the future intruded itself into past and present realities. The check came, prostrated itself as if apologetically, and went.

"Well, I was meanin' to mention," Boaz said, deftly tugging a cuff of his chocolate-suited arm, "that there was a flyer on my desk a couple of weeks ago. A police convention, a special thing, is gonna be held in New Haven. Next September. Around the twentieth or so. Some kinda connection with the old Winchester gun factory there. I didn't pay a whole lot of attention to it at the time, but—I should continue my education, shouldn't I? And maybe I could see you there?"

Nancy's delighted surprise was an easy read.

"By that time," Boaz added, "you and Annette probably will have endangered the entire eastern seaboard and might be in need of a little police help?" And he gave Nancy a grin, his first, crooked teeth and all.

(God, he's attractive, she thought.) "Oh, please come. That would be so great if you could. Please."

They both then had brief physical arguments with their coats

in the tiny room. Boaz was sleeking back the hair over his right
ear when Nancy asked, "Do you ever go to the Green Mill? Great
club, Dina says . . ."

"You mean Capone's old hangout? In Uptown? No, not
lately . . ."

Boaz found he'd developed a sudden interest in going, though
maybe not an interest in staying there for long.

". . . but I am prepared to spend a week of Sundays there if you
want to go."

Everything was shifting from the quotidian to the extraordi-
nary again. It was only apparently as usual that Boaz scanned up
and down the street before looking back over his shoulder for his
partner. She was pulling on her gloves and chatting amiably with
a couple near the window. Her smile widened as she turned to
him. Firmly, she took his arm at the door.

Epilogue

Six months later:

☞ Boaz, with a detailed memory of their long Sunday night together, propped up a postcard from Nancy on his cluttered desk at the station. Her note, affectionate and breezy, let him know she was almost packed to spend late June and part of July in Europe. "I hear some Valaida Snow is still to be found in Denmark. Another investigation! I'm on my way, Bo!"

On the front of her card was the chubby young Count Basie in Kansas City, Jo Jones at his right. Boaz jotted a reminder in his notebook to send a card to her tinily printed Copenhagen address. His convention reservation in New Haven had been long confirmed.

☞ Tadeusz Owsiany, the sanitation engineer who'd found Irene Foster's body, was about to start a new job. The morning after the alley incident, his worried wife had said to him, "I think—I mean, you comin' home in the middle of the day and all—don't you think you oughta maybe not go back?"

The terrible day before, her man had not eaten his midafternoon meal. He'd come home at 3:30, then put his elbows up on the kitchen table and cried. In late February he'd finally taken his wife's advice, quit the job, and entered training. In July he'd begin work as a hospital orderly.

☞ Annette Lisordi, like Nancy, was packing, but mostly books and a few sticks of furniture. A bottle of Piper Sonoma champagne, a rite-of-passage gift from Nancy, was chilling in Annette's refrigerator. Earlier that spring, Annette had accepted with pleasure a tenure-track appointment offered by Brandeis.

She had also, against the counsel of Emory friends ("You run into these people over and over again, Annette!"), allowed herself an expressive letter to the Purdue department chair. The "egregious bullying and contempt for women" displayed by the spread-eagled Professor Bunt was only part of her description. Concluding that "a whole new valley had been reached" by their hiring committee, she noted that if her interview experience had been similar to that of other candidates, then the fact that Purdue had been able to hire only two lines out of nine this year was "an outcome that makes for no surprise." A "cc:" at the bottom of her letter indicated a copy was being forwarded to the Purdue humanities dean. Strapping reinforced tape onto another box, Annette Lisordi was a cheerful new prof.

☞ Joan Mellish, drafting a section of her next colecture with Jason (a guest-speaker event scheduled at Harvard, to be entitled "The Colors of Excrement and the Palette of Creativity"), was interrupted by a phone call from New York. It was an insider friend for whom she'd done a few favors. Swearing her to secrecy, he confided that her name was now shortlisted for a MacArthur Foundation "genius award."

☞ And back in Chicago, the Rames murder trial had not, after six months, seated a jury, due to machinations surrounding the defense attorney's insanity plea. Deborah Rames was still in custody in Cook County Jail when Nancy's plane took off for London.

Four years later, however, in the maximum-security region of Dwight Correctional Center, Rames was serving the front end of four consecutive life sentences. She had avoided the usual fate of poisoners, thanks in part to an intervention by the matron. Safe within rigid structure, refocused, Doctor Rames had become, in fact, respected as only Murder One commands respect in prison, and as only the profession of teaching commands respect in that institution, as well. She has developed and continues to conduct two daily classes, both having already shown a certain measure of success. Her 8:00 o'clock class is "Basic Literacy." At 10:00 A.M. is "Introduction to Good Books."